More Praise for *The*

"[The] real quest in *The Physics of Sorr...* sadness, to allow it to be a source of empathy and salutary hesitation. . . . Chronicling everyday life in Bulgaria means trying to communicate Bulgarian sadness, which is—to the extent that these things can be disentangled—as much a linguistic as a metaphysical dilemma."
—Garth Greenwell, *The New Yorker*

"Both an intellectual game and a very human story, *The Physics of Sorrow* captivates." —Elizabeth C. Keto, *The Harvard Crimson*

"Gospodinov launches himself into the premiere league of European authors. . . . [He] rises above the lowlands of novelistic commercialism and convention, saving not only himself but literature as well—and with it, the entire world." —*New Journal of Zurich*

Praise for *Time Shelter*

"Mr. Gospodinov, one of Bulgaria's most popular contemporary writers, is a nostalgia artist. In the manner of Orhan Pamuk and Andreï Makine, his books are preoccupied with memory, its ambiguous pleasures and its wistful, melancholy attraction."
—Sam Sacks, *Wall Street Journal*

"[An] antic fantasy of European politics. . . . 'History is still news,' Gospodinov writes, cunningly drawing attention to the violence that the past wreaks on the present."
—*The New Yorker*, Best Books of 2022

Also by Georgi Gospodinov

Time Shelter
The Story Smuggler
And Other Stories
Natural Novel

The Physics of
Sorrow

A Novel

Georgi Gospodinov

*Translated from the Bulgarian
by Angela Rodel*

Liveright Publishing Corporation

*A Division of W. W. Norton & Company
Independent Publishers Since 1923*

Copyright © 2011 by Georgi Gospodinov
Translation copyright © 2015 by Angela Rodel

First published in Bulgaria as *Fizika na tagata* by Janet 45 Publishing.

First published as a Norton paperback in 2024

For information about permission to reproduce selections from this book, write to Permissions, Liveright Publishing Corporation, a division of W. W. Norton & Company, Inc., 500 Fifth Avenue, New York, NY 10110

For information about special discounts for bulk purchases, please contact W. W. Norton Special Sales at specialsales@wwnorton.com or 800-233-4830

Manufacturing by Lakeside Book Company
Production manager: Delaney Adams

ISBN 978-1-324-09489-0 (pbk)

Liveright Publishing Corporation
500 Fifth Avenue, New York, N.Y. 10110
www.wwnorton.com

W. W. Norton & Company Ltd.
15 Carlisle Street, London W1D 3BS

1 2 3 4 5 6 7 8 9 0

Contents

Epigraphy   3

Prologue   5

I. The Bread of Sorrow   7

II. Against an Abandonment: The Case of M.   55

III. The Yellow House   69

IV. Time Bomb (To Be Opened after the End of the World)   115

V. The Green Box   147

VI. The Story Buyer   175

VII. Global Autumn   197

VIII. An Elementary Physics of Sorrow   231

IX. Endings   269

Epilogue   273

The Physics of
Sorrow

Epigraphy

O mytho é o nada que é tudo.[1]

—F. Pessoa, *Mensagem*

There is only childhood and death. And nothing in between . . .
—Gaustine, *Selected Autobiographies*

The world is no longer magical. You have been abandoned.
—Borges, *1964*

. . . And I enter the fields and spacious halls of memory, where are stored as treasures the countless images . . .
—Saint Augustine, *Confessions, Book X*

Only the fleeting and ephemeral are worth recording.
—Gaustine, *The Forsaken Ones*

I feel a longing to fly, to swim, to bark, to bellow, to howl. I would like to have wings, a tortoise-shell, a rind, to blow out smoke, to wear a trunk, to twist my body, to spread myself everywhere, to be in everything, to emanate with odors, to grow like plants, to flow like water . . . to penetrate every atom, to descend to the very depths of matter—to be matter.
—Gustave Flaubert, *The Temptation of St. Anthony*

---

1 Myth is the nothing that is everything.

. . . mixing
memory and desire . . .

—T. S. Eliot, *The Waste Land*

Purebred genres don't interest me much. The novel is no Aryan.

—Gaustine, *Novel and Nothingness*

If the reader prefers, this book may be taken as fiction . . .

—Ernest Hemingway, *A Moveable Feast*

Prologue

I was born at the end of August 1913 as a human being of the male sex. I don't know the exact date. They waited a few days to see whether I would survive and then put me down in the registry. That's what they did with everyone. Summer work was winding down, they still had to harvest this and that from the fields, the cow had calved, they were fussing over her. The Great War was about to start. I sweated through it right alongside all the other childhood illnesses, chicken pox, measles, and so on.

I was born two hours before dawn like a fruit fly. I'll die this evening after sundown.

I was born on January 1, 1968, as a human being of the male sex. I remember all of 1968 in detail from beginning to end. I don't remember anything of the year we're in now. I don't even know its number.

I have always been born. I still remember the beginning of the Ice Age and the end of the Cold War. The sight of the dying dinosaurs (in both epochs) is one of the most unbearable things I have seen.

I haven't been born yet. I am forthcoming. I am minus seven months old. I don't know how to count that negative time in the womb. I am as big as an olive, weighing a gram and a half. They still don't know my sex. My tail is gradually retracting. The animal in me is taking leave, waving at me with its vanishing tail. Looks like I've been chosen for a human being. It's dark and cozy here, I'm tied to something that moves.

I was born on September 6, 1944, as a human being of the male sex. Wartime. A week later my father left for the front. My mother's milk dried up. A childless auntie wanted to take me in and raise me, but they wouldn't give me up. I cried whole nights from hunger. They gave me bread dipped in wine as a pacifier.

I remember being born as a rose bush, a partridge, as ginkgo biloba, a snail, a cloud in June (that memory is brief), a purple autumnal crocus near Halensee, an early-blooming cherry frozen by a late April snow, as snow freezing a hoodwinked cherry tree . . .

I are. We am.

I. The Bread of Sorrow

The Sorcerer

And then a sorcerer grabbed the cap off my head, stuck his finger straight through it and made a hole about yea big. I started bawling, how could I go home with my cap torn like that? He laughed, blew on it, and marvel of marvels, it was good as new. Now that's one mighty powerful sorcerer.

Come on, Grandpa, that was a magician, I hear myself say.

Back then they were sorcerers, my grandfather says, later they became magicians.

But I'm already there, twelve years old, the year must be 1925. There's the fiver I'm clutching in my hand, sweaty, I can feel its edge. For the first time I'm alone at the fair and with money to boot.

Step right up, ladies and gents . . . See the fearsome python, ten feet long from head to tail, and as long again from tail to head . . .

Daaang, what's this twenty-foot-long snake? . . . Hang on there you, where do you think you're going, you owe me a fiver . . . Well, I only got five and I'm not gonna waste it on some snake . . .

Across the way they're selling pomades, medicinal clay, and hair dyes.

Dyyyyyyye for your ringletsssss, brains for your nitwitssss . . .

And who is that guy with all the sniffling grannies gathered around him?

. . . *Nikolcho, the prisoner of war, finally made it back home, and heard that his bride had married another, Nikolcho met her at the well and cut her head clean off, the head was flying and crying, oh my Nikolcho, oh why* . . . Time for the waterworks, grannies . . .

And the grannies bawl their eyes out . . . *Now buy a songbook to find out what terrible mistake he made, slaying his innocent wife* . . . A songbook hawker. Geez, what could that mistake have been? . . .

People, people, jostling me, I clutch the money, just don't let anybody steal it, my father had said when he gave it to me.

Stop. Agop's. Syrup. Written in large, syrupy pink letters. I swallow hard. Should I drink one? . . .

Come and get your rock candyyyyyy . . . The devil is tempting me, disguised as an Armenian granny. *If you're in the know, here is where you'll go* . . . So what now? Syrup or rock candy? I stand in the middle, swallowing hard, completely unable to decide. My grandfather in me cannot decide. So that's where I get the indecisiveness that will constantly torment me. I see myself sitting there, scrawny, lanky, with a skinned knee, in the cap that will soon be punctured by the sorcerer, gawking and tempted by the world offering itself all around me. I step yet further aside, see myself from a bird's-eye view, everyone is scurrying around me, I'm standing there, and my grandfather is standing there, the two of us in one body.

Whoosh, a hand grabs the cap off my head. I've reached the sorcerer's little table. Easy now, I'm not going to cry, I know very well what will happen. Now there's the sorcerer's finger coming out the other side of the cloth, man oh man, what a hole. The crowd around me roars with laughter. Someone smacks my bare neck so hard that tears spring into my eyes. I wait, but the sorcerer seems to have forgotten how the rest of the story goes, he sets my torn cap aside, brings his hand to my lips, pinches his fingers and turns them and, horror of horrors, my mouth is locked. I can't open it. I've gone mute, the crowd around me is now roaring with laughter. I try to shout something, but all that can be heard is a mooing from somewhere in my throat. Mmmmm. Mmmmm.

Harry Stoev has come to the fair, Harry Stoev has come back from America . . .

A husky man in a city-slicker suit rends the crowd, which whispers respectfully and greets him. Harry Stoev—the new Dan Kolov, the Bulgarian dream. His legs are worth a million U.S. dollars, someone behind me says. He puts 'em in a chokehold with his legs, they can't move a muscle. Well, that's why they call it his death grip, whispers another.

I clearly imagine the strangled wrestlers, tossed down on the mat one next to the other, and start feeling the shortage of air, as if I've fallen into Harry Stoev's hold. I rush to escape, while the crowd takes off after him. And then from somewhere behind me I hear:

Step right up, ladies and gents . . . A child with a bull's head. A never-before-seen wonder. The little Minotaur from the Labyrinth, only twelve years old . . . You can eat up your fiver, drink up your fiver, or spend your fiver to see a marvel you'll talk about your whole life long.

According to my grandfather's memory, he didn't go in here. But now I'm at the Fair of this memory, I am he, and it irresistibly draws me in. I hand over my fiver, say farewell to the python and its deceitful twenty feet, to Agop's ice-cold syrup, to the story of Nikolcho the prisoner-of-war, to the Armenian granny's rock candy, Harry Stoev's death grip, and sink into the tent. With the Minotaur.

From this point on, the thread of my grandfather's memory stretches thin, yet doesn't snap. He claims that he didn't dare go in, yet I manage to. He's kept it to himself. Since I'm here, in his memory, could I even keep going if he hadn't been here before me? I'm not sure, but something isn't right. I'm already inside the labyrinth, which turns out to be a big, half-darkened tent. What I see is very different from my favorite book of Greek myths and the black-and-white illustrations in which I first saw the Minotaur-monster. They have nothing in common whatsoever. This Minotaur isn't scary, but sad. A melancholy Minotaur.

In the middle of the tent stands an iron cage about five or six paces long and a little taller than human height. The thin metal bars have begun to darken with rust. Inside there is a mattress and a small, three-legged stool at one end, while at the other—a pail of water and scattered hay. One corner for the human, one for the beast.

The Minotaur is sitting on the stool, with his back to the audience. The shock comes not from the fact that he looks like a beast, but that he is in some way human. Precisely his humanness is staggering. His body is boyish, just like mine.

The first down of adolescence on his legs, feet with long toes, who knows why I expected to see hooves. Faded shorts that reach his knees, a short-sleeved shirt . . . and the head of a young bull. Slightly disproportionate to the body, large, hairy, and heavy. As if nature had hesitated. And just dropped everything right in the middle between bull and man—nature got frightened or distracted. This head is not just a bull's, nor just a human's. How can you describe it, when the tongue is also pulled in two directions? The face (or snout?)—elongated; the forehead—slightly sloped backward, but nevertheless massive, with bones jutting out above the eyes. (Actually, it is not unlike the forehead of all the men in our family. At this point I unwittingly run my hand over my own skull.) His lower jaw is rather protruded, the lips quite thick. The bestial always hides in the jaw, it's where the animal leaves us last. His eyes, due to the elongated face (or snout) that flattens out on the sides, are wide set. Over the whole facial area there is some brownish fuzz, not a beard, but fuzz. Only toward the ears and neck does this fuzz congeal into fur, the hair growing wild and in disarray. And yet he is more human than anything else. There is a sorrow in him, which no animal possesses.

Once the tent fills up, the man makes the Minotaur-boy stand. He gets up off the stool and for the first time looks at the crowd in the tent. His gaze wanders over us, he has to turn his head, given his obliquely set eyes. They seem to rest on me for a moment. Could we be the same age?

The man who herded us into the tent (his master and guardian) begins his tale. An odd mix of legend and biography, honed over the course of long repetitions at fairs. A story in which eras catch up with one another and intertwine. Some events happen now, others in the distant and immemorial past. The places are also confused, palaces and basements, Cretan kings and local shepherds build the labyrinth of this story about the Minotaur-boy, until you get lost in it. It winds like a maze and unfortunately I will never be able to retrace its steps. A story with dead-end corridors, threads that snap, blind spots, and obvious discrepancies. The more unbelievable it looks, the more you believe it. The pale and straight line—the only way I can retell it now, lacking the magic of that tale—goes roughly as follows.

Helio, the boy's grandfather on his mother's side, was in charge of the sun and the stars; in the evening he locked up the sun and drove the stars out into the sky, like driving a herd out to pasture. In the morning he gathered up his herd and let the sun out to graze. The old man's daughter, Pasifette, the mother of this boy here, was kind and beautiful, she married a mighty king from somewhere way down there in the islands. This was long ago, even before the wars. It was a rich kingdom, the Lord God himself (their god, that is, the local one) drank whiskey with the king of the islands, they set store by each other, God even gave him a big bull with a pure white hide, which was a downright wonder to behold. So the years went by and God demanded that same bull as a sacrifice. But Old King Minyo (Minos, Minos . . . somebody yelled out) was feeling stingy and decided to pull a fast one on God and slaughtered another bull, again fat and well fed. But can you really pull a fast one on God? God found out, hit the roof, started blustering, saying, don't pull this while-the-grass-grows-the-horse-starves business on me, now you'll see who you're messing with. He fixed it so that Minyo's meek and loyal wife, Pasifette, sinned with that very same handsome stud of a bull. (Here a buzz of disapproval sweeps through the crowd.) And from this a child was born—a man in body, but a bull in countenance, with a bull's head. His mother nursed him and cared for him, but that laughingstock King Minyo just couldn't stomach the disgrace. He didn't have the heart to kill the little baby-Minotaur, so he ordered it to be locked up in the basement of the palace. And that basement was a real labyrinth, a master stonemason made it so that once you go in, there's no getting out. That mason must've been from around these parts, one of our boys, since here we've got the best, while those Greeks are lazy as sin. (A buzz of approval sweeps through the tent.) But afterward that poor old mason didn't earn a red cent from the whole business, but that's another story. They tossed the little boy inside, at the tender age of three, torn away from his mother and father. Just imagine what his poor angelic little soul must've suffered in that dark dungeon. (At this point, people began sniffling, even though they themselves did the exact same thing with their little snot-nosed brats, fine, so it wasn't for eternity, they'd lock them up between the thick cellar walls only for an hour or two.) They tossed him there in the dark, the storyteller went on, the little guy cried day and night, calling for his mother. In the end, Pasifette begged one of those master masons who had made the labyrinth to sneak the boy out secretly, while they put a young bull in his place. But that's not in the book, some know-it-all in the crowd chimes in. Let's keep that between us, the storyteller says emphatically, so that old Cretan King Minyo doesn't find out about the switch, 'cause he still doesn't have the slightest inkling. And so they secretly freed the little boy with the bull's head and again secretly loaded him onto a ship bound for Athens (the same one going to take the seven Athenian lads and lassies, supposedly for the Minotaur). The little Minotaur gets off in Athens, there an old fisherman finds him and hides him in his hut, looks after him for a year or two, and gives him to one of our boys, a shepherd, who goes down south in the winter to graze his herd of cattle, all the way to the Aegean. He took him, saying since he'll never be able to live out in the open among people, hopefully the cattle will take him in as one of their own. Well now, that very same shepherd personally passed him on to me a few years back. The cows don't want him neither, he said, they don't accept him as their own, they're scared of him, my herd's scattered, I can't keep him with me any longer. Since then we've been going around to fairs with the poor little orphan, abandoned by his mother and father, not man enough for men, nor bull enough for bulls.

While he tells this story, the Minotaur bows his head, as if the story has nothing to do with him, only making a soft throaty sound from time to time. The same as I made with my locked lips.

Now show 'em how you drink water, the master orders and the Minotaur, with visible displeasure, falls to his knees, dunks his head into the bucket and slurps noisily. Now say hello to these good people. The Minotaur is silent, looking down. Say hello to these people, the man repeats once again. Now I see that in one hand he is holding a staff with a sharp spike on one end. The Minotaur opens his mouth and growls out what is more likely a deep, raspy, unfriendly Mooooo . . .

With that, the show ends.

I turn around before leaving the tent (last), and for an instant our eyes meet again. I will never be able to escape the feeling that I know that face from somewhere.

Outside I realize that my mouth is still locked shut, and my cap is torn. I dash toward the stand, but there is no trace of the sorcerer. That's how I left the memory, or rather, that's how I left my twelve-year-old grandfather. With locked lips and a torn cap. But why would he hide his visit to the Minotaur in his story?

Moooo

I didn't ask anything then, because he would've realized that I could get inside other people's memories, and that was my biggest secret. And I hated the Yellow House, where they would've taken me, just like they'd taken Blind Mariyka, because she saw things that would happen.

Nevertheless, I very secretly managed to find out something from Grandfather's sisters, seven in number, who came to see him every summer until the end of their lives, skinny, dressed in black, dry as grasshoppers. One afternoon I cornered the eldest and chattiest of them and casually began asking her what grandpa had been like as a child. I had bought her candy and lemonade in advance—they all were crazy about sweets—and thus got the whole story.

It was then that I learned that as a boy, my grandfather had suddenly gone mute. He had come back from the village fair and could only moo, he couldn't utter a single word. Their mother took him to Granny Witch to "pour him a bullet." She took one look at him and declared—this child has had quite a fright, I'll have you know. Then she took a bit of lead, poured it into an iron mug, heated it up over the fire until it melted and started sizzling. In "pouring a bullet," the lead takes on the form of whatever has frightened you. The fear enters the lead. Afterward you sleep with it under your pillow for several nights and then you throw it into a river, into running water, to carry the fear far away. Granny Witch poured the bullet three times and all three times a bull's head appeared, with horns, a snout, everything. Some bull at the fair had scared him, said Grandpa's sister, they'd go there to sell animals from the neighboring villages, buffalo, cattle, sheep, whole herds. For six months he didn't utter a word, only mooed. Granny Witch came nearly every day, burned herbs over him like incense, they held him upside down over the crumbs of dinner to make the fear fall out of him. They even slaughtered a young calf and made him watch, but his eyes rolled up into his head, he fainted and didn't see a thing. It cleared up on its own after six months. He came into the house one day and said: "Mom, come quick, Blind Nera has calved." They had a cow by that name. And so his lips were unlocked. Of course, most of the details came from my smuggled entry into my great-aunt's memory. Her name was Dana. She was hiding one other story, whose corridors I had already secretly slipped into.

The Bread of Sorrow

I see him clearly. A three-year-old boy. He has fallen asleep on an empty flour sack, in the mill yard. A heavy bee buzzes close above him, making off with his sleep.

The boy opens his eyes just a crack, he's still sleepy, he doesn't know where he is.

I open my eyes just a crack, I'm still sleepy, I don't know where I am. Somewhere in the no-man's-land between dream and day. It's afternoon, precisely that timelessness of late afternoon. The steady rumbling of the mill. The air is full of tiny specks of flour, a slight itching of the skin, a yawn, a stretch. The sound of people talking can be heard, calm, monotone, lulling. Several carts stand unyoked, half-filled with sacks, everything is sprinkled with that white dust. A donkey grazes nearby, his leg fettered with a chain.

Sleep gradually recedes completely. That morning in the darkness they had come to the mill with his mother and three sisters. He had wanted to help with the sacks, but they wouldn't let him. Then he had fallen asleep. They're surely ready to go by now, they've finished everything without him. He gets up and looks around. They are nowhere to be seen. Now here come the first steps of fear, still imperceptible, quiet, merely a suspicion that is rejected immediately. They're not here, but they must be inside or on the other side of the mill, or they're sleeping in the shade under the cart.

The cart isn't there, either. That light-blue cart with a rooster painted on the back.

And then the fear wells up, filling him, just like when they fill the little pitcher at the well, the water surges, pushing the air out and overflowing. The stream of fear is too strong for his three-year-old body and it fills up quickly, soon he will have no air left. He cannot even burst into tears. Crying requires air, crying is a long, audible exhalation of fear. But there is still hope. I run inside the mill, here the noise is very loud, the movements hasty, two white giants pour grain into the mill's mouth, everything is swathed in a white fog, the enormous spider webs in the corners are heavy with flour, a ray of sunlight passes through the high, broken windows, and in the length of that beam the titanic dust battle can be seen. His mother isn't here. Nor any of his sisters. A hulking man stooped under a sack almost knocks him over. They holler at him to go outside, he's in the way.

Mommy?

The first cry, it's not even a cry, it ends in a question mark.

Moommy?

The "o" lengthens, since the desperation is growing as well.

Mooommy . . . Moooooooommy . . .

The question has disappeared. Hopelessness and rage, a crumb of rage. What else is inside? Bewilderment. How could this be? Mothers don't abandon their children. It's not fair. This just doesn't happen. "Abandon" is a word he doesn't yet know. I don't yet know. The absence of the word does not negate the fear, on the contrary, it heaps up ever higher, making it even more intolerable, crushing. The tears begin, now it's their turn, the only consolers. At least he can cry, the fear has uncorked them, the pitcher of fear has run over. The tears stream down his face, down my face, they mix with the flour dust on the face, water, salt, and flour, and knead the first bread of grief. The bread that never runs out. The bread of sorrow, which will feed us through all the coming years. Its salty taste on the lips. My grandfather swallows. I swallow, too. We are three years old.

At the same time, a light-blue cart with a rooster on the back raises a cloud of dust, getting farther and farther away from the mill.

The year is 1917. The woman driving the cart is twenty-eight years old. She has eight children. Everyone says that she was a large, fair, and handsome woman. Her name also confirms this. Calla. Although in those days it's unlikely that anyone had deduced its meaning from the Greek—beautiful. Calla and that was that. A name. It's wartime. The Great War, as they call it, is nearing its end. And as always, we're on the losing side. The father of my three-year-old grandfather is somewhere on the front. He's been fighting since 1912. There's been no news of him for several months. He comes back for a few days, makes a child, and leaves. Could they have been following orders during those home leaves? The war is dragging on, they're going to need more soldiers. He didn't have much luck with future soldiers, he kept having girls—seven in all.

Surely when he returned to his regiment they would arrest him for every one of them.

Several pieces of silver hidden away for a rainy day have already been spent, the barn has been emptied, the woman has sold everything she could possibly sell—the bed with the springs and metal headboard, a rarity in those days, her two long braids, the string of gold coins from her wedding. The children are crying from hunger. All she has left is an ox and a donkey, which is now pulling the cart. With the ox, she struggles to plow. Autumn is getting on into winter. She has managed to beg off a few sacks of grain and is now on her way back from the mill with three bags of flour. Her daughters are sleeping in the cart amid the sacks. Halfway home they stop to let the donkey rest.

"Mom, we forgot Georgi."

A frightened voice comes from behind her back—Dana, the eldest. Silence.

Silence.

Silence.

Thick and heavy silence. Silence and a secret, which will later be passed on year after year. What is the mother doing, why is she silent, why does she not turn the cart around immediately and race back to the mill?

It's wartime, they're human, they won't leave a three-year-old child all alone. He's a boy, someone will take him in, look after him, there are barren women hungry for children, he'll have better luck. Words that I try to find in her thoughts. But there is only silence there.

We forgot him, we forgot him, the daughter chants behind her back through tears. Never mind that the word is different—we've abandoned him

Yet another long minute goes by. I imagine how in that minute the faces of the unborn look on, holding their breath. There they are, craning their necks through the fence of time, my father, my aunt, my other aunt, there's my brother, there's me, there's my daughter, standing on tiptoes. Their, our appearance over the years depends on that minute and on the young woman's silence. I wonder whether she suspects how many things are being decided now? She finally raises her head, as if waking up, turns in her seat and looks around. The endless plains of Thrace, the scorched stubble fields, the changing light of the sunset, the donkey that is chewing some burned grass, indifferent to everything, the three sacks of flour which will run out right in the middle of winter, three of her seven daughters, who wait to see what she will say.

The sin has already been committed, she has hesitated.

She considered, if only for a minute, abandoning him. Her voice is dry. If you want, you can go back. Said to Dana, the eldest, thirteen. The decision is shoved off onto another. She doesn't say "we'll go back," she doesn't say "go back," she doesn't move. And yet, my three-year-old grandfather still has a chance. Dana leaps from the cart and dashes back down the dirt road.

We, the as-of-yet unborn, craning our necks through the fence of that minute, draw our heads back and breathe a sigh of relief.

Dusk is falling, the mill is miles away. A girl of thirteen is running down a dirt road, barefoot, the evening breeze flutters her dress. Everything around is empty, she runs to tire her own fear, to take its breath away. She doesn't glance aside, every bush resembles a lurking man, all the frightening stories she has listened to in the evenings about brigands, bogeymen, dragons, ghosts, and wolves run in a pack at her heels. If she dares turn around, they will hurl themselves on her. I run, run, run in the still-warm September evening, alone amid the fields, on the baked mud of the road, which I sense more intensely with every step, my heart is pounding in my chest, someone is there crouching along the road, but why is his arm twisted up

like that so strangely, oh it's just a bush . . . There in the distance
the first lights of the mill . . . There I should find my three-year-old
brother . . . my grandfather . . . myself.

The mother, my great-grandmother, lived to be ninety-three, passing from one end of the century to the other, she was part of my
childhood, too. Her children grew up and scattered, they left her,
grew old. Only one of them never left her and took care of her until
her death. The forgotten boy. The story of the mill had entered the
secret family chronicle, everyone whispered it, some with sympathy
for Granny Calla and as proof of how hard the times had been, others as a joke, yet others, such as my grandmother, with undisguised
reproach. But no one ever told it in front of my grandfather. And he
never once told it. And he never parted from his mother.

A tragic irony of the kind we usually discover in myths. When
the story reached me on that afternoon, the main heroine was no
longer with us. I remember how at first I felt anger and bewilderment, as if I myself had been abandoned. I experienced yet another
pang of doubt in the justness of the universe. That woman lived to
a ripe old age under the care of that once-abandoned three-year-old
boy. And perhaps that was precisely her punishment. To live so long
and to see that child before her every day. The abandoned one.

I Hate You, Ariadne

I never forgave Ariadne for betraying her brother. How could you
give a ball of string to the one who would kill your unfortunate,
abandoned brother, driven beastly by the darkness? Some heart-
throb from Athens shows up, turns her head—how hard could that
be, some provincial, big-city girl, that's exactly what she is, a hay
seed and a city girl at the same time, she's never left the rooms of

her father's palace, which is simply a more luxurious labyrinth.

Dana returns to the mill all alone in the darkness and rescues her brother, while Ariadne makes sure that her own brother's murderer doesn't lose his way. I hate you, Ariadne.

In the children's edition of *Ancient Greek Myths*, I drew two bull's horns on Ariadne's head in pen.

Consolation

Grandma, am I going to die?

I'm three, I'm standing next to the bed in the middle of the small room, with one hand I'm clutching my ear, it hurts, with the other I'm tugging on my grandmother's hand and crying as only a scared-to-death three-year-old child can cry. Inconsolably. My great-grandmother, that very same Granny Calla, now over ninety, having seen plenty of death, having buried more than one loved one, an austere woman, is sitting up in bed with tousled hair, no less frightened than I am. It's midnight, the witching hour, as she called it. Grandmaaaa, I'm dying, Grandmaaa, I howl, holding on to my ear.

You're not going to die, my child. Good God, the poor little thing, so he knows about dying, too . . .

My mother runs in and catches sight of us like that, embracing and crying in the dark. I can imagine that composition clearly— a boy of three, barefoot, in short pajamas and a desiccated ninety-year-old woman in her nightgown, who, incidentally, will pass away in only a few days. Crying and talking about death. Perhaps death was hovering nearby, perhaps children can sense it? Hush now, child, you're not going to die, my great-grandmother repeated then, to console me. There's an order to things, my child, first I'll die, then your grandma and your grandpa, then . . . And this made me bawl all the harder. A consolation built on a chain of deaths.

My great-grandmother died exactly one week later. Just like that, out of nowhere, she lay in bed for a day or two and passed away on New Year's Eve. That was the first death I remember, even though they didn't let me watch. She was lying on the bed in the room, small and waxen, like an old woman-doll, I thought to myself then, even though dolls never get old. In the middle of the room, reaching almost to the ceiling, stood the Christmas tree, decorated with cotton, silver tin-foil garlands, and those fragile ornaments from the '70s, which lay all year carefully wrapped in a box in the wardrobe. Each of those shiny colored orbs during that unforgettable New Year's Eve reflected my dead great-grandmother.

I was more worried about my grandfather, who was sitting at her feet, crying quietly. This time abandoned for good.

Much later my grandfather would lie in that same bed one January night and take his leave of us, since he had a long road ahead of him. Mom is calling me to help her with the sacks . . .

Trophy Words

Szervusz, kenyér, bor, víz, köszönöm, szép, isten veled . . .

I will never forget that strange rosary of words. My grandfather strung them out on the long winter evenings we spent together during my childhood vacations. Hello, bread, wine, water, thank you, beautiful, farewell . . . Immediately following my grandmother's quick and semi-conspiratorially whispered prayer would come his *szervusz, kenyér, bor . . .*

He always said that he used to be able to speak Hungarian for hours, but now in his old age all he had left was this handful of words. His trophy from the front. My grandfather's seven Hungarian words, which he guarded like silver spoons. My grandmother was certainly jealous of them. Because why would a soldier need to know the word for "beautiful"? And she simply could not accept calling "bread" by such a strange and distorted name. God Almighty, Blessed Virgin, what an ugly word! Those folks have committed a terrible sin. How can you call bread "*kenyér*," she fumed, in dead seriousness.

Bread is bread.

Water is water.

Without having read Plato, she shared his idea of the innate correctness of names. Names were correct by nature, never mind that this nature always turned out to be precisely the Bulgarian one.

My grandma never failed to mention that the other soldiers from the village had brought real trophies home from the front, this one a watch, that one a pot, yet another a full set of silver spoons and forks. Stolen, added my grandfather, and they had never even taken them out to eat with, I know their type.

But my grandmother and Hungary were not at all on friendly terms, between them that spirit of understanding and cooperation, as it was called in the newspapers back then, just didn't work out. Quite a while later I came to understand the reason for this tension.

I found it strange that my grandfather didn't like to talk about the war. Or at least he didn't talk about the things I expected to hear and had seen in movies, the constant battles, artillery fire, kurrr-kur-kurrr (all our toys were machine guns and pistols). I clearly remember asking him how many fascists he had killed and bloodthirstily awaited the tally. Even though I already knew that he couldn't chalk up a single kill to his name. Not one. And to tell you the truth, I was a bit ashamed of him. Dimo's grandfather from the other neighborhood had shot thirty-eight, most point-blank, and had stabbed another twenty in the gut with his bayonet. Dimo took a step forward, thrust the invisible bayonet a foot into my stomach and twisted it. I think I gave him a good scare when I dropped to the ground pale and started throwing up. It's awful getting stabbed in the stomach with a bayonet. I barely survived.

Live Medicine

The slugs slowly drag themselves across the newspaper, without letting go of it. Several are timidly clinging together, body to body. My grandfather grabs one with two fingers, closes his eyes, opens his mouth and slowly places the slug inside, close to his throat. He swallows. My stomach turns. I'm afraid for Grandpa. And I want to be able to do as he does. My grandfather has an ulcer. The slugs are his living medicine. They go in, make their way through the esophagus and stop in the soft cave of the stomach, leaving their slimy trail there, which forms something like a protective film on top, a thin medicinal layer that seals off the wound. He learned this recipe on the front. Whether the slugs come out the other end alive and well afterward, or die as volunteers, plugging up the embrasure of the stomach lining . . .

A huge hand lifts me up and sets me at the opening of a red, warm and moist cave. It is not unpleasant, even if a bit frightening. The red thing I have been placed on constantly twitches, slightly bucking and rising, which forces me to crawl farther in toward the only available corridor. At the entrance there is a soft barrier, it isn't difficult to overcome. It's as if it opens on its own, in any case it reacts when I touch it. Now there's the tunnel, dark and soft, which I sink into, horns forward, like a slow bull. I leave a trail behind me to mark the way back. I feel safer with it. The path down is easy, short in any case. The tunnel soon broadens and ends in a wider space, a rather soft cave different from the first one I passed through. At one end I notice a brighter spot, sore and radiating warmth. I pass over it slowly, leaving a little slime. I don't like this place at all, though. It's cramped, dark, and musty, claustrophobic, as if the walls of the cave are shrinking and pressing in on me. But the scariest part is some strange liquid that the walls themselves are pouring over me and which is starting to sting. I don't have the strength to budge, as in a nightmare where you keep moving more slowly and slowly and slow . . .

To feel for everything, to be simultaneously the swallowed snail and the snail swallower, the eaten and the eater . . . How could you forget those few short years when you could do so?

Sometimes, while writing, he feels like a slug, which is crawling in an unknown direction (in fact, the direction is known—there where everything goes), leaving behind itself a trail of words. It's doubtful whether he'll ever follow it back, but along the way, without even meaning to, the trail may turn out to be healing for some ulcer. Rarely for his own.

Have a Good Trip

And yet, my grandfather did have his secret from the war. On that January night, when he wanted the two of us to be left alone, the door to the unspoken opened just a crack . . . He called me in, the eldest of his grandsons, the one who bore his name, I was 27. We were standing in his room, low-ceilinged, with a little window, where he had grown up with his seven sisters, where I had spent all my summer vacations as a child. He could hardly speak due to the recent stroke. It was just the two of us, he went over to the wooden sideboard, rummaged at length in one of the drawers, and there, from beneath the newspaper lining the drawer's bottom, he pulled out an ordinary sheet of notebook paper, folded into four, quite rumpled, and yellowed. Without opening it, he pressed it into my hand and signaled to me to hide it. Then we sat there, embracing, as we had when I was a child. We heard my father's footsteps in front of the house and let go. Two days later, my grandfather passed away. It was the end of January.

Lots of people came to see him off. He probably would've been anxious if he had seen them. The sons and daughters of his seven sisters arrived from all over, laid some meager winter flower by his head and placed their order for the beyond. The dead man is something like express mail in these parts. Okay now, Uncle, give Mom our best wishes when you see her. Tell her we're fine, that little Dana is graduated this year, everything is tip-top. Oh, and also tell her that her other granddaughter left for Italy. For now she's just washing dishes, but she's got high hopes. Well, okay then, Uncle, have a good trip. Afterward the nephew giving these instructions kisses the dead man's hand and moves away. He returns again shortly, apologizing, he'd forgotten to say that they'd sold the house in the village, but it was bought by good people, all the way from England. Well okay, goodbye again and have a good trip. Have a good trip. In these southeastern regions people don't say "rest in peace" . . . they just wish you a good trip. Have a good trip.

Side Corridor

A friend told me how as a child she was convinced that Hungary was up in the sky. Her grandmother was Hungarian and every summer she came to visit her daughter and her beloved granddaughter in Sofia. They always met her at the airport. They would arrive quite early, craning their heads upward like chicks until their necks grew sore, her mother would tell her: your grandma will show up any minute now. The grandmother from Hungary who came out of the sky. I like this story, I immediately tuck it away in the warehouse.

I suspect that when the Hungarian grandmother passed away she simply stayed up there in heavenly Hungary, waving from some cloud—except that now she no longer lands.

The Chiffonier of Memories

Four months later, in the middle of May, I was driving to Hungary in an old Opel. I had suggested to the newspaper I was working for that I write a story about Bulgarian military cemeteries from the World War II. The largest one is in Harkány in southern Hungary.

The boss agreed and here I am on the road through Serbia. Harkány, once a village, now a small town, is close to the site of the Battles of Drava. I soon left the highway and chose a more varied route through Stracin, Kumanovo, Prishtina, then I turned toward Kriva Palanka, through Niš, Novi Sad . . . I wanted to take all the roads my grandfather had trudged on foot through the mud in the winter of 1944. I had carefully studied the available military maps for the movements of the 11th Sliven Infantry Regiment, 3rd Infantry Division, First Army. I drove, and in my pocket sat that folded sheet of paper. A Hungarian address was written on it.

I reached Harkány. There would be time for the military cemetery. Before that I wanted to find a house. I wandered for a while before I found the street written on the paper. Thank God the street name hadn't been changed during those fifty years. I parked the car at the very end of the street and set out to find the house. It was only now that I stopped to think that, in fact, I had no idea what I was expecting from this late visit. My grandfather had lived here, billeted during those couple of calm weeks before the battles. Happy and worried at the same time. There's the house, built before the war. It's larger than my grandfather's, I note with a certain envy, more Central European. It has a big garden with blooming spring flowers, but my grandma's tulip's are prettier, I tell myself in passing. At the far end of the garden there is an arbor, sitting inside it is a woman my grandfather's age, with white, well-groomed hair, with no kerchief. I realize there's no telling who she may be. Over fifty years, houses change their inhabitants, people move, they die. I push open the front gate, a bell above it announces my arrival. A man in his 50s comes out of the house. I greet him in English— I could've done it in Hungarian, thanks to my grandfather's lessons, but I keep that to myself for now. Thank God, he speaks English, too. I explain that I am a journalist from Bulgaria, I even show him my press badge from the newspaper and say that I'm writing an article about Bulgarian soldiers who fought in this region during World War II. Have you been to the cemetery? The man asks me. I say that I haven't been there yet. I'm interested in what the people living here know, what they remember. He finally invites me into the arbor with the elderly woman.

This is my mother, he says. We hold out our hands. A light, distrustful handshake. Her memory is failing, he explains. She can't remember what she ate for dinner last night, but she remembers the war, there were Bulgarian soldiers here, I think they were even quartered here in the house. Then he turns to her and obviously tells her who I am and where I've come from. She only now notices me. Her memory is a chiffonier, I can sense her opening the long locked-up drawers. A long minute, she has to wade back through more than fifty years, after all. The man seems ill at ease with this silence. He asks her something. She turns her head slightly, without taking her eyes off me. It could pass as a tick, a negative response, or part of her own internal monologue. The man turns to me and says that at the end of January she suffered a brain hemorrhage and now her memory is no longer quite all there.

The end of January, you say?

Yes, the man says, slightly puzzled. What difference could that make to a foreigner?

My grandfather fought in this region, I say.

The man translates. I can't explain how, but I'm sure she recognizes me. I'm the exact age now that my grandfather had been back then. My grandma also said that I am the spitting image of him—the same bulging Adam's apple, lanky and slightly hunched, with the same distracted gait and slightly crooked nose. The old woman says something to her son, he jumps up, apologizing that he hasn't offered me anything to drink and suggests cherry cake and coffee. I accept, since I want to stay here longer and he darts into the house. We are finally alone, sitting across from each other at the rough-hewn table in the arbor. The table is quite old—I wonder if my grandfather sat in this very arbor? Spring has gone berserk, bees are buzzing, nameless scents waft through the air, as if the world has just been created, without a past, without a future, a world in all its innocence, before chronology.

We look at each other. Between us lie almost sixty years and a man whom she remembers at twenty-five, and whom I saw off a few months ago at eighty-two. And no language in which we can say everything.

She had been a beautiful woman. I try to see her with my grandfather's eyes from January of 1945. Amid all the ugliness, mud and death of the war you enter (I enter) the European home of a girl of twenty-something, blonde, with lovely skin and large eyes. Inside there is a gramophone, something you have never seen, music unlike any you've ever heard is playing. She is wearing a long, urban dress. It is calm and bright throughout the whole house, a sunbeam passes through the curtains, falling precisely on the porcelain bowl on the table. As if the war had never been. She is reading in a chair by the window. Some sound draws me out of the picture. Her glasses have fallen to the ground, I hand them to her. Crossing over half a century instantaneously is frightening. That beautiful face suddenly wrinkles and ages in seconds. First I thought of showing her the paper from my grandfather. Then I decided that I shouldn't. We've had these few minutes alone (how clever of her to send her son away).

In front of her stands the grandson of that man. So everything has worked out as it should. Finally, here is the living letter, sent with such delay. So he survived. He returned to his wife and his infant son, the son grew up and had a son . . . And now here is the grandson, sitting in front of her. Life had taken a turn, she had been forgotten, gotten over, everything worked out as it should . . . A long-deferred tear trickles from her eye and gets lost in the endless labyrinth of wrinkles on her palm.

She grasps my hand, without taking her eyes from mine, saying slowly in impeccable Bulgarian: *hello, thank you, bread, wine* . . . I continue in Hungarian: *szép* (beautiful). I said it as if passing on a secret message from my dead grandfather and she understood. She squeezed my hand and let it go. The last two Bulgarian words I heard from her were "farewell" and "Georgi." My grandfather and I had the same name. Her son reappears with the coffee, he immediately notices that his mother has cried, but doesn't dare ask. We drink coffee, I ask him what he does, it turns out he's a veterinarian (like my father, I was about to say, but take a sip of my coffee instead).

Is your grandfather still alive, he asks politely. He passed away in January, I reply. I'm really sorry to hear that, my condolences . . . I could clearly see that he did not suspect anything. She had decided to spare him that. Or perhaps I have imagined everything. I've avoided looking at him the whole time, so as not to discover too much of a likeness. After all, the world is full of men with crooked noses and bulging Adam's apples. I got up to leave and kissed the woman's hand. At the front gate he shook my hand just a second too long and for an instant I thought he must know everything. I quickly let go and headed around the corner to the car. I opened up the sheet of paper from my grandfather. A baby's hand from 1945 had been traced in pencil above the address. Who could say whether it was the same one I had just shaken goodbye?

The Good Man Flees When One Pursues

A few years ago I had to get a new passport and take care of a few formalities at the town hall. I filled in my personal data—divorced, tall, college-educated . . . I turned in the form at the window, the woman compared it to the information she had in the computer, looked at me, and said coldly: "Why are you hiding a child?" This statement echoed loudly enough, I could sense how everyone filling out forms around me suddenly looked up, it even seemed that they drew back slightly. I myself stood there like someone caught at the scene of a crime. I've noticed that I can more easily make excuses for things I have done, but when I am accused of something that has never even crossed my mind, I freeze up, guilty. As the saying goes, the wicked man flees though no one pursues. However, for me the opposite was always truer: the good man flees when one pursues.

I kept silent longer than was probably acceptable before managing to utter that I have only one daughter. In that time—how unsure one is of his own innocence!—I calculated all my past relationships. I recalled one girlfriend who claimed to be pregnant every time we were on the verge of breaking up. You have a twelve-year-old son, the woman at the window announced unceremoniously. I stood there thunderstruck. All that was missing was for her to add "congratulations." Can I see? I asked. She turned the monitor toward me and, thank God, it wasn't me, just a case of identical names. The woman didn't even apologize, turning around angrily in her chair, disappointed that I'd gotten away so easily. If she had known that I would spend the rest of the day going over in my mind all the women I had been with twelve years ago, even listing them by initials on a piece of paper, rating on a scale from 1 to 10 the potential risk of having a child I didn't know about with each of them . . . If she had only known that, she would have been somewhat satisfied.

The Cellar of the Story

But perhaps the story went like this.

March 1945. The war is coming to an end. A battle for a small Hungarian town, ferocious, the upper hand constantly changing, street by street. A Bulgarian soldier is seriously wounded and loses consciousness. His regiment is pushed back, the city remains temporarily (for a few days) in German hands. The soldier comes to in a cellar, lying on an old bed, above him stands the woman who has bandaged him up. She had managed to drag his body from the sidewalk straight through the little basement window, which is at street level.

She signals to him not to move, but he couldn't even if he wanted to, he's lost a lot of blood. In very bad German, the enemy's language, he manages to exchange a few words with the Hungarian woman. Days go by, weeks, a month. Sometimes he loses consciousness, then wakes up again, still on the cusp between life and death. She continues bringing him food every day, applying compresses, changing his bandages . . . By the second month he has visibly improved, it's clear that he'll survive. The woman tells him that the little town is still in German hands and that the war has dragged on.

She lives alone, a widow, childless, she's the same age as the soldier, around twenty-five. She falls in love with the wounded man. And because of him, she decides to change the entire course of the war. The Germans have not surrendered, they've come up with a secret weapon that has slowed everything down, the front has been pushed back east. Once she even fakes a search of the house. The man in the cellar only hears someone stomping the floor above him with roughshod boots and hurling the chairs to the ground, some containers fall, the sound of a broken dish . . . He grips his machine gun, ready to shoot the first ones to enter the cellar, but he remains undiscovered, thank God.

The closed space of that little room starts driving him mad. The sole small window has been boarded up with sheet metal. Through a single thin crack—good thing the sheet metal is bent—a bit of light gets in, just enough to distinguish day from night. He can't stop tormenting himself with the question of how a practically finished, a practically won war could so suddenly change its course. And how long he will remain unnoticed by the Germans in this basement.

We should note that he, too, has secretly fallen in love with the woman taking care of him, but he does not yet want to admit it to himself. There, in his home country, he has a wife and child, who certainly think him dead. One night his rescuer stays with him, she merely touches his face and that is enough.

It was unexpected, as always happens after a long wait, they embraced, their breaths quickened, they uttered some fragmented words, passionate, tired, amorous, each in his own language. He didn't understand any of that crazy Hungarian, she didn't understand any of that crazy Bulgarian. Afterward silence fell, in which the two of them lay side by side. Languor and happiness on her part. Languor, happiness, and some unclear alarm (but clear guilt) on his. He tells her, in Bulgarian, that he has a wife and little boy, whom he left when the child was only a week old. Both to salve his conscience that he said it, yet also for her not to understand because it was in Bulgarian. He didn't know that when it comes to understanding things they shouldn't, women have another literacy altogether. The Hungarian woman got up suddenly and went upstairs. For several days he did not see her at all.

One afternoon a sudden blow smashed through the window of the cellar. The man leapt up—he always slept with his weapon by his side—and hid in the corner. The light pouring in stung his eyes. Soon a boy's tousled head poked through the window. The man crouched behind a huge barrel. Only then did he see the heavy rag ball a meter away from him. The boy muttered something, crawled like a lizard through the narrow window and slipped inside. The man held his breath. The boy was so close that he could feel the warmth of his sweaty body. The boy grabbed the ball, tossed it through the window, pulled himself up on the ledge and wriggled out.

Along with dust and the scent of cat urine, the wind blew a scrap of an old newspaper through the window. And even though it was in Hungarian, he could still make out *Hitler Kaput* and see the photo of the Russian soldier raising a flag over the Reichstag.

He understood everything. He battered down the door and went up the stairs with his carbine. The light stung his eyes, and he hung on to the furniture as he walked. The woman was standing in front of him. She told him that he could shoot her or stay with her. She told him that she loved him and that they could live together, she also told him that he wouldn't get very far with that rifle and his military uniform, that the world was no longer the same a whole month after the end of the war. Yes, it turned out that it was already June. She spoke softly, mixing Hungarian and German. He, mixing German and Bulgarian, replied that she was his savior and without her he would now be rotting on the Hungarian steppe. He also said that he would like to live with her until the end of his days (that was in Bulgarian), but that he had to go back to his son, who by now must be more than six months old, but that even if he tried, he would never be able to forget her. And both of them knew that once they parted, they would never see each other again. And that if they embraced now, they would never let each other go. Fortunately for his son, who was nine months old, each of them swallowed back their desires. In the end, they just said awkwardly: well, okay then, farewell. She filled him a backpack with whatever there was to eat and burst into tears only when the bell above the front gate jingled behind him.

The town of H. and his village in Bulgaria were separated by exactly 965 kilometers and two borders. He walked only at night, first, so as not to meet people, and second, because during the day his eyes continued to ache terribly from the light. He walked back along the same route he had trod with his regiment half a year earlier. He hid in abandoned shacks, burned out villages, he slept by day in old foxholes, trenches, and pits dug by bombs. In the end he had decided to leave his weapon and uniform with the Hungarian woman, so as not to attract attention. She had given him a real knitted sweater—this June happened to be cold and rainy—and a good hunting jacket with lots of pockets, left over from her late husband. And so, without a weapon, without epaulets or ID papers, he retraced the path of the war, always heading east, hiding from everyone. On the thirty-fourth day, in the middle of July, he reached his village. He waited until midnight and slipped like a thief into his own home. His parents were sleeping on the second floor, his wife and son were most likely downstairs, in the room next to the shed. This scene of recognition is clear. Fear, horror, and joy all in one. The dead husband returns. Here he was already proclaimed a fallen hero, awarded some small medal, his name had even been chiseled into the hastily erected memorial on the village square, alongside the names of his fellow villagers who had died to liberate the homeland. His reappearance, like all resurrections, only upset the normal course of life.

What now? Bulgarian joy is quickly replaced by fretting. They woke up the parents and they all started asking the risen one how it had all happened and what are we going to do now? That he's safe and sound is all very well and good, but it creates some mighty big headaches as well. The resurrected soldier was so exhausted that he couldn't explain a thing. As the third rooster crowed and day began to break, the family council made the only possible decision—to stick him in the cellar, both so he could sleep and so that no one would see him. Thus the returning Bulgarian soldier spent his first night at home—as well as all the following days and nights over the course of several months. He simply exchanged one basement for another.

Those were troubled times. The communists were roaming the country, killing for the slightest infraction. The soldier's family was in any case on the list of village high-rollers, thanks to their three cows, herd of sheep, and nice old-fashioned cart with the rooster painted on the back. But what sin could the soldier possibly have committed? I'll tell you what. First of all, he lied to the authorities about his heroic death, for which he had been crowned with a medal and glorified on the village memorial. The other thing that would earn him a bullet straight away was separation or desertion from his army unit. To disappear from your regiment for four months, without death as an alibi, and then to return a month after the end of the war without the weapon and uniform issued to you likely goes beyond the imagination of even the most merciful political commissar. What could the soldier possibly say in his own defense? The truth? Admit that he had spent four months in a Hungarian town with a lonely young widow, hiding in a basement long after the town had been liberated by his countrymen? Who, in fact, were you hiding from, comrade corporal?

The resurrected man's wife continued to wear black. To her, he told almost the whole truth. He simply added thirty or so years to the compassionate Hungarian lady's age and everything fell into place. The elderly Hungarian woman had lied to him about the continuation of the war and a German siege, because her motherly heart had wanted him, the Bulgarian soldier, to replace the son of the same age that she had lost.

His wife was a decent and reasonable woman, she was glad that her husband had returned alive and did not wish to know more. Even when she carelessly opened that envelope which the postman, her brother's son, had furtively pressed into her hands, with only a baby's handprint and an unreadable address, she didn't say anything, but painstakingly sealed it up again, gave it to her husband and continued wearing her widow's weeds.

A year later, half-blind from staying in the dark, the man came out of the cellar and went to give himself up. He gave them the scare of their lives. His beard and hair had gone white during that year, they could hardly recognize him. Where did you come from, the mayor asked him. From the other world, the soldier said and that was the most precise answer. He quickly told some poorly patched together story about how he fell prisoner to the Germans during the attack on H., how he was sent to work in the salt mines behind German lines, how they worked there, slept there—in the end the Germans were forced to beat a hasty retreat and dynamited the entrance to the mine. Of the thirty prisoners, he was the only survivor and found a hole to crawl out of. But from that long stay in the dark he had badly damaged his eyes and so, half-blind, he had traveled for months before reaching his home village. The mayor listened, his fellow villagers who had gathered around in the meantime listened. The women bawled, the men blew their noses noisily so as not to bawl themselves, while the mayor grimly crumpled his cap. Whether the people really swallowed that story or whether they wanted to save him is unclear, but in any case they all decided to believe it, and the mayor helped arrange things with the higher-ups in the city. They quietly reissued the dead man's passport, cut off his wife's widow's pension, only his name remained on the memorial. And so as to do away with any lingering doubts, the mayor ordered the local bard to make up a song about the soldier who happily returned home a year and some after the end of the war. The song was a heroic one, according to all the rules of the time, telling at great length and breadth about "his dark suffering in the mine so deep" and how Georgi the Talashmaner (from the name of the village) "tossed the boulder to make his way, to see the sun" with Herculean strength. This was followed by his almost Odyssey-length return and the blind hero's miraculous orientation toward his beloved homeland and the village of his birth.

Risen Georgi (that's what they called him in the village) lived a long life, he saw well in the evenings, but by day was blind as a mole. He came out of the basement, yet the basement stayed inside him. During that year and a half, several lives had happened to him and it became ever harder for him to remember which of them was the real one.

Perhaps he had perished in that little Hungarian town after all? Was that Hungarian woman who changed the course of the war to keep him really young, or was she an old woman who had lost her son? How did he manage to escape from the German mine? And that which gave him no peace until the very end—the child's hand, traced on an ordinary white sheet of notebook paper and sent in a postal envelope.

(Both versions end with the same small child's hand, traced on a piece of paper. But stories always end in one of two ways—with a child or with death.)

A Place to Stop

Let's wait here for the souls of distracted readers. Somebody could have gotten lost in the corridors of these different times. Did everyone come back from the war? How about from the fair in 1925? Let's hope we didn't forget anyone at the mill. So where shall we set out for now? Writers shouldn't ask such questions, but as the most hesitant and unsure among them, I'll take that liberty. Shall we turn toward the story of the father, or continue on ahead, which in this case is backward, toward the Minotaur of childhood . . . I can't offer a linear story, because no labyrinth and no story is ever linear. Are we all here? Off we go again.

A Short Catalogue of Abandonments

The history of the family can be described through the abandonment of several children. The history of the world, too.

The abandoned child with the bull's head, thrown into Minos's labyrinth . . .

The abandoned Oedipus, the little boy with the pierced ankles, tossed on the mountainside in a basket, who would be adopted first by King Polybus, later by Sophocles, and in the end by his later father, Sigmund Freud.

The abandoned Hansel and Gretel, the Ugly Duckling, the Little Match Girl, and the grown-up Jesus, she wants to go to her grandmother's house, he to his father's . . .

In this line come—even without legends to back them up—all those abandoned now or in the past, and all those who shall be abandoned. Having fallen from the manger of myth, let us take them in, in this inn of words, spread beneath them the clean sheets of history, tuck in their frostbitten souls. And leave them in hands, which, as they turn these pages, shall stroke their frightened backs and heads.

How many readers here have not felt abandoned at least once? How many would admit that at least once they have been locked in a room, a closet, or a basement, for edification? And how many would dare say that they have not done the locking up?

In the beginning, I said, there is a child tossed into a cellar.

The Basement

For a long time, I used to watch the world through a window at sidewalk level. The apartments changed, but every one of them had one such low window. We always lived in the basement, the rooms were cheapest there. My mother, father, and I had just moved into yet another basement. Actually, into another "former basement," as the landlord said. There's no such thing as a former basement, my father replied sharply, and the landlord, not knowing how to take this, just laughed. In these parts, when somebody feels uncomfortable, he starts laughing, who knows why.

It's temporary, my father said, as we carried in the table. It was the mid-70s, I knew that we were defined as "extremely indigent," I knew that the extremely indigent were those who inhabited a space of less than five square meters per person, and we were waiting our turn for an apartment on some list. Clearly, the list was quite long or someone was cutting in line, because we continued to live in that basement room for several years. On the "ground floor" (which was, in fact, underground), there was a long corridor and just one other room, always locked. I didn't ask why we didn't rent it as well, I knew the answer, we're saving money for an apartment. Plus, we had to maintain that cramped five square meters per person so as not to slip from the category of the extremely indigent. The long corridor played the role of entrance hall and kitchen, but it was so narrow that it had room for only two chairs, a hotplate, and something like a little table. When my mom and dad fought, my dad would go out there to sleep, on the table. He also listened to Radio Free Europe there, secretly, on an old taped-up Selena. I was very proud that my father listened to that station, because I knew it was forbidden. Actually, I was proud that I was part of the conspiracy. When you share a single room, you can't keep too many secrets.

In fact, the house where that basement apartment was located was downright beautiful. Three stories with big, light windows looming up above. Thousands of shards of glass from beer bottles, green and brown, had been stuck into the deliberately rough plaster, following the fashion of the times, and they sparkled like diamonds in the sun. And the third floor formed a slight semi-circle, almost like a castle. What would it be like to live there, in that round room, with its round windows and curved balcony? A room without edges. From up above you could probably see the whole city and the river. You could see everyone who passes by on the street, and full-length at that, not just as strange creatures made solely of legs and shoes. At school, I never failed to mention that I lived in that house with the rounded tower. Which was the truth. Of course, I didn't specify which floor.

At the same time, my father dreamed of an apartment with a living room, fully furnished with a drawing-room suite, he could see himself sitting in the large, square armchair with his paper, legs propped on the footstool. He had seen this in a Neckermann catalogue, which some family friends had briefly lent us. My mother dreamed of a real kitchen with cupboards, where she could line up the little white porcelain jars of spices she would some day purchase. I would suspect that same West German Neckermann was responsible for that dream as well.

. . .

Feet and cats. Indolent, slow, cat-length afternoons. I would spend the whole day glued to the window, because it was the lightest place. I would count the passing feet and put together the people above them.

Men's feet, women's feet, children's feet . . . I watched the seasons change through the change of shoes. Sandals, which gradually closed up, transforming into fall shoes, which later crept up the leg, exquisite ladies' boots, the stylish ones made of pleated patent leather, the workers' coarse rubber boots that took out the trashcans, the villagers' galoshes, arriving for the market on Thursday, the blue or red kids' boots, the only colorful splotches amid the overwhelming brown and black. And again the gradual spring easing, the undressing of shoes down to the bare summer soles, ankles and toes, shod only in sandals and flip-flops. The flip-flops were something like swimsuits for feet.

During autumn, the window became piled with yellowish-brown fallen leaves from the sidewalk, making the light in the room soft and yellow. Then the late autumn wind would scatter them. The rains would come—and the eternal puddle out front. I could sit and watch the drops falling into it for hours, forming fleeting bubbles, whole armadas of ships, which the drops would then smash. How many historic sea battles unfolded in that puddle! Then the snow would bury the little window and the room would become a den. I would curl up into a ball like a rabbit under the snow. It is so light, yet you are hidden, invisible to the others, whose footsteps crunch in the snow only inches away from you. What could be lovelier than that?

The God of the Ants

He was six when they started leaving him home alone. In the morning his mother and father would light the gas heater, constantly telling him to keep an eye on the flow of gas inside the little tube. Two gas heaters on their street had exploded. They left him food in the refrigerator and went out. A typical 1970s childhood. Left on his own all day, with that early unnamed feeling of abandonment. The half-dark room frightened him. He would spend the warm autumn days outside. He would sit on a rock by the gate, on the sidewalk, like a little old man, counting the people passing by, the cars, the makes of the cars. He'd try to guess them from the humming before they appeared from around the curve. Moskvitch, Moskvitch, Zhiguli, Trabant, Polski Fiat, Zhiguli, Moskvitch, Moskvitch . . . When he got tired of that, he would rest his head on his knees and stare at the stone slabs of the sidewalk. Each slab was crisscrossed uniformly by vertical and horizontal lines, and in the furrows they created ants would run, meet and pass one another. This was a whole other, quasi-visible world. It looked like the labyrinth from that book with the illustrations. He would sit like that for hours, thinking up stories for every ant. He observed them with the skill of a naturalist, without knowing the word, of course. He would study them, devoting to them hours of the time he was so generously allotted. Each ant was different from the others.

Sometimes he would imagine that he was the God of the Ants.

Most often he was a kind God, helping them, dropping crumbs or a dead fly down to them, nudging it with a stick toward their home so they wouldn't have to struggle to carry it.

But sometimes he grew wrathful without reason, like the real God, or he simply felt like playing and so would pour a pitcher of water into the corridors of the labyrinth. He made a flood for them.

Other times he would pour salt at the ends of the flagstone, he had discovered by chance that they detested salt, and they would stagger through the corridors of that temporary prison, frightened senseless. When they met, they would quickly press their feelers together, as if passing on some very important secret.

His other discovery, divine and scientific, was that ants hate the scent of humans. If you trace a circle around an ant with your finger, it will run up against that invisible border as if you had built a wall.

He had already noticed this ability of his, he considered it a terrible defect to be able to experience that which happened to others. To *emplant* himself—the word would come later—into their bodies. To be them.

One night he dreamed that he, his mother, and his father were walking down the street and suddenly a giant finger, whose nail alone was as big as a cliff, thumped down and began circling around them. And as if it wasn't terrifying enough that this finger could crush them at any second, just like that, out of carelessness, it also reeked toxically to boot. A stench you could ram into and crack your skull on.

But in the winter things change, you can't stay outside all day. The room grows ever dimmer, the stove smells like gas, while scary things peek out from under the bed or creak inside the worm-eaten wardrobe. The only salvation then is the window. He would climb up to it in the morning and get down only to eat his slice of bread at lunchtime and to pee.

A Place to Stop

I'm thinking about the first person, which easily recedes into the third, before returning again to the first. But who can say for certain that that boy there forty years ago was me, that that body is the same as the one here? Even the ants from 1975 are not the same. I don't find any similarities between the body of a six-year-old, with that thin, pale-pink skin and invisible blond fuzz on his legs. No preserved sign of identification, no trace, except the vaccination scar with which our whole generation is marked. That nearly invisible scar on the shoulder, which over the years has treacherously grown and begun to creep downward.

A detour within a detour. A friend of mine told me a story about how after an amorous night, when she was lying exhausted on the floor with her younger lover, he suddenly asked her (with certain sympathy) what that scar on her arm was from (it had already left her shoulder). She then realized with horror that he didn't have that vaccination brand anywhere on his shoulders. Those who came after us are no longer marked in that way, she said, he seemed like an alien to me, like a clone. She got up, got dressed, and they never saw each other again.

Ant-God

Most likely all dreams, when being retold, should begin with the opening statement, revealing and startling in its simplicity, which I heard from Aya, who was then four: I dreamed that I was awake.

And so, I dreamed that I was awake. I was standing in front of huge curtains with nameless colors that flowed into one another—like I said, huge, but light and ephemeral. It was made clear to me in the dream that concealed behind them was "the beautiful face of God," in those exact words. I draw aside the first curtain. (It seems that between curiosity and fear, curiosity always takes the upper hand, or at least that's how it is in dreams.)

Behind it there was a second one. I draw it aside.

A third.

A fourth.

I notice that every subsequent curtain becomes ever smaller and smaller. Hence whatever it was hiding is ever smaller as well. I keep drawing them aside until finally only one is left, the size of a child's handkerchief. I stop myself. Should I really draw this curtain? Could God possibly be so small? Perhaps the Antichrist is tempting me in my dreams?

I draw it aside. Behind it stands a big black ant. And I somehow know that this is God. But he has no face. The discovery is terrifying. How can you pray to and trust in someone who has no face? Someone who is that small? The revelation that the Ant-God gave me in the moment of awakening, without opening its jaws, went more or less like this: God is an insect who watches us. Only small things can be everywhere.

Crumbling Language

I learned the alphabet from the cemetery in that town languishing in the sun. I could put it this way, too—death was my first primer. The dead taught me to read. This statement should be taken absolutely literally. We went there every Thursday and Saturday. I stood reverentially before the hot stone crosses. I was as tall as they were. With a certain dread, I dragged my finger along the grooves, reading more through my skin, I memorized the half-moon of *C*, the door of *H*, and the hut of *A*. Language seemed warm and hard. It had a crumbling body. Only a bit of dust and fine sand remained on my fingers from the stone. The first words I learned were:

rest
eternal
here
memory
born – died
God

And names, so many names, cemeteries are teeming with names.

Atanas H. Grozdanov
Dimitar Hadzhinaumov
Marincho — 5 years old
Dimo Korabov
Georgi Gospodinov
Egur Sarkissian (Granny Sarkistsa's son)
Calla Georgieva

. . .

What happened to the names after their owners died? Were they set free? Did the names continue to mean something, or did they disintegrate like the bodies beneath them, leaving only the bones of consonants?

Words are our first teachers in death. The first sign of the parting between bodies and their names. The strangest thing about that cemetery was that the names repeated themselves. I stood for a long time in front of a headstone with my name, freed up by someone who had used it for only three years.

Years later, I make a point of visiting the cemeteries in the cities where I am staying. After paying my respects to the central streets, the cathedral on the square, and solemnly passing by the memorial to the relevant king on horseback (will today's presidents jut out above granite limousines tomorrow?), I hasten to inquire after the city cemetery and sink down the walkways of that parallel city-and-park rolled into one. Death is a good gardener. I understood this even back then, at age six, amid the furiously blooming roses, lilies, aromatic bushes, the plums, wild apples, tiny cherries, and rotting pears of the village cemetery.

The crematorium at Père Lachaise resembles a cathedral with a chimney. Adorno says that to write a poem after Auschwitz is barbaric. But can you have crematoriums at all, even in cemeteries?

The dead taught me to read. I write this sentence again and realize that it says more and different things than I had intended. The people who taught me to read are no longer with us. The things which I have read since then were written primarily by the dead. That which I am writing out now are the words of a person who has set off . . . I did not know that so much death dozed beneath language.

G

After the primer of the graveyard I ran up against the real primer for first grade and felt simultaneously enlightened and confused. Every letter was connected to a word and a picture.

What word starts with the letter *G*?

God—I hastily called out, what an easy question. But something wasn't right, the teacher blanched, she was no longer so smiley. She came over to me as if afraid I might say something more. Where did you learn that word? Uh, in the graveyard. Then one of the girls in the front rows said: "Government, Comrade." That was the right answer. And the teacher latched on to that lifeline, excellent, my girl. While I felt so lonely with my God. Strange that you can't have two words with one and the same letter, as if G's curving back was too slippery to hold two such truly grandiose words.

The word "government" begins with G. There is no God in our government! That's just gobbledygook, the teacher accented every G, we'll learn about that later in the upper grades. Are we clear on this?

But he's there in the graveyard . . .

This here is a school, not a . . .

Geez, all these problems just from a single word, I'm going to start hating school before long.

That evening, my mother and father had a serious talk with me. The comrade teacher had told them everything. Well, okay, but there is a God, right? It was as if I had asked them the most difficult question in the world. Look here, my mother started in (she was a lawyer), you know that there is, but you don't need to go throwing his name around left and right, he gets angry if you mention him for no reason in front of strangers.

And as a rule, just keep your mouth shut, my father added.

God was the first secret. The first of the forbidden things that you could only talk about at home.

There's no God in Bulgaria, Grandma, I blurted out as soon as we got home and I caught sight of her pouring oil into the icon lamp on the wall. My grandmother crossed herself quickly and invisibly. She surely would've snapped at me for such talk, but she saw my father in the doorway and merely said: Well, what is there in Bulgaria anyway, there's no paprika, no oil . . . Only she could combine the country's physical and metaphysical deficit like that. God, oil, and paprika.

She would read the Bible furtively, she had wrapped it in a newspaper so it wouldn't show. She would read at random, dragging her arthritis-gnarled index finger along the lines and moving her lips. Thus, I heard the whole Apocalypse in whispers, in the late afternoons of my childhood, under the quiet Jericho trumpets of the flies buzzing around the room.

My grandmother knew she shouldn't talk about such things in front of people, so as to protect my father, who could get into trouble. My father knew that he shouldn't talk about other things and locked himself up with the radio in the kitchen, so as not to screw up my life (that's what my mother said). I knew that I shouldn't talk about anything I'd heard at home, so the police wouldn't come and screw up my parents' lives. A long chain of secrets and lies that made us a normal family. Like all the others. That was the greatest trick of the whole conspiracy—being like the others.

Invisible Ink

At five I learned to read, by six it was already an illness. The indiscriminate guzzling of books. Some kind of literary bulimia. I would read whatever I found and soon reached my mother's bookshelf and that purple volume with a hard cover and a large title reading "Criminology." The first chapter began with the sentence that before the socialist revolution of September 9th, criminology did not exist. While the following one, already having forgotten this, stated that the study of bourgeois criminology was necessary for two reasons: first, to denounce its reactionary essence, and second, to recover everything of value within it . . .

The denunciation was the most interesting part. Only there, between the lines and the distorted quotations, could you understand what was going on in the world after all.

Bourgeois criminology had nevertheless discovered several "minor" things, such as the lie detector, forensic psychology, dactyloscopy. I liked the title *Finger Prints* (1897) by some Francis Galton or other, a bourgeois criminologist.

At the root of revolutionary criminology, of course, stood Lenin. It was obvious that the criminal was in his blood. At the same time, he had laid the foundations of all the other sciences and all text-books confirmed this ab-so-lute-ly (to use one of his favorite words). "Language is the most important means of human communication" was written above the blackboard in the classroom. That genius of the banal.

But the most interesting things in that purple textbook on criminology were the parts on forensic photography, weapons and . . . invisible ink. "Invisible inks are solutions of organic or inorganic substances: fruit juices, onion, sugar solutions, urine, saliva, quinine . . ."

This repulsed and attracted me at the same time. I had never imagined spies as bedwetters writing with urine, syrup, and spit. Scribbling your secret messages in various secretions? Ugh. On the other hand, though, the very accessibility of invisible ink was a welcome discovery. I had everything I needed at hand. For starters, I decided to forgo urine, I went down to the cellar, grabbed a jar of canned peaches, opened it and with the end of a matchstick slowly wrote out the two most secret pages in my diary.

Here I will show part of what was written with invisible fruit ink:

What, so you don't see anything? That means it really is invisible. If only I could write a whole novel in such ink.

Side Corridor

After all the evidence that the history of the past four billion years is written in the DNA of living creatures, the saying that "the universe is a library" has long since ceased to be a metaphor. But now we will need a new literacy. We've got a lot of reading ahead of us. When Mr. Jorge said that he imagined heaven as a library without beginning or end, he most likely, without suspecting it, was thinking about the endless shelves of deoxyribonucleic acid.

I am books.

Dad, What's a Minotaur?

We bang around like Minotaurs in these basements, to heck with their . . . friggin' housing fund and lists. My father made heroic attempts not to curse in front of my mother and me, not unlike his attempts to quit smoking. I was sure that he secretly made up for it, smoking up all those skipped cigarettes and cursing out all those unsaid curses. My father's line following his stumble over the nozzle of our Rocket vacuum cleaner would have important consequences for me. I knew what "friggin" and "housing fund" were, just as I knew about "extremely indigent," "Pershing," and so on, but I didn't know what a Minotaur was. Nor whether it was one of the good guys (our guys) or the bad guys. At that time, I divided everything into those two categories. I discovered with surprise that adults did, too. The world was divided in two—good vs. bad, ours vs. yours. We, as luck would have it, had ended up our side, hence that of "the good guys." However, I had heard my father say in the evenings after the news: "Come on now, how is that idiot Jimmy Carter to blame for the fact that I live in a basement and that there's no lids for the canning jars?!" My mother, who was always more sensible, would shush him. Did they think I would let something slip in front of the local cop who lived two doors down? And they really did draw Jimmy Carter like an idiot in caricatures, with huge teeth, a star-spangled top hat clapped over his eyes, chomping on a winged rocket rather than a cigar.

I've gone down other corridors again, I keep getting mixed up when I turn back. Past time is distinguishable from the present due to one essential feature—it never runs in one direction. Where did

I start? Good thing I'm writing this down, otherwise I'd never find the thread again . . .

We bang around like Minotaurs in these basements . . . That was the line . . . and it immediately entered my as-of-yet unassembled catalogue of epiphanies, of all those revelations, which as a rule appeared in the most unexpected and even inconvenient of moments. My father tripped over the nozzle of the vacuum cleaner because he didn't see it, because it was cramped, we lived underground, the afternoon was overcast, the window was low, and the sun failed to reach down there.

Dad, what's a Minotaur? I asked. My father pretended not to hear me. Dad, is the Minotaur on our side? I think this question irked him all the more. The next day he brought me that old complete edition of Ancient Greek myths from somewhere. I never set the book down again. I entered into the Minotaur then and don't recall ever coming out. He was me. A boy who spent long days and nights in the basement of the palace, while his parents worked as kings or slept with bulls.

Never mind that the book makes him out to be a monster. I was inside him and I know the whole story. A huge mistake and calumny lie hidden there, exceptional injustice. I am the Minotaur and I am not bloodthirsty, I don't want to eat seven youths and seven maidens, I don't know why I've been locked up, it's not my fault . . . And I am terribly afraid of the dark.

II. Against an Abandonment: The Case of M.

In the basement of the palace in Crete, Daedalus built a labyrinth of such confounding galleries that once you went inside it you could never find the exit again. Minos locked up his family's shame, his wife Pasiphaë's son, in this underground labyrinth. She conceived this son by a bull sent by the god Poseidon. The Minotaur—a monster with a human body and a bull's head. Every nine years the Athenians were forced to send seven maidens and seven youths to be devoured by him. Then the hero Theseus appeared, who decided to kill the Minotaur. Without her father's knowledge, Ariadne gave Theseus a sharp sword and a ball of string. He tied the string to the entrance and set off down the endless corridors to hunt the Minotaur. He walked and walked until he suddenly heard a terrible roar— the monster was rushing toward him with its enormous horns. A frightful battle ensued. Finally, Theseus grabbed the Minotaur by the horns and plunged his sharp sword into his chest. The monster slumped to the ground and Theseus dragged him all the way back to the entrance.

—Ancient Greek Myths and Legends

Dossier

Most honorable members of the jury, living and dead, from all times and geographies, ladies and gentlemen collectors and tellers of myths, and you, most honorable Mr. Minos, the present judge from the underworld.

Over the course of 37 years I have been preparing this case, "The Case of M.," and writing arguments in his defense. I began at nine, with my grandfather's indelible pencil in his old soldier's notebook, which he had long since ceased using. (This does not, however, justify my unauthorized appropriation of the notebook. As we see, in the beginning there is always a crime.)

The first version reads as follows:

The Minotaur is not guilty. He is a boy locked up in a basement. He is frightened. They have abandoned him.

I, the Minotaur.

That was the whole text. Written in large capital letters on two pages from the notebook. I include it with the other materials related to the case. In broad terms, that is the basic thesis. Over the years I have merely added further evidence. And I have collected the signs which have come to me on their own.

It is striking that I have not found any compassion for the Minotaur in the whole of the classics. No departure from the established facts, from the monstrous mask once placed on him. Monster is the tamest word bandied about when it comes to the Minotaur in ancient writings. Doesn't Ovid in Metamorphoses call him a "double-natured shame" and "disgrace from his abode" . . . Nothing but a disgrace and a freak. Didn't he suspect that only a few months later he himself would be sent to the Pontus—the depths of the subcelestial Roman labyrinth, from which he would never find his way back. Not all roads lead to Rome when you are in the labyrinth of the provinces, my dear Ovid.

The funny thing is that he is much kindlier toward the Minotaur in one of his earlier books, *Heroides* or *Epistulae Heroidum*. I prefer the translated title "Heroines," as it best captures the heroin of despair. There, the abandoned Ariadne writes to Theseus, who is already sailing for Athens. And there, for the first time, this accessory to the Minotaur's murder, motivated by love, seems to regret what she has done: you would have died in the winding labyrinth unless guided by the thread I gave you, Theseus. You said that as long as we both shall live, you'll be mine. Well, look, we're alive, and if you're alive, too, that means you're nothing more than a low-down despicable liar. I never should've given you that damn thread, and so on. But the important thing for our case is that in the next line she calls the Minotaur her brother for the first time: "Club that killed my brother, the Minotaur, condemn me too!" Let me note for this honorable court that the monster has been recognized as a brother by another human being.

"My brother, the Minotaur," let us remember that.

"He had the face of a bull, but the rest of him was human," said the gentle and all-knowing Apollodorus (or Pseudo-Apollodorus) at some point during the second century B.C. I believe he's the only one who didn't use disparaging epithets against our client.

What does cunning Plutarch do? So as not to sin through his own words, he prefers to speak of the Minotaur through the mouth of Euripides. The latter called him: "A mingled form and hybrid birth of monstrous shape." And also: "Two different natures, man and bull, were joined in him." This second statement sounds relatively neutral, which in our case can be taken as compassionate, thus the Minotaur's human nature can again be seen here.

Unlike him, Seneca, practically an age-mate of Christ, uses language in his *Phaedra* that would make even Roman soldiers blush.

Wretched whore, Hippolytus screams at Phaedra, you've outdone even your mother Pasiphaë, who gave birth to a monster, displaying her wild lust to all. But why should I be surprised, you were carried in the same womb where that two-shaped infamy sloshed around . . . It went something like that, to use the jargon of the time.

Does the prosecution object? If it is because of the language, let me note that the words are not mine, while the translation is quite precise. It has nothing to do with our case? You're mistaken. We're talking about the abandonment and forcible confinement of a child, branded by his origins, for which he is not to blame. This is followed by slander, abasement, and the public circulation of lies . . . Yet it can be seen, albeit between the lines, in casual suggestions and hints, that the Minotaur's human nature has been recognized. Despite the fact that his human rights have been taken away. I ask that this be duly noted, your honor, and that you allow me to continue.

The poet Virgil, that favorite of Augustus, sideswipes the victim in passing with the following two lines: "the Minotaur, hybrid offspring, that mixture of species, proof of unnatural relations . . ."
His every word drips with revulsion.

Speaking of Virgil, we can't help but mention Dante. In *The Inferno*, the Minotaur is placed at the entrance to the seventh, bloodiest circle: "on the border of the broken bank / was stretched at length the Infamy of Crete." Dante is even more merciless than his guide, Virgil. After being exiled to the labyrinth, after dying under Theseus' sword, our defendant was tossed in among the bloodsuckers, tyrants, and those who have sinned against the laws of nature. But isn't the Minotaur merely the fruit of such sin, not a perpetrator, a victim, the most long-suffering victim?

(By the way, that seventh circle was guarded by centaurs. The centaur, with its animal hindquarters and human torso is the mirror image of the Minotaur.)

If literature constantly returns to the Minotaur's monstrous birth, then visual art is hypnotized by his death. In all the ancient images we have, in all the frescoes, vase-paintings and illustrations of myths and legends, the scene is one and the same—Theseus kills the Minotaur. He is about to be stabbed or is already dead, Theseus dragging him by the horns. Put together, it looks like a series of techniques for close-quarters combat with a sword.

Theseus grasps the Minotaur by one horn and jabs at his chest with the double-edged sword.

The Minotaur has laid his unnaturally large head in Theseus's lap, exposing his neck to the sword's blow.

Theseus is behind the Minotaur's back, holding his neck with his left hand, while driving his short sword somewhere into the soft tissue beneath the rib cage with his right. The body is human. You're killing a human being, Theseus. The sword goes in smoothly. Yes, in all these scenes the supposedly terrifying body of the Minotaur is vulnerable, there's no hiding this fact.

On the bottom of one of the kylixes, those shallow glasses for wine, the Minotaur is even beautiful, he looks more like a Moor, with sensual lips and handsome nostrils, he is kneeling, imprudently exposing his body to Theseus's sword, while the latter's right foot steps upon the Minotaur's groin.

In several preserved frescoes on wine vessels we see Theseus dragging behind him the Minotaur's mild-mannered corpse . . . He scarcely defended himself, as the other lawyer-by-correspondence in the case, Mr. Jorge, shall also testify.

In some of the scenes the murder is even more brutal, harsher, and more barbarian—committed with a heavy staff, a gnarled wooden mace, a crude prototype of today's bat. The murder of an ox or bull, as they still do it in the village slaughterhouses, is a blow with the butt-end of an axe to the forehead.

Only childhood and death. And nothing in between. Except darkness and silence.

Ladies and gentlemen, I beg that all this be taken into consideration.

Viruses

Billy goats and lilies courted all around me
I cried out afeared—Dear Lord have mercy!
Such a sin simply cannot be.
God's right hand He placed in between.
O, world, from a second Sodom ye are redeemed!

—Gaustine of Arles, seventeenth century

A few words about Daedalus's unnatural craftsmanship, which made possible that which nature had forbidden. He crafted a wooden cow, covered it in real cowhide and stuffed Pasiphaë, Minos's wife, who was crazed with lust for the bull, into its empty womb. He put the cow on wheels and took it to the meadow where the bull normally grazed. What happened next is clear. "The bull came up and had intercourse with it, as if with a real cow. Pasiphaë gave birth to Asterios, who was called Minotauros," as Pseudo-Apollodorus tells it.

However, the myth keeps mum about another hidden consequence. Could the Trojan Horse have been born from the Cretan wooden cow? Again hollow, on wheels, but quite a bit larger, fitting a whole thirty armed soldiers in its womb—not to seduce, but to subjugate. A cow giving birth to a horse, a woman giving birth to a man-bull—Daedalus slips a Trojan horse into the history of species. And a few millennia later, yet another new heir will crop up, without a wooden body, without any body at all—the Trojan horse, a malicious computer virus. It pretends to be a useful program, lies low for a day or two before unleashing its fury—erasing files, opening doors, smashing defenses, letting foreign eyes into your virtual Troy. And all of that—born of Daedalus's unnatural craftsmanship. Which goes against the natural order that the mysterious Gaustine from the seventeenth century insisted upon.

> *There is Order here and God makes no mistake,*
> *Fly and ram, tulip and oak do not copulate.*

Myth and Game

Shall we talk about the Minotaur and videogames? Just enter any one of the games that have multiplied in recent years. Clichés and classics. The Minotaur looks like your average B-movie thug.

Short-legged and beefy, with a short, thick neck, hairy, with the terminator's trapezoidal face and absurd little horns. And sometimes, as an added bonus, a crooked boar's tusk. As if the rest wasn't enough, they had to go and cross the bull with feral pig.

My dearest Ovid, Virgil, Seneca, Plutarch, Euripides, and you, Mr. Dante "Inferno" Alighieri (to spell out your nickname, too), come see what mythology has become. See the character you so despised. You've contributed greatly to his present image. Behold him and weep, you proto-gamers from antiquity. Some day we can play a round, when we get together in real time. In real time, ha ha ha . . . We'll play "The Minotaur in the Labyrinth" or *World of Warcraft* or *God of War* or . . . some 3-D game. Then, however, only the Minotaur will be three-dimensional, while we'll all be two-dimensional shades (we'll be in the Kingdom of the Shades, after all, right?), pathetic cartoons with faded colors from the beginning of the digital era.

The Madonna with Minotaur

A child is sitting in his mother's lap. She is holding him in her left arm, she has most likely just nursed him and is now waiting for him to burp. The child is naked. The scene is iconic, so well known and repeating in all images after the birth of the Christ Child. There is one difference, however, which makes this drawing unique. The child has a bull's head. Little horns, long drawn-out ears, wide-set eyes, a snout. The head of a calf. Pasiphaë with the Minotaur Child. Centuries before the Virgin Mary.

The image is one of a kind. It was discovered near the erstwhile Etruscan city of Volci, in present-day Lazio. It can be seen in the collection of the Parisian National Library. Someone dared to recall the obvious, which the myth would quickly forget. We're talking about a baby. Carried and delivered by a woman. We're talking about an infant, not a beast. A child, who will soon be abandoned (sent to the basement). Most likely Minos needed time, months, even a year or two, to decide what to do, how to hide this marked child from the world. If we peer at the faces of the mother and the son, we can see that both of them already know.

Perhaps this is the very moment of separation? Her left arm no longer embraces him, but pulls away, waving farewell gently behind the child's back.

Later the myth will transform the child into a monster, so as to justify the sin of his abandonment, the sin against all children, whom we will abandon in the future.

Child-Unfriendly

The absence of children in Greek mythology is striking.

If we agree that antiquity is the childhood of mankind, then why is that childhood so devoid precisely of children? Apparently where everybody is acting childish, real children are unwelcome. Insofar as they exist, they are most often devoured by their fathers. Any left undevoured will devour their fathers. That's how it's been since the beginning of time, since Chronos and his children.

It's clear that Time always devours his children. But there is time where there is light, where lightness and darkness, day and night alternate. So it turns out that the only place hidden from time is the absolute darkness of the cave. That's where the child Zeus was hidden away. It was the only place where Chronos (Time) did not rule.

The Minotaur, too, is hidden away in the dark underground labyrinth. And since time does not pass there, he remains a boy forever.

We were also locked up in the basement, that late urban cave, like momentary Minotaurs amid the jars of pickles and jam.

I had an aunt who always threatened to eat me up every time she came to visit. Huge and hulking, a distant offshoot of the Titan's line, she would stand in front of me, spread wide her enormous arms with their rapaciously painted nails, bare her teeth malevolently, two silver caps sparkling, and would slowly step toward me with a deep growl coming from her belly. I would curl up into a ball, screaming, while she shook with laughter. She didn't have any children, she must have devoured them.

Devoured Children in Greek Mythology (an Incomplete Catalogue)

In the beginning, of course, there were Chronos's children, devoured by the old man himself: Hestia, Demeter, Hera, Hades, Poseidon. And one long stone, wrapped in swaddling clothes in place of Zeus.

Zeus, who swallowed up his wife Metis, because of Athena (as of yet unborn and hence also swallowed up), who was hidden in her womb. She was then born from his head in full battle array.

Itys (Ityl)—the young son of the Thracian king Tereus, killed by his mother and aunt and served up as a meal to the unsuspecting father. Ovid recounts this in the sixth book of his Metamorphoses in lurid detail: the child trustingly embracing the murderess, the blow of the sword, some of the warm body boiled up in pots, other parts roasted on hissing spits . . . And in the end the feasting Tereus "gorged himself with flesh of his own flesh."

There's more . . . The story of the child Pelops, Tantalus's son, who was hacked to pieces by his father, stewed up, and offered to the gods. And only grief-stricken Demeter ate part of his shoulder in her melancholy haze.

Here, too, figures that murky story with Lycaon, the king of Arcadia, who served up his grandson Arcas to Zeus in order to test him.

You won't find the youths and maidens devoured by the Minotaur in this list—I don't believe in that part of the myth. Besides, bulls are herbivores.

P. S.

And one wacky echo in modern times.

It's an ordinary baking pan, large, with indelible traces of endless use. The rice has been washed and lightly steamed, amid the white—little balls of black pepper. You can clearly see that the stove has been switched on, the oven door is open, and two hands are carrying the tray toward it. There's just one unusual detail—that's no chicken or turkey on top of the rice, but a baby, naked and alive. I almost said raw. It's lying on its back, its arms and legs in the air. It is clearly only a few days old and weighs no more than a middling turkey.

I own this photo (black and white) and the story, bought as a package deal. The woman who received this photo in the mail just about fainted. "Here is your new grandson. Isn't he sweet?" The letter was from her daughter in Canada, who had sent the first photo of the long-awaited baby. Back when she was little, they used to teasingly tell her: "you're so sweet, I'm going to eat you up. With rice, with rice . . ." It was a family saying. And now, twenty years later, the daughter had decided to literalize the joke.

A myth, deboned, mocked, yet still scary.

The Voice of the Minotaur

The defendant has the floor.

Silence.

Does the defendant have anything to say in his own defense, or does he prefer to remain silent?

The Minotaur's voice has not been preserved anywhere in all of recorded antiquity. He doesn't speak, others speak for him. There where everything animate and inanimate refuses to shut up, where the voices of gods and mere mortals, of wood nymphs and heroes, of crafty Odysseuses and naïve Cyclops are constantly swarming, where even the despised Centaurs have the right to speak, only one remains silent. The Minotaur. No voice, no sound, no whimper or threat, nothing anywhere. Not even in the hexameter of Homer, that Minotaur among poets, who in the long nights of his blindness wandered through the labyrinths of history. Nor in Ovid, the exile, who knew very well the fate of an outcast, nor in Vergil, nor in Pliny the Elder, nor in Aeschylus, Euripides, or Sophocles . . . no one gives voice to, no one preserves the voice of the Minotaur. It's easy to feel sorry for Icarus, it's easy to sympathize with Theseus, with Ariadne, even with old King Minos . . . No one pities the Minotaur.

Does the defendant have anything to say? Otherwise . . .

He does. Why shouldn't he be worthy of the heroic hexameter?

The Minotaur's Speech in His Own Defense
(a Fragment)

Some words I have for you o'er which so long I've mused
In night's embrace, O Minos, Hades' judge most cruel
My tongue has longed to say just once: O father mine!
Yet I discern your scorn and swallow back my cries.
Forsooth! The truth outshines your deepest, darkest fears
Your blood I share—a freak by birth, my lineage's clear.
Your father's likeness true, I'm kin to all you all
The first true bull in our damned house was Zeus; recall
how he seduced the fair Europa, dam to you
from Grandpa Zeus I got my bullish form so true.
His very spit and image, to my curving horns,
As Cretans crones in tales so love to wail and mourn.
A god was he, while I am but a freak; but know
O Minos, father dear, you wanted bulls like snow
so white far more than my sweet mother ever hath
and now you cringe disgusted by your son their calf . . .

Minos: The court will now break for a recess . . .

Moooo . . .

Take away the defendant . . .

Moooooo . . .
oooooooooooooooooooooooooooooooooooooooooooooooooooooooo
oooooooooooooooooooooooooooooooooooooooooooooooooooooooo
oooooooooooooooooooooooooooooooooooooooooooooooooooooooo

III. The Yellow House

Asylum

A yellow, peeling building, far past the last houses, long and low, with barred windows, the fence girded with barbed wire. An "asylum for the mentally ill," as they officially called the place, which everyone in that Podunk southeastern town simply called the nuthouse. Rumor had it that the fence was electrified at night and that several people had been fried. I was afraid, yet at the same time it was precisely this fear that drove me to hang around nearby.

One evening, passing by there, I heard a chilling howl. There was something excessive and inhuman in that howling or bellowing, something from the mazes of the night Ooooooooohhh . . . That endless Oooohh dug tunnels in the silence of the early November evening. It was Sunday. The fallen leaves blanketed the whole street, still emitting a faint scent of rot and acetone, which preceded the corpse of autumn. Only the light above the gate scattered the damp dusk. The nurse had gone home, while the head doctor only came once a week in any case. The porter more or less had to be there, but he was probably dozing drunk in the doctor's office. In this case, that saved the howler, who would otherwise undergo the traditional ice-cold shower under the garden hose. It was said that they sprayed them with water directly in their rooms ("cells" is the more precise term) through the bars of the window, as a natural curative procedure for cooling down demons. The head doctor had long since made peace with the fact that he would end his career here in this Podunk town. And he didn't worry about any inspections or sanctions, just as a man who finds himself in hell is freed from the fear that something worse could befall him.

I walked around the yellow house on that Sunday evening, the gloomy corridors of that howl sucking me in ever deeper. I was afraid to enter it, whatever was inside was not fit for the human eye and ear. But my body continued to move mechanically in a circle, I sensed that I was beginning to slip away from myself. Just a bit more and I'll enter the corridors of the scream, I'll crawl along the furrows, I'll emplant myself in the body of the screamer.

Just then a hand grabs me firmly by the shoulder; startled, I return to myself like a snail withdrawing into its shell. My father.

Neither of us can hide our surprise at seeing the other in this place. Neither of us has any business being here. And neither of us asks the other what brings him here at this hour. We turn toward the city without a word and sink into the November evening, far from that cry.

I knew that I would never again free myself from the tunnel of that Oooooooohhh. The howl would pursue me throughout the years with varying degrees of doggedness. Appearing and dying away in unexpected situations. Sometimes it would quiet down, I would lose it in my happiest moments, in joyful gatherings with people amid their deafening chatter . . . But in the next moment of silence it would inevitably appear. And ten years later, when I came down with that constant ringing in my ear, I knew that that howling-bellowing-crying thing was now settled in there for good. In the very center, in the cave of the skull, from there to the tympanic membrane, the hammer and the anvil, in the very labyrinth of the inner ear, as the doctors put it.

The Diagnosis

Much later, already in my student years, I got up the courage to tell an older doctor friend of mine about the "emplanting" that had seized me in childhood. The doctor thought for a long time and finally offered a rare diagnosis, perhaps made up on the spot, which went more or less like this: pathological empathy or obsessive empathetic-somatic syndrome. According to him, the illness was exceedingly rare and incurable, but it peaked in childhood. Over the years the attacks became easier to control and lost their most acute manifestations, without disappearing entirely. Just as in epilepsy, he said, we never know where the person wanders when he is in such a fit.

In my case, there were no fits per se, my body remained completely calm, if slightly stiff, like a person lost in thought or deeply absorbed in some story. When I fell into such a state, I didn't blink, my pupils stopped moving, my mouth hung half-open, my breathing switched to some automatic regime, while I (part of me) shifted into someone else's story and someone else's body.

I accepted this with a mixture of fear, a vague sense of guilt, and satisfaction. I had put quite a lot of effort into hiding this ability or illness as much as I could. Only my grandmother could always recognize it: "Eh, he's gone off again." It often happened against my will. As if right where another felt pain, in that cut, that wound, that point of inflammation, a corridor would open that sucked me inside. In stories, especially those told by loved ones, there was always some blind spot, a momentary gap, a weak point, incomprehensible sorrow, longing for something lost or that had never taken place, which pulled me inside, into the dark galleries of the unspoken. There were such secret galleries and corridors in every story.

For his own peace of mind, the doctor sent me for an MRI, into that enormous white capsule where they cut your brain into thin slices and peer at all its secrets. Relax and think pleasant thoughts, the nurse said . . .

Two hours later I entered the office of the doctors who would analyze the image, but I could sense from afar their poorly disguised consternation. The picture hadn't come out. Maybe it was due to the machine, it was old, after all. Actually, this was the first time something like this had happened to them, absolutely nothing could be seen, just a dark-black plate. This didn't come as a surprise to me. I know nothing can be seen, because inside is darkness, an un-illuminable, centuries-deep darkness. My skull is a cave. I didn't tell them that, of course.

Sometimes—at the same time—I am a dinosaur, a fish, a bat, a bird, a single-celled organism swimming in the primordial soup, or the embryo of a mammal, sometimes I'm in a cave, sometimes in a womb, which is basically the same thing—a place protected (against time).

Side Corridor

The tendency toward empathy is strongest between the ages of seven and twelve.

The most recent research is focused on the so-called mirror neurons, localized in the anterior portion of the insular cortex (insula). To put it simply, they react in a similar fashion when a person feels pain, sorrow, or happiness, or when one observes these emotions in another person. Some animals also experience empathy. The connection between shared emotional experiences and mirror neurons has not been well studied; experiments are in the works. Researchers believe that the conscious cultivation of empathy, including through the reading of novels (see S. Keen), will make communication far easier and will save us from future world cataclysms.

—*The Journal of Community and Cortex*

My Brother, the Minotaur

Still, what was my father doing that night near the yellow house? Okay, so it was part of his job—going wherever they called him. Almost all the town's residents kept animals in their yards. But what would a veterinarian be doing at a home for the mentally ill? He must have been coming from there, where else would he have appeared from in that wasteland?

Suddenly the whole picture came together in my head with staggering clarity. I say "suddenly," but in fact the separate pieces of that puzzle had been elaborated carefully and at length with the fastidiousness intrinsic to a child's imagination. Now everything came together so easily, frighteningly easily within me.

That inhuman howl really was inhuman, and it wasn't Ooooh, but Moooo. And it came from a half-man, half-bull locked up in there. (I'd already seen one such boy in my grandfather's hidden memory.) The human doctor hadn't been able to do anything for the human, so they had decided to treat the bull. Of course, they called the best (and only, incidentally) veterinarian in town: my father.

There was another, darker version of the story, also fine-tuned at length during those lonely childhood afternoons. That half-human-half-bull boy was not just anybody, but my "stillborn brother," whom I'd heard them whispering about. Actually, he'd been born alive, but with a bull's head and they'd put him in the home. They had abandoned him. With the best of intentions. So he wouldn't disturb his healthy brother. I remember that I wrote all that down in my most clandestine (read: secretly illegible) handwriting, rolled the sheet of

The Physics of Sorrow 73

notebook paper into a scroll and shoved it in my secret box under the bed.

Or maybe I wasn't even their son at all, instead they had adopted me, despairing of giving birth only to kids with bull-heads?

This was one of the basic fears of my childhood. If this were true, then I could easily be abandoned again. We could be abandoned again, my Minotaur brother and me.

I remember that I devoted the next few days to finding some crack, some door left slightly ajar, through which I could enter into the cave of this secret. I asked my father—ostensibly off-the-cuff and cautiously—what kinds of diseases cows came down with. Had he ever seen Siamese twin calves and what would he do in such a case? Would they kill one to save the other? My father gave absentminded replies. Once, however, he nevertheless let his guard down and launched into some story about a cow who was in labor for fourteen hours right on New Year's Eve when he had been a kid and . . . I didn't hear any more of the story, I simply slipped down the corridor the story had opened up to me. I stopped at the entrance . . . It definitely wasn't right to sneak into a father's secrets. There was something indecent and unnatural about it, you could see things you'd rather not see. I could still hear his voice, he was carried away with his story, I could still turn back. I told myself, I'll do it only this one time. I pushed on ahead, then quickly ducked into a side corridor of his story, I was no longer interested in it, his voice died away. I wandered aimlessly through my father's childhood, look how alike we are, skinny, in baggy clothes, probably hand-me-downs, look, there he's stealing eggs out from under the chicken, they're still warm, I can feel them, my grandma, his mother (now mine, too), sees me, I run with the eggs toward the general store, if I manage to sell them to Grandpa Angel the shopkeeper, I'll get a candy bar for each one. I run and run, go into the store, thank God there are no other customers. Grandpa Angel, here are three eggs for candy bars, I wheeze breathlessly, he looks at me, does your mother know, yes, she sent me, he takes the eggs, holds them up to the sunlight, well now, these eggs here are stolen, heeey, how did you know, he gives them back to me, at that moment my mother is coming up the street, I grab the eggs, stuff them in my pocket and dash out, but I trip on the crumbling steps and fall. Careful with those eggs, Grandpa Angel laughs. I feel the yoke seeping over my crotch.

I leave that incident before retribution comes, I turn down another corridor, change direction. I tell myself that I'm not going to lend an ear to things that don't concern me. At the last minute, I veer away from a girl my father is kissing, I'm kissing, behind the stone wall of the house. She's attractive, but she won't become my mother. He's attractive, too. I'm attractive as well, as long as I'm him. Tall, with curly hair, I feel women's eyes on me as we pass. That one looks foreign. That one is familiar from somewhere. That one . . . Wait, now there's my mother. The answer to the riddle that brought me here should be somewhere around here. I need to turn down some corridor and look on from there, but I can't move. She's in pain. The pain is terrible and I can't stand aside, it sucks me in. Something alive is being torn apart . . . I'm tearing her apart . . . Finally, a baby's cry, that cry comes from me, I am myself, that wrinkly, wet, bluish hunk of meat. Tossed out, choking, shaking all over.

Something gives me a good hard shake and pulls me back down those dark corridors—light, words, my father's face . . . What's wrong . . . What's wrong . . . I've been trying to wake you for ten minutes now . . .

I feel bruised from the journey . . . Everything's fine, Dad, I'm here . . . I was born to my own mother, what a miracle.

My father dragged me out, before I managed to see whether there was someone else there, if someone else came out after me. I was left with the uncertain feeling that I wasn't alone in that cave.

I was born to my own mother and father, but that doesn't make me any less a Minotaur. I continued spending long days alone, at the window, paging through a book.

Nippers

Just as in antiquity, the children of socialism were also invisible. Little nippers hanging around at the grown ups' feet. Prepared for life, without entirely being a part of it.

Run down to the cellar for some pickles! Go and play in the other room, we're talking to our guests! Hightail it out of here, I've got work to do! Don't make me start up the spanking factory . . . Patriarchy and industrialization rolled into one.

Three months at the village every summer, with their grand-mothers, in the fresh air and sunshine, to get toughened up, drink milk straight from the sheep, and eat raw eggs. You take a warm egg out from under the chicken, your grandma wipes it on her apron, pokes a hole in it with a thick needle, sprinkles a little salt inside and you suck it up through the hole with all your might under her fond gaze. Drink up, drink up, an egg is equal to a shot, she would say. That's what some famous doctor who had passed through the village thirty years ago and had spent the night had said. One egg, he said, is equal to a shot, take it from me.

I would find out much later that this pedagogical regimen of "fresh air and sunshine" was also crucial for German children of the 1930s, so they would grow up healthy, energetic and in fine fighting form. I wonder if they stuffed them full of raw eggs, too?

While rereading ancient Greek myths from that already dog-eared book on those endless summer afternoons, I made the following discovery. Zeus turned out to be exactly like us from the late 1970s. A child sent deep into the countryside, to be looked after by his grandmother Gaia (and kept far from his father), to drink goat's milk (his goat was divine, of course), and to grow up hale and hearty.

I will always remember milk from an ordinary mortal sheep, straight from the udder and still warm, with a few shiny turds floating in it, to be blown off to the side with the foam. Only in childhood is immortality possible. Perhaps because of that milk and the raw eggs.

But there's a very slow, creeping fear, too. I've been abandoned. They've left me here, they've gone back to the city, they're gone.

Mother Bean

Mother Bean had a green body and two little beans for eyes. We were really afraid of her. Don't go into the bean patch, my grandma would holler when she saw us in the garden, or Mother Bean will come after you! We never did see her, but she was always in the back of our minds as we carefully skirted the rows planted with beans.

In the vineyard, on the other hand, lived Mother Vine, guarding her children. For that reason we didn't dare trample through the rows, snitching grapes left and right.

Once my grandma caught us committing true genocide on a colony of red ants that was crawling across the paving stones in front of the house. Then we heard about Mother Ant for the first time, huge and with sharp claws yea big.

Everything had a mother, only we didn't. We had grandmothers.

The Minotaur Syndrome

The 1970s. Our mothers were young, studying—first, second, third year, working—first, second, third shift. We were there in the empty apartments, ground floors, basements, lost in boredom and fear, roaming amid the vague anxieties of the one left on his own. Is there a Minotaur Syndrome?

I didn't have fish, a cat, a turtle, or a parrot, because that was the last thing we needed, as my mother wisely noted. In any case, we were constantly moving to new rental apartments, awaiting the great day when we would receive an apartment of our own. The only thing I had was Laika, the dog, whose homeless soul was howling through the cosmos. And my brother, the Minotaur. They lived illegally in my five square meters of living space, invisible to my mother and father, and to the landlords.

A Private History of the 1980s
And then . . .

A History of Boredom in the 1980s needs to be written. This is the decade that produced the most boredom. The afternoon of the century.

When I heard the word "boredom" for the first time, I was six and felt anxious because I didn't know what it was. You must be bored being alone all day, one of the neighbors, Auntie Pepa, said to me. I imagined it as a slight illness, some sort of malaise, like a stuffy nose, a cold, or an allergy to poplar fluff. That's why I answered evasively: uh no, nothing's wrong, I'm fine. Where I came from, boredom was unheard of, they never used the word. There was always something that needed doing, the animals would never let it take root, they would mow it down as soon as it cropped up. But here, in the town of T, it thrived everywhere. It shimmered like a haze above the hot asphalt, chipped away at the houses' fading ochre, lulled the sunflower-seed hawker to sleep in the shade of the park, purred like a cat or brought on one of the deafening sneezing fits of Uncle Kosta from across the street.

Catalogue of Collections
    Napkins
    Empty packs of cigarettes
    Matchboxes
    Pins and stamps
    Pocket calendars
    Winking postcards
    Wrappers from imported candies, paper and tinfoil
    Wrappers from chocolate bars, paper and tinfoil
    Gum wrappers (minus the gum)
    Empty bottles of whiskey, cognac, Campari . . .

Clearly, the things in this collection are abandoned, empty, used up. Somebody has smoked Marlboro Reds and Rothmans Blues, eaten imported chocolate candies, chewed some gum, and downed a Metaxa brandy. Only a few bottles, boxes, and wrappers are left for us. The collectors of emptinesses and abandonments.

There's my first cassette tape player, a Hitachi mono, we bought it from some Vietnamese people in exchange for my grandfather's old donkey. To the very end, my grandpa thought it was a bit like trading a horse for a chicken, as the saying goes. The horse being the donkey, and the chicken—the tape player.

Our history and literature textbooks—we got a kick out of adding finishing touches to the painfully familiar photographs inside. A moustache and a pirate's skull cap on top of the general secretary of the communist party's head, which was a round and bald as an egg. And on the poet-revolutionary Hristo Botev's heroic face—may the gods of literature forgive me!—I drew round, John Lennon-style glasses. The glasses completely transformed the fearsome Botev into a slightly bewildered, bearded hippie of Bulgarian revolutions, which are as a rule unsuccessful.

The world was simple and ordered, simply ordered. On Wednesday—fish, on Friday—Russian TV.

In East German cowboy movies, the redskins were the good guys, the proletariat of sorts, since they were the reds.

The television listing for Monday, November 18, 1973 or 1983 (it's not clear from the scrap of newspaper):

- — - —— - — - —— - - — - —— -

17:30 — Discussion of decisions made by the July Plenum of the Central Committee of the Bulgarian Communist Party. 18:00 — News. 18:10 — For Pioneers: "The Little Drum." 18:30 — "Children of the Circus," a film. 19:00 — "Beautiful and Comfortable," a program about economics. 19:20 — For the People's Army: "At Attention with a Song," concert. 19:40 — Advertisements. 19:45 — Melody of the Month. 19:50 — Good night, children! 20:00 — Around the World and At Home. 20:20 — Sports Screen. 20:30 — Televised theater: "Wedding Anniversary" by Jerzy Krasnicki. 21:40 — Winners of International Concerts. 22:00 — News.

- — - —— - — - —— - - — - —— -

I can't explain why, but this listing always plunges me into melancholy. The last news at 10 P.M. and that's it. Only sssssssssssssss and snowflakes after the national anthem.

Here's the green canvas bag from the gasmask, filled with the exhausting fear of the atomic and neutron bombs, of air raid sirens being tested. I remember the bomb shelter under the school gym, where once a month we hid "on alert." Ragged breathing in the dark, the back-up lighting generator that didn't work anyway, the chaos, the scent of sweat and fear, the subsequent boasts of one fellow student who claimed to have "bombed," i.e. grabbed the tits (in the jargon of the day, may it rest in peace) of our chemistry teacher in the dark—by accident, he had been aiming for a different target.

While I was putting on my gasmask during our military training drills in school—which took me a whole seventeen seconds—the major kept shouting: "That's it! You're dead . . ." And he shoved the stopwatch in my face.

It's not easy living thirty years after your death.

The end of our training coincided with the end of that for which we had been trained.

The Sexual Question

Was there sex in socialism? And socialism in sex? At the start of our erotic Bildungsroman stood *Man and Woman, Intimately*, translated from the German, the secret bestseller of that time, always well hidden on the highest shelf way in the back. Once the book disappeared.

Did anybody touch that book?

Which book?

You know which one.

We all read it behind one another's backs. It was at once a practical handbook, an intimate physician, and erotic literature.

And so we first discovered sex through medical discourse. Masturbation (or so it said there) was harmful to one's health, as was sex without love . . . But actually, for us, love without sex was no less torturous.

From a Catalogue of Important Erotic Scenes
Now as she ran up the steps toward Sonny a tremendous flash of desire went through her body. On the landing Sonny grabbed her hand and pulled her down the hall into an empty bedroom. Her legs went weak as the door closed behind them. She felt Sonny's mouth on hers, his lips tasting of burnt tobacco, bitter. She opened her mouth. At that moment she felt his hand come up beneath her bridesmaid's gown, heard the rustle of material giving way, felt his large warm hand between her legs, ripping aside the satin panties to caress her vulva. She put her arms around his neck and hung there as he opened his trousers. Then he placed both hands beneath her bare buttocks and lifted her. She gave a little hop in the air so that both her legs were wrapped around his upper thighs. His tongue was in her mouth and she sucked on it. He gave a savage thrust that banged her head against the door. She felt something burning pass between her thighs. She let her right hand drop from his neck and reached down to guide him, her hand closed around an enormous, blood-gorged pole of muscle. It pulsated in her hand like an animal and, almost weeping with grateful ecstasy . . .

The mythical page 28 from Mario Puzo's *The Godfather* was a revelation, a baptism-by-fire for a whole generation. I had copied it out longhand, just like most of my classmates, while some braver souls sliced it right out of the book with a razor blade.

Sex appeared to be a complicated acrobatic routine with hops, holds, lifts, thrusts, first with one hand, tongue, then with the other . . . I would never learn. But in any case, the very knowledge of that figural composition gave me the confidence of the initiated. At least in theory I knew what I had to do to reach that "grateful ecstasy" . . .

The other novel was French. Unlike the mute scene in *The God-father*, now there was an abundance of words, sighs, ellipses . . . From here we learned that you can talk during sex, too. *Bel Ami* by Maupassant. "I adore you, my little Made . . ." Please don't, I beg you . . . a quick thrill . . . wild and clumsy copulation . . .

Let's add the secret erotic stories that were distributed in mimeo-graphed copies and attributed to Balzac, about intercourse (that was the word used) between a woman and an animal (something like Pasiphaë with the bull), only in this case it was a dog or a bear, I don't remember anymore.

. . .

In all that scarcity, we found sources of erotica in unexpected places.

In classical painting, for example. An inexhaustible reservoir of naked female bodies, of course chubbier and more Baroque than we would have liked, but it was still something. We gazed at the cheap reproductions . . . Goya's "The Naked Maja," Botticelli's "Venus," Rubens's "Three Graces," Courbet's "Bather" . . . But Delacroix's "Liberty Leading the People" from our history textbook, with all the revolutionary zeal of her breast surging up out of her dress, became part of our own sexual revolution.

Underwear ads in old *Neckermann* catalogues.

The "golden girls" of Bulgarian rhythmic gymnastics.

All figure skating competitions.

Sculptures of the nude goddess Diana with her bow. The whole town of D., the erstwhile Dianopolis, was scattered with them. One afternoon, for a split second I caught a glimpse of a classmate of mine naked through the window of the house across the street; her name was also Diana. I already knew the myth and was afraid that the curse would catch up with me, that I would be turned into a stag that very minute, I felt my feet growing hooves, while enormous antlers would sprout out of my head any moment. A dog in the yard next door started barking at me right then, a sure sign that he'd sniffed out the stag in me . . .

Pantyhose packages showing long female legs.

Later we heard the rumor that sperm was very beneficial for female skin, and one of the older kids from our neighborhood bragged that he was often called upon to make "deliveries." It's the Bulgarian Nivea, he liked to say.

I've kept a whole bag full of love letters from that time. Should I add them here? It's unbelievable how many letters were written back then. For a moment I wondered what would happen if I sent them back to the girls who wrote them? If I scrounged up their addresses and started dropping them in the mail one by one? I think V., the writer of the longest and most amorous missives, is happily married in Mexico.

V. wrote on both sides of the sheet, there was never enough room, so she would keep writing on the envelope, on the inside. One time I received a whole seven letters from her at once. She had mailed one, then wanted to add something more, and so on. She went to the post office every half-hour. I was in the army when I got them. The soldier who went to pick up the mail from the nearby village waved the seven letters over his head from afar. Everyone from the base came outside, each expecting a letter in that abundance. He started reading off the names on the envelope; actually, it was only a single, solitary name, seven times. I felt so guilty looking at the others' faces after each letter—sorrow, which quickly changed to quiet hatred. Because of all the injustice in the world. Seven letters can't arrive and be all for the same person.

Now I see that some of their opening lines were literally taken from the little tome *Love Letters of Great Men*. An innocent deception that I only now have discovered. This explains the lofty style—"My love, I believe that fate is sheltering us . . ."—after which it launches without transition into everyday life: "Most of the lectures are lame, and some of the professors couldn't care less . . ." "Do you remember Petya, whom I introduced you to? . . . She's snagged herself an Italian, if you can believe it . . ."

Or this: "I want us to be as happy again as we were on March 8 and 9!!!" With three exclamation marks.

What I wouldn't give to remember what happened on March 8 and 9.

Overheard on a train: "During socialism, we made lots of love, because there wasn't anything else to do."

The Cook Book of Silences

To the "List of Unwritten (and Impossible) Stories from the 1980s," I'll add yet another: A Short History of Keeping Mum.

From her silence, my mother made wonderful fried zucchini, baked lamb, *banitsi* . . .

Everything can be said with a few dishes. Only now do I realize why my mother and grandmother were such good cooks. It wasn't cooking, but storytelling.

The labyrinths of their *banitsi* were as delicious and winding as Scheherazade's fairytales. Here is the missing Bulgarian epos, the Banitsi Epos.

. . .

Our next-door neighbors at the time enjoyed pleasant but slightly strange marital relations. They argued every Saturday afternoon. It had become a ritual, part of the weekend spectacle. I remember once how, when their Saturday fight didn't take place, we were honestly worried. My mother in full seriousness urged my father to go over and make sure nothing had happened to them. My father replied that he couldn't go and ask: "Why aren't you fighting?" Especially since no one had ever asked them why they fought in the first place. He went over there in the end, of course. My mother always emerged the victor. No one answered the door. It turned out they were out of town.

In fact, all of their arguments followed one and the same script. The husband would grab his suitcase, a splendid hard-sided brown suitcase, hollering that this time he was leaving for good. He would step out the front door, set his suitcase on the ground, sit down next to it and light up a cigarette. The woman would start cooking and after an hour or so the anesthetizing scent of Saturday dinner—chicken with potatoes, beef stew, or lamb with green onions, depending on the season—would start wafting through the yard, it would smell so nice and homey that the man would slowly pick up his suitcase and simply step over the threshold back into the house, returning from the brink of his latest Saturday flight. Resigned and hungry.

Returning to the Town of T.

The Metaphysics of Dust
I've fallen asleep on the windowsill. I wake up from the sun shining through the dirty glass, a warm afternoon sun. Still in that no man's land between sleep and afternoon, before I return to myself, I sense that soaring and lightness, the whole weightlessness of a child's body. Waking up, I age within seconds. Crippling pain seizes my lower back, my leg is stiff. The light in early September, the first fallen leaves outside, the worry that someone may have passed by on the street and seen me.

I climb down from the window carefully, unfolding my body, instead of simply jumping down. The room, lit up by the autumn sun, has come alive. One ray passes right through the massive glass ashtray on the table, breaking the light down into its constituent colors. Even the long-dead, mummified fly next to it looks exquisite and sparkles like a forgotten earring. The Brownian motion of the dust specks in the ray of light . . . The first mundane proof of atomism and quantum physics, we are made of specks of dust. And perhaps the whole room, the afternoon and my very self, with my awkward three-dimensionality are being merely projected. The beam of light from the old whirring film projector at the local movie theater was similar.

I recalled the darkness, the scent of Pine-Sol, the whirring of the machine. Everything in the movie theater was made from that darkness and a single beam of light. The headless horseman arrived along the beam, as did the great Rocky Mountains, the Grand Canyon; horses and Indians, whooping Sioux tribes, geometrical Roman legions, and ragged Gypsy caravans headed for the heavens kicked up dust along it, Lollobrigida and Loren came down that beam, along with Bardot, Alain Delon and his eternal rival Belmondo, oof, what an ugly mug . . . I remember how, when the movie was boring—less fighting, more talking—I would turn my back on the screen and peer into the beam coming from the little window at the back of the theater. It swarmed with chaotically dancing particles. But this wasn't your average, ordinary dust wiped off the furniture in every home. This magical dust made up the faces and bodies of the most attractive men and women in the world, as well as horses, swords, bows and arrows, kisses, love, absolutely everything . . . I watched the specks of dust and tried to guess which would turn into lips, an eye, a horse's hoof or Lollobrigida's breasts, which flashed by for an instant in one scene . . .

I pass my hand through the beam of light in the room, stir up the specks of dust, and quickly close my fist, as if trying to catch them, that's what I did as a child . . . I would wave my arms, charging into battle against them . . . From today's point of view, the battle was lost, they've won. My one small consolation is that soon I, too, will be with them. Dust to dust . . .

The House

I'm here incognito. The ironic thing is that I'm not making any particular effort. The surest refuge, if you want to remain unnoticed, is to go back to your hometown. I nevertheless try to keep up the conspiracy to some extent, going out only rarely. Before coming, I let it slip here and there that I was leaving the country for a good long while, I made up some writers' fellowship in Latin America. I got my regular dose of snarky comments on two or three literary websites, to the effect that the number of trips I've taken has significantly outstripped the number of sentences I've published in recent years. Completely justified accusations. I grabbed my bags and took off. Or rather, I came back. I don't know which verb is more accurate in this case.

The house we'd once rented rooms in had stood empty for years. The old owners had passed away, their descendants were scattered all over the world. I managed to get in touch with the caretaker. I paid him for three months, although I didn't count on staying for more than two or three weeks. I planned on returning to Sofia incognito, where all those boxes and my gloomy birthright of a basement awaited me.

Still, the caretaker couldn't help but ask what had brought me here and why I wanted to rent this particular house. I had an alibi ready, of course. If nothing else, in this line of work I could always come up with a story that sounded believable. I put my money on the tried-and-true spiel about a scholar who had chosen an isolated place to finish up an important study.

But still, what made you choose these parts, of all places? The locals run away from here as fast as their legs can carry them.

That's exactly the reason, I'm looking for peace and quiet. I passed by here some years back, treated my broken leg at the Baths. This is a wonderful place you've got here, just wonderful, I repeated. His suspicions melted away. If you praise the place where someone lives, it's like he personally deserves the credit for it, and you're already one of the gang, you're in. I again stressed that I would have lots of work to do and would like to remain undisturbed. The caretaker assured me that I had picked the right place. My neighbor to the left was an old deaf woman, while the house to the right had been empty for many years and rats and hobgoblins had the run of the place. They say, he went on, that you can catch sight of a faint light flickering through the rooms from time to time. That's the soul of Blind Mariyka, who was the last one to live there. The man fell silent, perhaps afraid I would back out of the deal, before adding that he, of course, didn't believe in such nonsense.

I remember that neighboring house very well. Back then, Blind Mariyka was alive and Lord knows why we were so terrified of her.

During the day she would stay hidden inside her room, only in the evenings would she come out into the yard and wander amid the trees with her arms stretched out wide. Some said she saw better at night than during the day, since the darkness within her and the darkness outside got along. Just like with moles. Folks in these parts don't mince words.

Otherwise, everything was the same. The street still bore its old name, that of a Soviet commander, the room was the same, with a table, a bed, and an old oil stove. Even the now-faded orchids on the wallpaper hadn't changed.

A family of swallows had built a nest under the eaves of the house. They had three little ones. In the evening I would deliberately leave the light on outside. It lured flies and moths, which the swallows would catch. Soon I found myself wondering if what I was doing was right. I was helping one species kill another more easily. Yes, the swallows had babies that needed more food. Children are a bullet-proof alibi. But most likely those flies and moths I was victimizing had children, too. Why should the little swallows be more precious than flies' larvae? Are not the murder of a fly and the murder of an elephant both murders equally?

I had come back to that house in T. for a specific reason. I pull up the floorboard to the right of the window. That's where the bed had been. As a child, I had hidden a secret stash box there. Afterward we had moved quickly and I hadn't been able to take the box. I told myself that one day, I would come back for it. That box gave rise to all those later boxes and crates, they all stemmed from it and at the end of the day, without it my collection would never be complete.

The End of the Indians

Let's have a moment of silence for the dead Indians and those of us from their tribe. I need to add them to that catalogue of disappeared things. Along with those extinct pagers, videotapes, and Tamagotchis. When we watched *Winnetou*, we all become Winnetou. After *Osceola*, the neighborhood was filled with Osceolas. It was the same thing all over again with Tecumseh, Tokei-ihto, Severino, and Chingachook, the Great Snake . . . I know that now these names mean nothing to those who were born later. Batman, Spider-Man, and the Ninja Turtles have managed to get the upper hand over the Indians and their whole mythology, dishonestly at that, never once going directly into battle against them. They finished up what the pale faces had begun two centuries ago.

The story I want to tell takes place after the showing of one of these old East German cowboy films. I remember that we always came out of the movie theater dazed, as if after a battle with the Whites. For at least an hour afterward, we always had one foot still in the film, half-Indians, half-third-graders. It was almost a physical sensation. And so, after one of these films, we went to a bakery near the movie theater to get our usual *boza* and *tulumbichka*. We needed quite some time to pull ourselves together after the battles, to climb down off our horses and reenter the dull Bulgarian world. We got in line at the bakery. Finally, it was time for the first of our gang, let's call him our "chief," to order, and he ordered his *boza* and *tulumbichka* with dignity. The woman at the counter, however, was chatting with someone and didn't hear him. Our chief stood in front of the display case with a stony expression on his ten-year-old face. When the woman finally looked at him and somewhat rudely snapped, "Come on, squirt, tell me what ya want, I don't have all day," he spat out coldly: "Chingachook does not like to repeat himself." No one had expected this. It definitely took guts to spout off such a line and the long pause, during which only the ceiling fan could be heard, underscored the magnificence of the moment. A second later, however, the woman and several of the regular customers burst out laughing as if on cue. That was really low (super-duper low, as we would have said back then), worse than if they'd smacked us around or thrown us out. Chingachook couldn't take it and dashed outside. We also "spurred our horses."

None of us made fun of Chingachook afterward; on the contrary, we admired his courage in a world that didn't give a shit about you. Especially if you're a kid in third grade.

The epilogue to this story is far more depressing. Strolling around the town of T. now, years later, I came across a carnival shooting gallery. I could have sworn that it was the same trailer from my childhood, faded and rusted out. Even the rifles were the same, the butts were just more worn than ever. This had once been the most magical place for us. Only here could we see all the foreign treasures that were otherwise locked away (I now know that they came from Yugoslavia). It was an Ali Baba's cave with candy cigarettes, color postcards of Gojko Mitić, Claudia Cardinale, Brigitte Bardot, pocket calendars of naked women, decks of cards, pictures of a woman who would wink at you, depending on which angle you looked at her from, pens with a boat floating inside it, scented Chinese erasers, pistol-shaped cigarette lighters, cap guns, leather belts with huge metal buckles, Elvis Presley pins, Eiffel Tower key chains, old calendars with the whole Levski soccer team, glass canes full of colorful candy, sparklers, leather cowboy hats, plastic holsters, glass balls of every size and color, Bakelite ballerinas, porcelain Little Red Riding Hoods complete with a wolf . . . This whole porcelain-plastic kitsch emporium, which, I repeat, was once priceless to us, now looked run down and defeated. In every store, you could now see far greater treasures (and far greater kitsch). Right in front stood those brown, poorly molded Indians with their tomahawks, bows, spears, horses, and so on, which we would have given our right arms for back then. I went over to the trailer and suddenly recognized in the man behind the counter the once-proud Chingachook, aged and paunchy, calling out to a group of kids who were passing by unimpressed. The film was over.

I didn't say anything to him, I stepped back into the shadows of the chestnuts across the way and stayed there, watching. A short while later, a boy of around fifteen, most likely his son, came up to the trailer; they exchanged a few words and Chingachook left. I waited a bit, then went over to the boy. I paid for ten shots, picked one of the two rifles, and started shooting at the walnuts. With the first shot it became clear that the rifle's aim was off a few centimeters to the left. That old trick used in all shooting galleries, it downright warmed my heart.

"This rifle's aim is off," I said.

"Well uh, no, it shouldn't be," the boy blushed. "Try the other one."

"No, no, I've already figured out how far this one is off," I laughed. I broke a few walnuts, then took aim at the wolf that was hot on the rabbit's trail, then at the prince, who bowed and kissed the princess.

"Pick a prize, sir," the boy said, after I'd put the rifle back in its place.

I asked how much the Indians cost, I picked up a squatting brave shooting a bow and arrow, another on horseback, I caressed their edges, looking them over like a connoisseur. The boy stood there, staring in disbelief. I was surely the first one who had shown any interest in them. When I said that I wanted to buy all the Indians, he looked frightened. He didn't know what his dad would say, he was really attached to them. But they are for sale, aren't they, I asked more sharply. Yes, of course, they're for sale, the boy replied, looking around helplessly for his father. How much? The price, of course, was laughable. Look, here's what we'll do, I said, I'll pay for all of them, but only take half. I'll leave the others for your dad. And tell him not to give them away so cheap. They've got added value from the past. I'm not sure he understood me.

"Are you a collector?" The boy asked, while handing me the cheap plastic bag full of Indians.

"You could say that."

"Leave me a name or stop by again, I'm sure my dad would be happy to meet you. Nobody around here cares about Indians."

"Tell your father 'hello,'" I replied, walking away.

"What's your name?" The boy called after me.

I took a few more steps, I was under no obligation to answer, I could pretend that I hadn't heard him. Yet I turned around.

"Swift-Footed Stag is my Indian name." I waved and disappeared around the corner.

Side Corridor

Blind Man's Bluff. The easiest way to make a labyrinth—you just put on a blindfold and start walking. Suddenly the world is turned upside-down, the room you knew so well is different. A true labyrinth in which you stumble into things, get hurt, move about with moans and groans. It now occurs to me that this would be the Minotaur's favorite game.

When we were kids, my female cousins and I made a pact that no matter how old we got and how much we changed, even if we had kids of our own and become bigwigs or total losers, we would get together on one particular day every year to play Blind Man's Bluff. Until we really do go blind, they laughed. Those accidental brushes while trying to catch someone in the dark, the drawn-out process of recognition through touch were part of the innocent eroticism of that game. We played for the last time sometime toward the end of college. I only remember that I stumbled into the giant cactus in the living room and was pulling out needles for the next two days.

Juliet in Front of the Movie Theater

This is probably my third outing at most since I've been here.

I'm walking slowly down the dusky streets, meeting people whose faces mean nothing to me. Sullen, tired, expressionless. The early October twilight falls quickly, the scent of roasted peppers hangs in the air, everyone has gone home for dinner, I can hear lines from (one and the same) television show. I pass by the town movie theater, which has long since forgotten the scent of film reels. And suddenly behind me, a female voice spits out in a single breath: "Hi, hi . . . what are you up to? I'm leaving . . . Okay, goodbye . . . I won't be back anytime soon . . ."

A tongue-twister, followed by strange, soundless laughter. It was so unexpected that it really did make me jump. By the time I had summoned up a reply, even though there was clearly no need to do so, the woman had already passed me by. Juliet, crazy Juliet! I recognized her from behind, slightly stooped and always rushing. The same old-fashioned pink suit she'd worn for as long as I could remember, with big cloth buttons and a drooping hat like the Queen of England's.

Juliet from my childhood, Alain Delon's fiancée, who was always hanging around the local movie theater, they let her in for free, and she knew all the films by heart.

Once as a child, when I still possessed that ability in spades, I sensed the whole cacophony inside her. As if she herself were made of movie scenes, slightly blurred and changing at breakneck speed. Runaway trains swooped down on me, along with horses, amorous shivers, a few merciless kicks to the gut, faces, lines, a punch in the nose, low-flying planes, off-the-cuff remarks, sorrow, and euphoria . . . I slipped back out exhausted and dazed.

Blissful over her "romance" with Alain Delon, she was always explaining how he would come get her from T. to take her directly to Paris, *par avion*. She was illiterate and was constantly looking for someone to help her write letters to her beloved. Since I, too, was often hanging around the movie theater and was one of the few who didn't mock her, I became her go-to letter-writer, a local Cyrano de Bergerac. They all began with "To my heart's true love, Alain," then obligatorily moved on to a short critique of his latest film, with a detailed explanation of how she had deciphered all the signs he was sending her from the screen. Sometimes, she would allow herself brief, jealous admonitions, for example to watch out for that young Anne Parillaud, as well as for that ditzy M. D. (I silently replaced "ditzy" with "ritzy") . . . The letters always ended with assurances that she, Juliet, was ready, she didn't have much luggage and was waiting for him, so why didn't he drop her a line or two to let her know when he would be coming to get her? He could find her every afternoon in front of the movie theater. I would put the letter in an envelope, write "Alain Delon, Paris" on it, and she herself would drop it into the yellow mailbox. The return address was invariably "The Town of T., Juliet, in front of the movie theater." Clearly, these addresses only underscored the fame of both correspondents. Known to the world and to their town.

One day, however, the miracle of miracles occurred and Juliet received a letter from Alain Delon. Someone had left it at the box office of the movie theater. The fact that the postmark on the envelope bore the name of the neighboring city and that the letter was written in Bulgarian were negligible details. I had the honor of being its first reader. Juliet no longer trusted anyone else.

"My dear Juliet," the local wags had written, with all of their small-town cruelty, "I get your letters regularly and I was forced to learn Bulgarian so I would be able to write back to you. I don't always manage to reply, because I'm swamped with work and women, but I don't pay any attention to the women due to my eternal devotion to you, my dearest child, my darling fiancée. Never stop waiting for me, gather up your dowry, be sure to throw in a swimsuit, I'll swing by T. to take you directly to Sardinia. Your ever-loving, Delon."

They had reeled her in like a sardine, but she was darting around in such joy that I didn't have the heart to insist that the letter was a forgery. She snatched the envelope out of my hands and stuffed her nose into it, as if trying to catch a whiff of Delon's cologne, then she hugged me, tucked the letter in her bosom and set off to make the rounds of the city, mad with happiness, spreading the good news and saying her goodbyes.

Now nothing could shake her certainty that Delon would come, and she spent all her afternoons in front of the movie theater with a shabby little bag holding her dowry and swimsuit. Years passed, the movie theater closed down in the '90s, Delon himself grew mercilessly old, but Juliet never missed an afternoon, hanging around the agreed-upon place. I've rummaged through my personal archives and old newspapers from those days, I can't find any pictures or any sign of her, the town's sole aristocrat. Her brother, Downtown Gosho, had wrested the title of town madman from her, what inequality in madness as well! Gosho himself, good-natured and harmless, was found drowned, entangled in the reeds of the Tundzha River. From a surviving picture of him, we can reconstruct a bit of his sister Juliet's luminous face as well.

Let me add Juliet's story to the time capsule that is this book. One day, Delon, old and forgotten, will learn that every afternoon in the town of T. for forty years (here Penelope shrinks in shame), a woman has been waiting for him in front of the long-defunct local movie theater with all her luggage in a small bag.

An Official History of the 1980s

In 1981, Bulgaria turned 1,300 years old. For two years running, we watched herds of galloping proto-Bulgarians and hordes of barbaric Slavs hidden in the bogs, breathing through hollow reeds like snorkels. Everybody had a friend or relative who was an extra in the crowd scenes in those historic epic films. Rumors flew about proto-Bulgarians with digital watches that carelessly appeared in some of the shots. At that time, digital watches were a big hit, to the delight of the Vietnamese wheeler-dealers we bought them from on the black market; you couldn't just take them off and leave them lying around somewhere. In a certain sense, the 1,300th anniversary passed like a film premiere. The true events of 1981, the ones we hadn't prepared for, were something else entirely.

Mehmet Ali Ağca shot the pope. Bulgaria was mixed up in it somehow and we all stood glued to our TV sets. Nothing brings a small nation together like the feeling that everyone is against it.

Bulgaria was not directly involved in the other important event. In December, we heard about AIDS for the first time. Which, in 1981, officially put an end to the '60s. All sexual revolutions were called off for health reasons. Since they had never really started here in Bulgaria, we didn't take their end as anything particularly tragic.

Brezhnev died the very next year. Did this have anything to do with the AIDS epidemic? I doubt it. It was a November day, cheerless and dreary, it was raining. They announced the news at school, the teachers looked more scared than sad. Yes, fear was stronger than grief. Who will protect us now? Classes were cancelled for the day. The next day, they brought the television set from the teachers' lounge out into the corridor and made us line up at attention to watch the funeral, in all of its dismal detail: the massive coffin heaped with flowers, the slow marches that echoed throughout the whole school. They had cranked up the volume to the max. The youngest kids, who were right in front of the television, looked on in bewilderment—it was most likely the first time they had seen a dead person. And so we confronted death head-on, in a cold school corridor, forcing ourselves to sniffle a bit for a person who had meant nothing to us. I was twelve and had kissed a girl for the first time the day before, albeit it in the dark during a game of spin-the-bottle at a birthday party. First kiss, first death.

That marked the beginning of the end. Soviet general secretaries started dying off every year or two, like an epidemic. The ritual was already worked out. School would be called off for a day. The next day, we would watch the funeral in the school hallway and the class presidents would cry, while those of us in the back rows would peg each other with rice launched from pens-turned-blow-darts. After so much repetition, death no longer made such an impression on us.

In fact, the whole period I was in puberty can be briefly described through the prism of the complex political context of the '80s.
First kiss (with a girl).
Brezhnev dies.
Second kiss (different girl).
Andropov dies.
Third kiss . . .
Chernenko dies.
Am I killing them?
First fumbling sex in the park.
Chernobyl.
A long half-life of exponential decay ensues.

Yellow Submarine

After numerous, careful listens to "Yellow Submarine," recorded in 1968, you can discover an encoded call to revolution, a conspiratorial message from the Beatles to the youth of Bulgaria. In the middle of the song (precisely one minute and 35 seconds from the beginning) in the background noise you can clearly hear the phrase "pusni mi verigata" or "let go of my chain," with the accent on the "u," uttered very quickly in impeccable Bulgarian. Just like that: *pusnimiverigata*. Unfortunately, we decoded it far too late, in the mid '80s, when all was already lost.

We all live in a . . . tum-tuh-dum-tuh-dumm . . . tum-tuh-dum-tuh-dumm . . . tum-tuh-dum-tuh-dumm

We all live in a . . . tum-tuh-dum-tuh-dumm . . . tum-tuh-dum-tuh-dumm . . . tum-tuh-dum-tuh-dumm

But no Yellow Submarine ever passed by the Yellow House.

Four Seconds from the '90s

I saw myself in a three-minute video from November 3, 1989, the only surviving one as far as I know, despite all the cameras that were there. For four seconds, I was twenty years old. Four long seconds, which gave me time to remember everything. God, how skinny and ridiculous I was, with my bulging Adam's apple, hair hanging in my eyes, my jacket, as cheap as only a student's could be. And there's Gaustine, too, the only shots of him, he never let himself be photographed. We're constantly looking around, curiosity and fear. It was the first protest rally in Bulgaria in forty years. Seen from today, the protest was completely harmless in its demands: stop some hydro-project from polluting the Rila Mountains. But the Wall hadn't fallen yet, nor had the regime in Bulgaria. I noticed the plainclothes people with cameras, who definitely weren't from the news station. Secret service agents use a different filming technique, they zoom in on individual faces so that they can be identified. Thanks to that I can be seen up-close for a whole four seconds. The cameraman overdid it a bit. Here and there I catch sight of familiar faces, a few people from the university, a poet. Their faces are anxious, their bodies tense, ill-at-ease, our clothes are almost identical, badly cut, mass-produced. Yes, unlike the '60s, which were truly sexy, colorful, they knew how to dress, the '80s, like communism as a whole, came to an ugly end.

Look, now on the recording you can see the plainclothes agents bursting in, driving a wedge in the rally to cause chaos. We spot them, my friend and I exchange a few words, then I turn my head to the right, directly toward the camera that is filming me. That happens during the third second. I try to enlarge the frame, but the recording is too grainy. By the fourth second, I'm already gone.

So I don't forget . . .

From a bookstore on Vitosha Boulevard, I stole the book *What to Cook During a Crisis*, so I could give it to the girl I was living with at the time. We didn't have anything to eat in our apartment besides two cans of beans, food aid from the Swiss Army's supplies, already past their expiration date. We would sit down in the evenings with the stolen cookbook.

What should we whip up for dessert?

Well, what do you say to pear cake?

We would open up to page 146, where the cake recipe was, and would start to read slowly, savoring the taste of every word. We would add half a cup of honey to the butter melted in a pan. We would carefully separate the egg yolks from the whites. We would then mix the yolks with half of the sugar, plus the oil, milk, flour, and baking powder. We would stir the ingredients very well with a wire hand mixer and pour them into the greased pan. We would put the pan in the oven and bake it until golden-brown. We didn't have any of the abovementioned things, except the pan, the oven, and the wire hand mixer. But we got so into it that afterward, you could see traces of flour on our hands.

Auntie Fannie, 70, from the Youth 1 neighborhood, requested a stomach X-ray at the local polyclinic because of the free oatmeal they gave out before the exam.

The cold and the power outages during the '90s. The dark foyer of the Globus movie theater, strangers' blind breathing backs . . .

Meetings across dark Sofia, as I make the rounds as a freelance nighttime reporter for some newspaper. A bear-trainer without his bear, wandering through the city. Some newly minted Mafiosi had rolled up in an SUV, asked him how much the bear cost, he had stood his ground, telling them it wasn't for sale, they whacked him over the neck, grabbed the bear's chain and tied it to the back of the SUV. They needed it, they said, to train their pit-bulls. They tossed fifty leva at him, and the bear went running off after the SUV, roaring. These little things don't even make it into the black chronicles of the '90s.

The story of Blind Tony, who is trying to find himself a wife on the bus to Students' Town with a single, endless recitative:

> *Yes, Tony am I, I'm a one-in-a-million guy,*
> *I'm looking for a wife, with whom to share my life . . .*

This is followed by an epic, adventure-filled tale about who he is and where he is going, how he has struggled to make a life for himself in the big city, a story about the future young family he'll found, plans for children and a peaceful old age . . . At the end, in the same rhythm and in rhyme, Blind Tony gives his exact address and telephone number.

The story of a college classmate of mine, who would spend several hours every day in the noisiest café near the university, desperately hoping to find someone to marry her before she went back to her hometown of B. There, her father would scream at her from the doorstep: "Did you get married yet, girl? What did we waste all that money on for these five years, only to have you come back an old maid? There's no man for you here!"

She would sit there, slowly sipping the biggest coffee in the world, waiting. Her secret desire for marriage was already painfully obvious. All the men avoided that table. Once she called me up in a panic, saying that she was in a very tight spot, her father was really sick and she wanted to bring home some man before he passed away. Just this once, she assured me. I agreed, we went to her hometown. They had laid out a huge table under the trellis, around which her closest aunts and uncles and a few neighbors were sitting in gloomy silence. They carried out her father, he looked like a very ill local Don Corleone. I went up to him, he looked at me for a full minute, tried to say something, coughed, and they carried him back inside.

Years later, I happened to end up at the bus station in the same town. An old woman peered at me and cried: "Hey, there's the boy! The same one who lied to our girl and left her at the altar, why didn't you get married, my boy . . ."

Books with their old socialist price tags from bookstores on the brink of going out of business, which we would sell in the courtyard of the university. *Zoo, or Letters Not about Love* by Shklovsky, a collection of Kafka's letters entitled *I Was Born To Live in Solitude*, all pocket editions, and Joyce's *Portrait of the Artist as a Young Man*, in hardcover, for a whopping 4.18 leva, but nobody bought it. *Once upon a time and a very good time it was there was a moocow coming down along the road and this moocow that was coming down along the road met a nicens little boy named baby tuckoo . . .*

These are just the little things that will fall by the wayside, everything else is there in the newspapers from that time. Yet despite everything, the '90s was the most lively, the best decade in which everything could have happened. We were young for the last time then. It was then that Gaustine appeared, a philosophy drop-out, with his ingenious projects (and flops), which occupy a whole separate notebook.

Why does Gaustine continue to be important to me? I've rarely had friends. Empathy predisposes you to closeness with people, but not in my case, when the weight of others' sorrows pressed down on me like a sickness. No women, no relationships, no friendships. But Gaustine seemed to be made of a different time and different matter. I don't know anyone like him—translucent, yet simultaneously opaque. I would pass through him like thin air or run into a glass wall. But despite this, or perhaps precisely because of it, he was the only one I could call a friend.

Gaustine's Projects

All the ways of earning money honestly had slowly evaporated. One day, we were hanging around the movie theater to see which new films were out. The tickets were unattainably impensive, we just gaped at the poster and a few photos in the display window.

Then Gaustine had an ingenious idea: we would retell movies. A detailed retelling over the course of thirty minutes for a minimal fee. His "Movies for the Poor" Project. Complete dumping of the film industry. And he got really worked up. Can you imagine what a move this is, what a historical reversal from the visual back toward the narrative? You stand in front of the movie theater, mingling with those folks hanging around outside, and strike up a casual conversation, saying how amazing the film was, but these movie theater types are motherfucking bloodsuckers for charging those prices; however, you've seen it already and would be happy to retell it to them in detail in exchange for an absolutely negligible 700 leva. Tickets cost ten times that amount. We gather up a group of fifteen or so and we're good to go.

Wait, wait, I interrupt him, when are we going to watch the movie?

We'll watch it afterward, after we get the money, Gaustine replies.

But then what will we tell them?

We'll make it up, he replies innocently. How hard could it be, you're a writer, right? You've got a title, a few lines from the poster and a couple photos in the display window. What more could you want?

He was something else. He wasn't even kidding. He had absolutely no sense of humor. Like all obsessed people. Like those who are off the beaten track, as my grandma would say. Like revolutionaries and women—according to Nietzsche.

Movies for the Poor. Like those Tamagotchi for the poor from that old joke. Tamagotchi, if anyone still remembers, were those pager-like (perhaps I need to explain what a pager is, too?) gadgets on which you could take care of your electronic pet, feed it at certain times, give it water, and play with it when it whined. And when you got sick of it, you'd ditch it for a few days, until it starved to death. Where have all those Tamagotchi gone? To all the old pagers. A person has no idea how much death he is capable of generating.

I know I'm getting sidetracked, but let's have a minute of silence for the souls of:

The pagers of yore

Tamagotchi

Videocassettes and the VCR

Cassette-tape players,

which buried eight-tracks,

which buried record-players,

Audiocassettes

Telegrams, with their whole accompanying ritual

Typewriters (allow me to add a personal farewell to my Maritsa, filled with cigarette ashes and coffee from the '90s.) Writing on a typewriter required physical exertion, a different type of movement, if you recall.

OK, the minute's over. What were we talking about? Movies for the Poor, yes, but first let me finish the joke. Since Tamagotchi also cost money, Tamagotchi for the poor also cropped up. And you know what they were? A cockroach in a matchbox. That's it. It may not be funny anymore, but I insist upon gathering up these odds and ends, all the things that have already passed away, they're gone, dead. Which I guess is the opposite of what is written: "to carry them through the flood alive and to go forth and multiply again" . . . I've gotten completely turned around. I don't know whether the things I've now chaotically and slightly hysterically saved from my own flood will be able to live, let alone go forth and multiply. I know that the past is as fruitless as a barren mare. But that makes it all the more dear to me.

That idea about movies for the poor didn't bear any fruit, either. Let me just say that we barely escaped unscathed after I tried to tell the first group the story of a film I hadn't seen.

The "Personal Poem" project also met a similar end.

There's no such thing as shameful work, Gaustine repeated this old chestnut one morning. You'll sit there like those street artists who draw people for money, you'll hold a pencil and paper, saying: Would you like me to write a poem for you? Every pretty girl has the right to a poem. (I think that was a quote). It'll only take ten minutes.

So there I was on a bench, in the park in front of Café Crystal downtown, with a few sheets of paper, a pencil, and a discreet sign in front of me offering "personal poem" services. Toward the end of the second uneventful hour, a woman of around fifty came up to me. This wasn't the way we'd imagined it. For some reason, we'd imagined all of our clients being twenty-year-old girls. She was plump and looked like a bad guy from a Soviet cartoon. She asked for her personal poem. The designated ten minutes passed. Nothing. My head was empty and hollow, like a basement in which you can hear only the minutes dripping and trickling away. I started feeling worse and worse for both of us. She started sweating, took out a tissue, can I move, yes, of course, I'm not drawing you, after all. Where should I look? It doesn't matter, slightly off to the side, you don't need to look at me, it's a bit distracting. She was either romantic or nouveau riche. And with every passing minute echoing in the void, my failure gleamed ever brighter. Finally, I decided to grab the bull by the horns. I raised my head, looked her straight in the eye and said: "Actually, you have such a strong aura today that it's very difficult for me to concentrate. Would you mind stopping by some other time?"

At that time, all the newspapers were writing about auras and aliens. And it worked, the woman, instead of slapping me across the face, beamed. She said I was a true poet, and that she had immediately recognized this. Only a natural born poet could catch auras. (As if auras were carp.) She announced that she lived nearby and invited me to her place for a glass of wine. I agreed mostly out of a sense of guilt. It turned out that she lived alone. She took out the bottle, sat down quite close to me on the couch, despite the abundance of open seats, and pressed her body up against me. I beg your pardon, I'm a poet, I shot out, quickly standing up. As if wanting to remind her that I work mainly with auras and that bodies do not enter into my sphere of competence.

Sssssmaaack! Her slap quickly sent that project, too, into the heap of Gaustine's great and misunderstood ideas.

He took the lead in the "Condom Catwalk" project himself.

All he needed to do was go to the people with the cash and explain what a goldmine he was offering. He came back crestfallen. We sat down, poured ourselves green cows (crème de menthe with milk) and he described in detail how as soon as he set foot in that obscenely rich agency, he knew that they wouldn't appreciate the idea.

A fashion revue for rubbers. A revolution, Gaustine was getting enthused.

A revue-lution, I chimed in.

That's good, remember it, he noted in passing before going on. No one has ever done that kind of fashion show, know what I mean? They've put everything imaginable on the catwalk, but never this accessory, Gaustine was getting worked up. Total minimalism. Condom producers will pour crazy cash into it. But they were like—how would the whole catwalk with condom-wearing models work?

First, the state would slap them with a huge fine for pornography, second, no TV station would broadcast that kind of fashion show. Or if they did, they would have to put little black squares right over the most central part of the event.

And lastly, heh heh heh, they were just rolling with laughter, who's gonna guarantee non-stop erections backstage, huh? Who? Do you have any idea what a huge job that'd be? Like changing tires in a Formula 1 pit stop. Ha ha ha . . .We're talking serious pumping!

Gaustine waited for the jokes to die down and told them coldly: Come on, take your wangs out of your mouths nice and slowly. In fact, the show won't involve live models.

What do you mean, the agency guys gaped at him.

To avoid all those problems, Gaustine said, we'll use African ritual figures. They all have large phalluses.

Large what? the dudes asked, confused.

Large, erect phalluses, Gaustine repeated calmly.

Cocks, the boss explained.

That way we'll add some art to the whole business, since only then is an erect phallus not pornography, Gaustine concluded his presentation.

They made him wait outside while they made their decision. They called him back in an hour later and turned him down. Because of the art thing. Who's gonna want to look at some African statues with boners? They had nothing against art (or porn either, probably), but in this case neither was worth their while.

So this idea, too, was sent to the repository of failures. Fine, put it down in the notebook, Gaustine said. Clearly we're ahead of our time. Some day they'll be fighting each other tooth-and-nail for that idea. And so he piled up his treasures in the future. I was merely the treasurer. In the end, writing, too, is the preservation of failures.

Now that would really make him mad. Something that hasn't happened yet is not a failure, I can hear him saying.

I believe that somewhere else, in some other time and place, he is an ingenious and successful inventor or a great swindler.

Here, in the brown notebook of failures, also rest Gaustine's other unrealized projects:

Vault for personal stories. We would hear out, preserve, and keep stories in full confidence for a certain period of time. If the client so desired, after his death, his story could be willed to his heirs.

Projections on the sky. (One of his most monumental projects.) An ultra-powerful apparatus would project upon the whole "screen" of the sky. In the beginning, he didn't have a clear idea of what exactly would be projected, yet the idea of that celestial open-air cinema filled him with excitement. Such a huge space can't just sit there empty and unused. Just imagine the whole hemisphere craning their necks and looking up at the same moment.

A month later the project had taken on much more concrete parameters. Let's project clouds on the clouds themselves, best of all when there's low, dense cloud cover.

And what will you project onto them?

Clouds, for example, for a start.

Clouds?

Clouds on clouds. Let's see how nature reacts to the duplication, to the tautology. And it'll be best if we project rain. Just imagine— cinematic rain from real clouds. At first, the audience will scatter, frightened. Like in *The Arrival of a Train in La Ciotat Station* in 1896. At the beginning and end of cinema stands a natural scare.

There's more . . . *Garden of Novels*. Classic novels will be planted in rich soil, watered and fertilized with manure to see which of them will bear fruit. A project for reestablishing balance—what is made of wood should once again return to the earth.

The project "A la Minute Architecture" is also here. Small wire sculptures recreating several seconds or a minute from the flight of the ordinary housefly; the wire should accurately reproduce all the twists and turns of the flight.

And the photo exhibition "Skies over various cities, photographed at three in the afternoon." And Lord knows what else . . .

Gaustine. His only successful project was his own disappearance. One evening he came to say goodbye, I asked where he was going, sure that he had come up with some new scheme. To 1937, he said simply. I took it as a joke. Drop me a line, I said. At that time the '90s were in full swing, the most interesting of times, but he disappeared. I had no idea (and still don't) what he had come up with. But when I got the first letter followed by two or three postcards, written in the old handwriting from the 1930s—yes, I think every decade has its own hand—I realized that this time, unlike all the others, he had managed to pull it off.

(I've told more about this in some "And Other Stories.")

I saw him one winter afternoon years later at a café in the London airport, holding a magazine in his hand and looking worried, as far as I could tell from a distance. My plane was about to take off, I just ran over to say "hi," I almost threw myself down on his table. He looked at me coldly, I noticed his white turtleneck sweater, of the type that had long since gone out of style, Are the gentleman and I acquainted? I stood there stunned for a few seconds, heard my name on the last call for my flight and dashed back to the gate. I had noticed that the magazine he was reading was *Time* from 1968, opened up to an article on the war in Vietnam. It was January 2007.

A late text message at 3 A.M. years later.

I found out that cat urine glows in the dark. I thought that might interest you.

There was no name, but it could only be from one person. At least now he was in some closer year (unless he was already a cat).

Recently the London *Times* mentioned a new invention designed for rich yet harried businessmen with a taste for pinching pennies (or leading double lives)—a tourist agency for virtual tourism. The agency also supplies souvenirs from the untaken trip. You receive all the material evidence of a journey, including stamps in your passport, photos, ticket stubs from the Louvre, for example, or shells from the Cote d'Azure. (Maybe even sandwiches from the Sandwich Islands.) They tell you how your very own vacation went, outfit you with a whole set of memories. It's enough to make you yourself believe that you've taken the trip. For a moment it crossed my mind that Gaustine was giving me a sign.

IV. Time Bomb
(To Be Opened after the End of the World)

The Aging of an Empath

Once I could be in everything, be everything. Now, in the ineptness of my mature years, I wanted to gather up everything, as a small compensation for that which I had lost.

The aging of an empath is a strange and painful process. The corridors toward others and their stories, which once were open, now turn out to be walled up. House arrest in your own body.

Earlier, I would at times feel the need to shut myself up in the dark, letting nothing awaken the empathy, to just sit like that in the healing darkness of the nothingness. To keep myself from scattering, to stop the influxes of other people's sorrows and stories.

The only thing I want now is to remember a few days with that physical intensity of childhood, when I lived out everyone else's story as my own. What was the diagnosis again—radical empathetic-somatic syndrome . . . I no longer emplant, I only have memories of such emplantings—but what memories! They soar like meteorites in the dark. Sometimes I am (again) the Minotaur, other times Laika the dog, I leave a woman during wartime, I see my nine-month-old father and am happy, they abandon my three-year-old self at a mill at the turn of the century, they kill me as a bull a century later in a bullfight in T . . .

When I sensed that this ability was starting to fade, that I was undergoing de-empathization, as my doctor might jokingly put it, I resorted to this pale substitute—collecting. I felt an urgent need to horde, to organize things into boxes and notebooks, into lists and enumerations. To preserve things with words. The empty space left behind by one obsession can always be taken up by another. Before, I could inhabit all the bodies in the world, now I'm happy if I manage to move from room to room within the house of my own body. I stay the longest (did I mention this already?) in the children's bedroom.

Who am I. A forty-four-year-old man, in a basement with thick cement walls, a former bomb shelter. I say I'm forty-four, but add to that the age of my grandfather, who was born in 1913, also add that of my father, born at the end of the second Great War, of Juliet in front of the movie theater, of the escape artist Gaustine, add the ages of yet more people, whom I've inhabited for longer or shorter stretches, two cats, a dog, a few slugs, two dinosaurs—their skeletons are in the Berlin Museum of Natural Sciences. Add to all that the incalculable age of one Minotaur, who has never left the home that is my body.

Sometimes I am forty-four, sometimes ninety-one, sometimes in the labyrinth of a cave or a basement, in the night of time, sometimes in the darkness of a womb, as of yet unborn.

Most often, I am ten.

I wonder whether I'll die as all those things at once? *I'll suffer mass extinction, he told them, I'll become totally extinct* . . . like in that kiddie song about dinosaurs, where do I know it from?

First Aid Kit for after the End of the World
And here's the first notebook with instructions, begun in the late '70s, when it became definitively clear that World War III was inevitable—and the end of the world along with it.

I open up to the first page, written in a difficult-to-decipher hand.

> *Human beings like hugs. If you happen to meet some surviving human being, open your upper appendages up wide and gently squeeze him. For best results, keep your arms like that as long as you can.*

(This is followed by a hand-drawn diagram of people hugging.)

> *This will calm the human being down a lot. He might even start crying with a clear liquid coming from his eyes. Human beings love to cry. It's no big deal, it can't kill you. It's more dangerous if a red liquid starts trickling out of somewhere, it's stickier, because of the erythrocytes, I think. You have to stop it immediately or it could result in death. Death is . . .*

I had stopped there. Not because I couldn't explain death. I was already twelve and knew what death is, I could have copied the definition from my biology textbook—the cessation of all the vital functions of an organism is called . . . But who knows whether the language of those who would find the notebook had developed according to the same logic, whether their words followed that logic and whether they even used language in the first place? Did the ones who would come know what "red" is, for example? Maybe they would use some other word for red, say "blue." Or "tomato." Or "ktrnt." Or maybe they wouldn't have any words for colors at all:

a) because eyes will have long-since become vestigial organs, they will use far more advanced senses.

b) they won't read letters, that'll be a bygone stage, they will be illiterate, which in their case might actually be some kind of supra-literacy . . .

In any case, I added down at the bottom:

If you find this, you'd best come looking for me, I'll explain everything in
real life (if I'm still alive). You can find me in the basement at the school
(the entrance is under the stairway) or in the bomb shelter under the Tobacco
Factory, which is three blocks from here.

I signed it, too. Then I decided that wasn't enough, so I wrote out
my full name and a short description of myself. *Bluish-green eyes,*
more greenish in the summer, light hair, tall, with a straight nose, no
visible identification marks. Just like in my grandfather's passport.
However, that "no visible identification marks" wouldn't have helped
much in recognizing me, so I added: high forehead with supercili-
ary protuberances (I had heard that from the school doctor during
a check-up) and a mole on the left side under my lower lip. I knew
that people who hadn't met in a long time recognized each other
by their moles. I also added, which now seems wise to me, that in
the year 2000, I would be a thirty-three-year-old man. And since
human beings live an average of seventy-five years—and men even
a bit less than that—that after 2050 I most likely won't be able to
be of any assistance. But until then I'll be at their disposal. Then I
signed it once again.

He places (I can see him clearly in my memory) the notebook with
the instructions in a round metal Singer tin, the most valuable thing
he owns. It's from "before the Ninth," as his grandfather liked to
say. Always, when someone wants to say that something is really
old, they say it is from "before the Ninth"—i.e. before September
9, 1944, the date of the communist coup in Bulgaria. It sounds like
"before Christ." And the strangest part of all is that his grandma
and grandpa are also from before the Ninth, it's downright unbelievable. The tin has some strange letters on it, with a big red S on the
lid and gold decorations winding around it. Years later, on all of

my travels I would recognize in the details of houses and pictures from the turn of the century that Secession style, which, thanks to that tin, had been part of my childhood. A tin for thread and fabric samples given as a free gift along with the sewing machine.

The Singer sewing machine itself had disappeared "after the Ninth" for some strange reason. That was another dark and muddled thing. What existed before the Ninth disappeared after the Ninth. Yet that tin for thread and fabric samples remained, it had somehow managed to smuggle itself from one system into the other, so he could keep all of his treasures in it. The metal was sturdy enough to survive one end of the world, that's why he put his notebook with instructions inside as well. Just in case, however, he put the Singer tin in a larger, round halvah tin. True, it didn't look nearly as nice, it was even a little rusty, but it would nevertheless be safer that way, with doubled armor. Besides, who would think to swipe an old halvah tin? Then he tore a sheet of paper out of the notebook, smeared it with a tube of half-dried-up Rila glue and stuck it on top of the halvah label. Then very slowly, in capital letters, he wrote out: "To Be Opened after the End of the World!"

Although he couldn't explain why, he knew that the end of the world was not the end. After that, something would have to survive, to start all over again.

He had read in an encyclopedia that the most important discoveries in human history were fire and the wheel. That's why the first thing he put in the tin was a box of matches. After some hesitation, he added his favorite toy car. First, they would figure out what a wheel was and how it worked, then they would produce a real car, following the prototype. The matches and the little red car formed the basis of this kit for surviving apocalypses. Then he added a bottle of iodine, a bandage, half a package of aspirin and that "Vietnamese wonder gel" with its fearsome ingredient "tiger balm," whose sharp, pungent scent cured everything—from colds to mosquito bites. A first-aid kit for after the end of the world. That would do for a start.

I race into the bomb shelter of the third person singular, I send another into the minefields of the past. I was that same person, who was once in first person, and now I'm afraid to ask whether he's still alive. Are they still alive, all those we've been?

Double Preparedness

1980. On the one hand, there was the apocalypse, the flood, the end of the world according to his grandmother and St. John. On the other hand, that toothy (and armed to the teeth) Jimmy Carter was lurking, with his cowboy hat, riding a Pershing missile, as he was drawn in his father's newspaper. At school, the slide projector was constantly showing shots of that atomic mushroom cloud and he already carefully skirted any mushroom that happened to sprout up in the garden, as if it might explode under his sandals.

The two apocalypses—his grandmother's and the school's official one—didn't coincide precisely, which only made matters worse. It clearly was a question of two different ends of the world, as if one weren't enough. And a person had to be ready for each of them if he wanted to survive.

The preventative measures were also different. His grandma stopped slaughtering chickens, leaving that sin to weigh on his grandfather's soul. According to her, a person had to constantly repent and avoid sins of any kind. To reduce his load, for some time he ceased his experiments with ants and tried not to hate so much that revolting creature Stefka, who sat in the desk behind him, who never missed a chance to make fun of him for blushing. He couldn't think of any other sins.

Defense against nuclear and chemical weapons was more complicated. You needed to put on your gas mask in no time flat. "In no time flat"—his Basic Military Training teacher's favorite phrase. Then immediately add your cloak, rubber gloves, rubber boots, and hightail it to the nearest bomb shelter. Or if the bomb shelter is too far away, fall flat on your face in the direction opposite the nuclear blast, and don't look at the mushroom cloud so as not to ruin your eyes. He knew everything, just as the rest of his classmates did, about the chemical weapons sarin, soman, mustard gas, and the havoc they wreaked. They had become experts on poison gases, chemical and biological weapons, atomic and neutron bombs, Pershing and cruise missiles.

So there wouldn't be any surprises, he practiced for both scenarios. Whatever happens, put on your gas mask and start praying. During one of the drills, he tried to say a prayer with his gas mask on his head, but only a quiet rumbling could be heard through the hose, while the eyepieces of the tight rubber mask fogged up.

"What are you babbling to yourself about, greenhorn?" His military training teacher barked at him—he was a major, wore a uniform, and they were all afraid of him. "When you prattle on, you only use up your oxygen more quickly."

Whoever managed to put on his gas mask in the allotted time—how many seconds was it?—would survive. Whoever didn't, like Zhivka the Gimp, whose left arm was deformed, would be toast.

During recess, he would sit by himself at his desk, calculating whether his mother and father would make the cut-off. If they didn't, why should he bother trying to survive? As for his grandma and grandpa, they didn't stand a chance, they were so slow. His grandma would first have to put on her glasses, she never knew where they were, then she'd have to find the bag with the gas mask, call to his grandpa, who was surely out somewhere with the cows . . .That definitely added up to more seconds than were allotted.

Side Corridor

A person wearing a gas mask resembles a Minotaur.

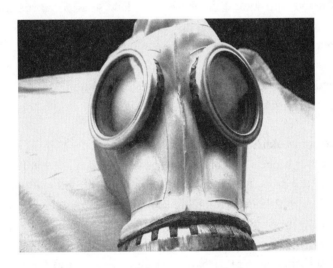

Death Is a Cherry Tree That Ripens without Us

Nothing will be destroyed by the bomb. The houses will remain intact, the school will remain intact, the streets and trees will still be there, and the cherry tree in the yard will ripen, only we won't be there. That's what they told us today in school about the aftermath of the neutron bomb.

—Notebook with instructions, 1980

Only now do I realize how precise that description is. The street is still there, the trees are still there, look, there's the cherry tree, except we're dead. Nothing is left of me, the erstwhile savior of the world. So that means somebody nevertheless dropped the neutron bomb. The absence of my grandmother, my grandfather, my father, my mother, and of that boy, about whom it's difficult for me to speak in the first person, only serves to confirm this.

No one has yet invented a gas mask and bomb shelter against time.

Time Shelter

The day after the Apocalypse, there won't be any newspapers. How ironic. The most significant event in the history of the world will go unreported.

But it's still beforehand. And I need to hurry . . . to finish my work.

A woman from Iran, sentenced to be stoned to death for adultery. Just don't do it in front of my son, the woman says, having managed to give an interview to a European newspaper. A girl from Afghanistan on the cover of *Time* with her ears and nose cut off. The photo is shocking, a big black hole gapes where her nose should be.

A huge fire near Moscow, the suffocating smoke blankets the city, the number of victims rises every day. Floods in Europe. A deluge in Pakistan . . .

I copy down the newspaper headlines. The dates say August 2010. I've read similar news in the Old Testament and in some of the medieval chronicles. It would be interesting to make a journal out of newspaper headlines only. Flood . . . Fire . . . Cut off . . . I carefully fold the newspaper in half, then once again, then once again, until it is as small as a napkin and all that can be read of the words are . . . od . . . fi . . . off. I stuff it into a box labeled "Fragile."

I'm trying to keep a precise catalogue of everything. For the time when "now" will be "back then," as we wrote in our school yearbooks, liberally doused with the tears of our youth, which didn't cost a thing. Good thing that the basement is big, an old bomb shelter, and despite all the stuff I've gathered up over the years, there's still free space to be found. I insisted on that when buying the place. A nice, big cellar, a whole underground apartment, with two hallways, walls that form niches and secret passageways. I quizzed the owner at length about the thickness of the walls, the year the place was built, any past flooding, and so on. He was quite surprised. He must've regretted not raising the price a bit. Are you planning on living down here? No, I replied. And the next day I moved the most basic necessities for living into the basement. I spend most of my time down here. I feel at home. I mostly use the floor above as an alibi. If you put some effort into appearing normal, you can save yourself a lot of time, during which you can be what you want to be in peace.

In recent days the newspapers have reported that they've found the diaries of Dr. Mengele, who lived to a ripe old age in Latin America. Written between 1960 and 1975 in ordinary spiral-bound notebooks. Full of notes about the weather, short poems and philosophical musings, biographical details. An alibi for life itself, with all of its innocent details.

January 1

I'm not a hermit, I have a television downstairs (I only watch the evening news), I subscribe to thirty-odd newspapers and magazines, so I'm certainly no hermit. I still need to follow the world closely, I'm gathering signs.

I read Aristotle's *Poetics* and listen to some surviving vinyl record.

It's January 1 of the final year, according to some calendar. It's too quiet, even for the afternoon of such a day. There aren't the usual calls, texted greetings. I turn off my phone, to have an alibi for that silence.

In the newspapers I processed a while back, it said that "unfriend" was the word of the year for 2009. It feels like that's all I've been doing these past ten years. Over time, friends have been disappearing in different ways. Some suddenly, as if they had never existed. Others gradually, awkwardly, apologetically . . . They stop calling. At first you don't get it. Then you start checking to see whether your phone battery has died. A sharp absence at five in the afternoon. At first it lasts around an hour, then it gets shorter. But it never disappears. Just like with the cigarettes you quit smoking years ago, but which you keep dreaming about.

In the dying light of the day I once again feel that inrush of obscure sorrow and fear, true savage fear, for which I have no name. I quickly put on my coat, pull on a hat with ear flaps, I could easily pass as either hip or homeless, that suits me fine, I'm invisible in any case.

If anyone wants to see what his neighborhood will look like after the end of the world, he should go outside on the afternoon of January 1. Indescribable silence. All available reserves of joy have been spent the previous evening. Dry and cold, the rock bottom has been laid bare. Metaphysical rock bottom. I've always wondered what is actually being celebrated—the end of one year or the beginning of another. Most likely the end. If we were celebrating the beginning, then January 1 would be the happiest day.

I stroll through the narrow, icy pathways between the apartment buildings, some empty wine bottle rolls from beneath my feet, along with the remains of explosive devices of every caliber . . . And not a soul outside. This is starting to look suspicious. As if someone, under the cover of New Year's fireworks, managed to blow everyone away. They detonated that neutron bomb. I'm the only survivor, behind the thick walls of my hiding place. I can't imagine there was anyone else cautious enough to have spent New Year's Eve in a bomb shelter. I wonder what's on CNN after the end of the world? I turn around to go check, and from the nothingness, two dogs and a bum jump out in front of me. The first living creatures . . . this year. I'm overjoyed to see them. Actually, this is their day, their New Year's is a day later. When the previous night's leftovers are thrown away and the dumpsters are overflowing like sad post-holiday malls.

To Be Opened After . . .

An alarm clock, safety pin, toothbrush, doll, matchbox car, ladies' hat, make-up kit, electric razor, cigarette case, pack of cigarettes, pipe, various scraps of cloth and fabric, one dollar in change, seeds for corn, tobacco, rice, beans, carrots . . .

What could hold a collection of such uncollectable things?

A suitcase, most likely. But who could be the owner of such a suitcase? The ladies' hat suggests a woman, the pipe and the electric razor a gentleman, even though that's no longer certain. Or the suitcase belongs to a little girl because of the doll, or perhaps a little boy because of the cars and all the odds and ends little boys tend to collect.

The list continues.

Novels, articles from *Encyclopaedia Britannica*, pictures by Picasso and Otto Dix, *Time, Vogue, Saturday Evening Post, Women's Home Companion*, and other magazines and newspapers from the late summer of 1938. All of that on microfiche. The Bible in hardcopy. Short letters from Albert Einstein and Thomas Mann. The "Our Father" in 300 languages (!) and two standard English dictionaries . . .

A museum's repository? A writer's den?

To be continued . . .

A fifteen-minute film reel containing: a sound film with a speech by Roosevelt apropos of the season (the year is still 1938); a panoramic flight over New York; the hero of the most recent Olympic games, Jesse Owens; the May Day parade on Red Square in Moscow; shots from the undeclared war between Japan and China; a fashion show in Miami, Florida, from April; two girls in full-length bathing costumes, gentlemen in afternoon attire . . . And a diagram showing the location of the capsule, with the precise latitude and longitude with respect to the equator and Greenwich.

A time capsule, yes. With the world's whole worrisome-cheerful schizophrenia, caught at a specific moment—on the eve of war, to boot.

That whole world was buried fifty feet underground on September 23, 1938, in perhaps the most famous capsule, designed by the engineers at Westinghouse Electric & Manufacturing Company for the World's Fair in New York. To be opened after 5,000 years. But exactly one year later, that world would be buried again (literally). This time without a ritual, without a capsule, and without a diagram showing the location.

At first, the engineers officially dubbed it the "Time Bomb," and it really did look like a bomb or a shell, with its elongated 228-centimeter body and rounded tip. Then they decided that was bad luck, so they changed the name, at least officially, but the fuse had already been set off.

In 1945 they wanted to open the capsule. Out of nostalgia for the lost, pre-war world? No. They wanted to add the most magnificent invention: a diagram of the atomic bomb. Then they decided against it. But twenty years later they couldn't help themselves and buried a second capsule in the same place, where, alongside information about the atom bomb and several newer weapons, they added a Beatles record, birth control pills, and a credit card.

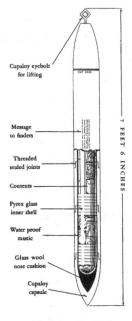

Cupaloy eyebolt for lifting

Message to finders

Threaded sealed joints

Contents

Pyrex glass inner shell

Water proof mastic

Glass wool nose cushion

Cupaloy capsule

7 FEET 6 INCHES

(Time bomb, 1938)

Voyager

The attempts to preserve time continue. The year is 1977. With the *Voyager* space shuttle, the strategy changes—the capsule can be buried in outer space. Until now, the direction had been down deep in the ground, now it's up deep in the sky. As far away as possible from earth, that dangerous place.

The golden plate contains a photograph of a five centimeter long fetus, a nursing mother, an astronaut in outer space (very similar to the fetus), a house, a supermarket, silhouettes of a man and a woman (the woman is pregnant and the baby is visible). But the best part are the sounds—the sound of rain, wind, a chimpanzee, a kiss, frogs, a crying baby being soothed, a tractor, a galloping horse, conversation around a campfire.

The shuttle is American, it was launched in the heat of the Cold War (such linguistic irony). We knew about *Voyager* only because there, on the golden plate, was a Bulgarian folk song. However, it also contained a greeting from the American president (we didn't know about that), that very same toothy Jimmy Carter, whom one neighbor woman of ours wanted to hack to bits with a cleaver like a chicken. So, in any case, now Jimmy Carter and that Bulgarian folk song were wandering amid the stars together. We were proud that our song of all things had been chosen. We later found out that it wasn't alone in the cosmos, but cheek-by-jowl with Azerbaijani bagpipes and a Georgian choir from the USSR, Aboriginal songs, Senegalese drums, Mozart, Bach, Beethoven . . . And we were slightly disappointed by this. Who knows why, but we imagined that all the aliens, when they stepped out in the evening onto their chilly celestial porches, liked best of all to play that Bulgarian folk song about a fierce rebel on their record players. (Small nations love being fierce.) I didn't understand any of the heavily dialectal lyrics of that song and was seriously worried about how the aliens would be able to understand it.

I hope they still haven't understood it, otherwise we'll lose them for good. Or maybe they gave it a listen and that's why they're late in coming. In short, Delyo, the hero of the song, threatens that if the Turks force two of his aunts to convert to Islam, he'll storm the village and *many a mother'll bawl / an' many a young bride'll howl / even the lil' baby in the belly'll cry out . . .*

That baby in its mother's womb, flying on the same disc with Delyo, better watch out.

Other Capsules, Other Testaments

The year is still 1977. The place is the city of Pleven.

"In the foundation of the Pleven Memorial Panorama, in the floor of the lobby, a capsule with a message has been buried. It will be opened in exactly one hundred years, when all of us will be living under communism," the chairman of the State Council, Comrade Todor Zhivkov announced during the placement of the capsule.

"Well, we won't *all* be living under communism," my father says and switches off the TV, "that guy thinks he's gonna live forever." I imagine how one hundred years from now, the new man, *Homo communisticus*, opens up the capsule and reads the instructions from his forefather, the now-fossilized *Homo socialisticus*.

And what was written inside? Slogans like "a firm right hand . . . the benefits of communism . . . to each according to his needs . . ." and other mumbo-jumbo, as we said back then.

This capsule-mania turned out to be catching. Everyone was racing to bury messages for the future. Our school's turn eventually came around. The capsule resembled a big glass test tube. I had the feeling I'd seen it in the chemistry lab. In front of the whole school, the principal read our message to the future Pioneer, who would live under communism, and then stuffed it inside. Then they added three drawings and three essays by students. There had been an essay contest on the topic: "How do I see myself in the year 2000?" In short, we saw ourselves as communists let loose in the cosmos. Communism had conquered the globe and was already being exported to nearby planets. We drew cosmonauts in their spacesuits with red stars on them, tethered to the mother ship with something like an umbilical cord or a rope and with a bouquet of daisies in one hand. Or make that poppies. Poppies were more fitting, since they had "sprung from the blood of fallen heroes." Later I would find out that poppies would always come in handy for other, more intoxicating uses as well.

They put those kinds of things in that capsule back then, and the Pioneer coordinator even suggested stuffing in the school flag as well, but the test tube turned out to be too small.

For the essay contest "How do I see myself in the year 2000?" held before the burial of the capsule, I wrote only a single sentence: "I don't see myself, because in the year 2000, the world will end. This is a fact." I can't say why I did it. I was immediately called before the Pioneer coordinator, who labeled it a "provocation." The main question was who had been telling me these "facts." Which only strengthened my suspicion that everybody knew what was going to happen, but they were keeping it under wraps as a state secret. I was old enough to know not to rat my grandma out. I lied, telling them I'd heard it from some fat Polish woman at the seaside. I purposely said "fat," so as to express my attitude toward this provocateur. Poles weren't like us, they lolled topless on the beach and sold Nivea hand cream on the sly. Let them go look for her.

It goes without saying that my early warning did not make it into the test tube.

In the meantime, I redoubled my efforts to fill my own capsule. In absolute secrecy, in step with the spirit of the times, as they said back then. In step with the spirit of the . . . Jesus, where did that come from? Remembering is never innocent, phrases from that time come back to me. There's suddenly a bad taste in my mouth. In step with the spirit of the times. In step with the spirit . . . I'll repeat it a few more times to make it meaningless.

Box Number 73

And one more "time capsule," one of the official ones. An ordinary paper envelope with red capital letters: "To be opened when he becomes a Komsomol member." Under socialism, they were given to every child right at birth. I have placed this fragile paper capsule in box number 73 and, contrary to the instructions, the envelope is only now being opened. Inside, the following was typed out:

Dear Young Man,

There are moments in a person's life that are never forgotten. Today, with trembling hands you untie the knot of your scarlet Pioneer's neckerchief, replacing it with a red Komsomol membership booklet. This is a symbol of the great trust the Party and our heroic and hardworking people have in you.

Be decent and daring in word and deed! Dedicate the drive of your youth and the wisdom of your mature years to that which is dearest to all generations—the Homeland!

Yet another stellar example of socialist-speak. I now see that it is a mouthful: *Be decent and daring in word and deed! Dedicate the drive . . .* What are all those Ds, why make the tongue scoot along on its ass? I wonder whether those suit-wearing fates handed my mother the envelope when she was still in the delivery room? While she was still in shock and didn't know which way was up, she was given diapers, a pot to boil bottles in, and a representative from the Regional Committee of the Communist Party came and handed her the letter. Don't worry about the kid, we've already preordained his fate, first he'll become a young Pioneer, then he'll put on his Pioneer's neckerchief, then he'll replace it with his Komsomol booklet, it's all written here. Set. In. Stone.

I was first thinking to toss out the envelope, but then decided to put it back in its place, in box number 73. There need to be such things inside, too.

I think I need to reinforce the box with added protection against such radioactive waste from the past. But what if only this capsule survives? What if it's discovered and a cult grows up around it? I shouldn't have gone there. I can see it ever so clearly.

Future Number 73

Many years after the apocalypse, life springs up again and after several millennia man makes a reappearance. These new post-apocalyptites develop more or less the same as earlier people did, not counting a few insignificant deviations (mutations), for example, the fact that they are incapable of abstract thought. Clearly, nature or God learned a lesson from the previous, less-than-smashingly successful experiment and has made some healthy adjustments.

Suddenly, the New Ones accidentally stumble across a buried but miraculously intact capsule with messages from before the apocalypse. The event is indescribable. Finally, some trace of their forefathers. But it is the most idiotic and laughable message imaginable (but they don't realize this). Some testament to their descendants, which should be opened 200 years later. Part of it has been worn away, but individual phrases have survived. They decipher it carefully. And devotedly, as stone tablets are read.

We must heed this testament and change our lives accordingly, that's how it is everywhere. Only one person resisted. On the contrary, he kept saying, we should do the exact opposite of what is written on the stone tablets if we want to avoid the fate that befell our forefathers. But no one listened to him. The Testament was circulated far and wide and every word was interpreted as specific instructions for action.

Every cliché (and a cliché is nothing more than an abstraction that has swallowed its own tail) becomes dangerous when it is made literal. Three empty, meaningless phrases from the distant twentieth century turned the life of a heretofore united and happy society, in which abstractions did not exist, upside down: . . . *Prepared and trained for the sea of life . . . The socialist family—the basic cell of our society . . . To spill your blood for the homeland . . .*

The sea wasn't far away. They immediately turned it into an Academy, where they began training the young and the old. The teacher would swim out in front, with the students around him in shoals, with their frail, knowledge-hungry bodies, flailing their arms and legs. The more frail and sickly among them quietly sank, falling back and left behind. The survivors felt at home in the water, their backs grew enormous, they knew everything about life in the sea. What erudite athleticism, what academic muscle . . . the non-drowned poets sang. On land they started to feel like beached whales. And life gradually returned to the sea. (What an evolutionary step backward.)

After that, true to the second line of the Testament, they filled the sea with wooden cells. Every newly married couple received one as a wedding present and lounged in it of their own free will.

Three times a year they celebrated the Day of the Great Bloodletting, on which they injured themselves, so as to offer up spilled blood to the Homeland. And since they had no idea or instructions as to what it was, they simply gathered up the blood in a huge container, which they soon dubbed accordingly: "Homeland."

There is no other surviving evidence of this civilization.

Carriers

A few years ago I decided to back-up my archive due to security concerns. I put the most important information on a disk, then hid the disk in a small box made of gopher wood, sealed with pitch on the inside and outside. I followed the Old Testament instructions, even though Noah's arks have gone through quite a few changes thanks to new technologies. The original was three hundred cubits long and fifty wide, with a height of thirty cubits, divided into three stories. Now it's a single disk.

At first, I was considering some fireproof box, but I decided it would be best to follow the description in that book. Pitched gopher wood keeps the water out and always floats to the surface, unlike a metal lockbox. The Book has thought of everything.

Of course, I don't count on disks alone. They're unreliable and if the least little thing goes wrong, the whole thing is shot. The more advanced the technology, the more irreparable the damages are. I read somewhere that paper, especially acid-free paper, turns out to be a far more reliable information carrier than any digital device. Its manufacturers say it'll last up to 1,000 years. That's surely more than we can say for this world. For this reason, I continue to rely on my boxes full of clippings and old-fashioned notebooks. Just in case the world turns analogue again. The likelihood is not at all negligible.

Since other capsules depicted the world like a postcard—kind, pretty, dancing, endlessly inventing various trinkets—the capsule in my basement had to contain the signs and warnings, the unwritten stories, such as "The History of Boredom in the 1980s," or "A Brief History of the Ephemeral," or "An Introduction to the Provincial Sorrow of Late Socialism," "A Catalogue of the Signs We Never Noticed," "An Incomplete List of Fears During 2010," or the stories of Mad Juliet, Malamko, Chingachook, the anti-historical person, my grandfather, the abandoned boy, the stories of all those coming of the void and going into the void, nameless, ephemeral, left out of the frame, the eternally silent ones, a General History of That Which Never Happened . . .

If something is enduring and monumental, what is the point of putting it in a capsule? Only that which is mortal, perishable, and fragile should be preserved, that which is sniffling and lighting matchsticks in the dark . . . Now that's what will be in all the boxes in the basement of this book.

Noah Complex

I imagine a book containing every kind and genre. From monologue through Socratic dialogue to epos in hexameter, from fairytales through treatises to lists. From high antiquity to slaughterhouse instructions. Everything can be gathered up and transported in such a book.

Let him write, write, write, let him be recorded and preserved, let him be like Noah's ark, there shall be every beast, large and small, clean and unclean, thou shalt take from every kind and every story. I'm not so interested in the clean genres. The novel is no Aryan, as Gaustine always said.

Let me write, write, write, let me record and preserve, let me be like Noah's ark, not me, but this book. Only the book is eternal, only its covers shall rise above the waves, only the beasts inside, between its pages swarming with life, will survive. And when they see the new land, they will go forth and multiply.

And what is written shall be made flesh and blood and shall be brought to life in all its perfection. And "the lion" shall become a lion, "the horse" will whinny like a horse, "the crow" will fly from the page with an ugly croak . . . And the Minotaur will come out into the light of day.

New Realism

I hadn't left the Underworld for a long time, so recently I decided to take a bit of a stroll. I waited for evening to fall, at this time of year it's almost dark by five in the afternoon. That makes my transition from the basement easier. Unfortunately the Christmas lights were already up and the darkness had retreated into the corners. I chose the darker streets, breathing in the cold air, and found myself in front of a gallery I used to enjoy going into. The gallery was still open, I had caught the last few days of an exhibit showing "The New Realism." There were no visitors at that hour, so I decided to go in.

I peered into the small glass containers, stuffed full of wine corks, useless odds-and-ends, into the traces of worn-away posters by Raymond Hains, Arman's long ribbons of paint, squeezed out of the tubes and stretched out like colorful snakes taxidermied in glass. I stood for a long time in front of the remains of a dinner by Daniel Spoerri, glued to the table and hung on the wall like three-dimensional pictures—a frying pan with dried grease, a table for two with two empty coffee cups, the grounds still in the bottom, two glasses and an empty bottle of Martini from the 1970s, a burned-down candle, only wax left in the holder, a crumpled napkin . . . Someone was here and has left. A conversation has taken place, something was said, something was left unsaid, they sat for a long time, the candle was burning, they were enjoying themselves, they got up and left. Did they have sex in the other room? Was the coffee before or after that? If you look even closer, you'll probably see lipstick on one of the glasses. From forty years ago.

Those people are most likely gone now. Only the coffee grounds remain. The new realism—new Noah's arks from the already-old twentieth century . . .

It was in the air. They all had a premonition of apocalypse in the late '60s and '70s, these new realists. Sometime around then, Christo started wrapping the world. As if getting ready to leave. Everything has to be packed up. We gather up our luggage, we take off. From the little wrapped rocking horse (his saddest work, in my opinion), to the bridge at Point Neuf. Come onnn, we're moving ouuut . . . They're going to knock down the house.

Memories of Moves

I've known it ever since my childhood, because of our frequent moves from apartment to apartment, that strange feeling when objects are removed from everyday use, the chair is no longer a chair, the table is not a table, the bed has been taken apart. The dresser is nothing but drawers and wooden shelves. The books are stuffed into white plastic bags stamped "crystallized sea salt," as if they were fish needing to be salted. I wonder if it will sting afterward when I page through them.

You stand amid all that chaos, mooning about, you don't know where to turn, the adults don't either, they're stressed out, waiting for the truck and smoking. Then everything is loaded up, but all of you are still fussing around, you don't want to shut the door, your mother goes to check for the twentieth time to make sure you haven't accidentally forgotten anything, your father has wandered off somewhere in the yard to water the two cherry trees and the rose bush, because who knows whether the new tenant will take care of them at all. I hug one of the cats, the other is hiding somewhere.

Farewell.

A new apartment.

New farewells.

The moves of my student years.

Moving out after divorce.

Moving to other countries.

Coming back.

A new apartment.

A whole life can be told as a catalogue of moves.

The Mother Capsule

After that exhibit, I go back home to my boxes and bags.

At every moment (including this one), somebody is burying a time capsule somewhere. The trend peaked in 1999. Then there was a certain drop in interest. The apocalypse of 2000 didn't come about. People were disappointed, which is understandable after all that waiting. In the meantime, Facebook cropped up, a new time capsule. Now you're a half-human/half-avatar, a strange sort of Minotaur, no a Min-avatar. I got distracted there, that's what Facebook does, it distracts.

What I wanted to say was that of the tens of thousands of capsules being buried in the ground annually, over ninety percent will be lost forever. The people who have buried them forget, die, move. A mother-capsule needs to be created, which would contain the coordinates of all the capsules buried around the world. And so that its coordinates wouldn't be forgotten, a special person needs to be hired whose only job is just that—to remember them.

Bundle and Bottle

The unlikeliest things can turn out to be time capsules. The largest is surely the city of Pompeii, which was preserved under ash. I prefer the smaller ones, myself. Like the bottle of brandy my grandfather set aside the day I was born. That bottle must be forty-four years old now. If I find it and open it, I'll have distilled the whole of 1968, at least for southeastern Bulgaria. The number of sunny days that summer, the early autumn rains, the humidity in the air, the quality of the soil, the vine diseases, the year's whole history written inside a glass bottle.

Or that bundle of clothes my grandma kept for "the end." A kerchief, an apron, a cherry-red vest, wool socks for winter, or pantyhose—in case it's summer—a pair of patent-leather shoes . . . A bundle to be opened on the day of her death. Even though she would open it every other day, to make sure moths hadn't chewed holes in the clothes or simply to look at them. That's a way of getting used to the idea of death, too. Once a month, she would put them on. She would replace her old black kerchief with the new one with its big, dark-red roses, her everyday brown woolen vest with the unworn red one, which had been given to her for some birthday. She would look at herself in the narrow rectangular mirror, bemoaning how pretty she had been back in the day, what a slender waist she had had. How can I show up there like this, she would cry. Only death awakened her vanity. More people were waiting for her there than here.

. . . and Hexameter

The unlikeliest things can turn out to be . . . Hexameter, for example. If something is said in hexameter, then historically and practically speaking, it has an infinite expiration date. The whole of the Trojan War is preserved in the capsule of hexameter. If that story had been stuffed into any other form whatsoever, it would have given out, gone sour, gotten torn up, crumbled . . . Hexameter turned out to be the longest-lasting material.

Hesiod, in his *Works and Days*, has left behind a true survival kit with instructions. If something happens to the world and people come who don't know anything, thanks to this book they will learn which month is good for sowing, which for plowing, when a boar or a bellowing bullock or a hardworking donkey should be castrated. It also includes these favorite instructions:

> One should not urinate facing the sun while standing erect, but
> One should remember always to do it at sunset and sunrise.

For everything, there should be a good book giving instructions. I add it to the box, too.

Bees and Bats

At the end of every year I open up the boxes, carefully look through all the publications from January to December, sometimes that is precisely what fills up my days until New Year's Eve, and I set aside only the most important things that need to be preserved . . .

I have my own system for sorting.

Often, the most important bits of news turn up on the pages of thin, irregular periodicals printed on cheap paper, such as *Modern Beekeeper*, *Gardening Time*, *Houseplant Diseases*, *Taking Care of a Small Farm*, *Bull and Cow: Newspaper for the Novice Farmer*, *Home Veterinarian*, *All About Cats*, and so on.

Sometimes those five lines from the "Strange News from around the World" column can turn out to be important, especially when they're describing the strange behavior of several colonies of bees in some remote North American town. The bees flew out of the hives in the morning and never came back. Now that's what I call a sign and a revelation, even though nobody noticed it at the time. People don't make the effort to read signs. They chalked up the bees' mysterious disappearance to the Varroa destructor, the Varroa mite to be precise, also called the "vampire worm," a tiny red tick that sinks its little hooks into the bee's body. I wrote a letter to the newspaper, explaining that this was something else entirely, that this was only the beginning, I even quoted Einstein, people are impressed when they hear Einstein: "If the bee disappeared off the surface of the globe, then man would only have four years of life left."

They weren't impressed.

It seems to me that the year was 2004, the winter of 2004, yes. A whole two years had to pass before people figured out that this wasn't some one-off case and that something strange was happening to all the bees around the world. Only in 2006 would those few lines from my beekeeping newspaper become front-page headlines in the *New York Times*, the *Guardian* and so on. And only then would they dub this strange disappearance of the most responsible and disciplined part of our holy family here on earth "Colony Collapse Disorder" (CCD). Hives are being deserted. One of the most domestic of creatures has lost its ability to find its way home, it gets lost and dies. Remember that diagnosis. Colony Collapse Disorder. The disintegration of the apian family . . . If this is happening to them, what is left for man and his unstable family? There's more apocalypse in that than in all the other hocus-pocus. The bees are the first sign. The buzzing angels of the apocalypse. We're expecting the trumpets of Jericho, but the only thing that can be heard is bzzzz . . . bzzzz . . . bzzzz . . . growing quieter and fading away. That's the signal. Don't you hear it? Just take out your iPod earbuds for a minute.

And what do we know about White Nose Syndrome? White Nose Syndrome in bats. We haven't even heard? No one counts dead bats. Look, if they were pigs or cows, everybody'd be worried. In 2006, ninety percent of the bat population in the caves around New York and San Francisco suddenly and somewhat inexplicably died . . . They stopped eating and hung comatose before finally flying out of the caves and falling to the ground outside with white noses . . . Small flying mice with white noses, miniature dead Batmans. I add this information to the box as well, it may turn out to be important.

I gather for the sake of the one who is to come. For the post-apocalyptic reader, if we may agree to call him that. It's not a bad idea to have a basic archive from the previous era. Today's newspapers will then be historical chronicles. Which is a good future for them. And a fitting testimonial to an epoch quickly yellowing and fading in its final days.

The newspaper is dated June 4, 2022. The headline is written in fat letters across the top: Strange Epidemic of Amnesia. And as a subtitle, in a smaller font: Colony Collapse Disorder in humans? The article reads more or less as follows:

> Rules and habits established over centuries are ceasing to work. We are seeing ever more cases in which people leave their homes in the morning to go to work, yet are in no state to find their way home in the evening.
>
> C. S. (39) had a normal morning, just like thousands of others before it. Toast, eggs and bacon, the big mug of coffee, joking around with the kids, kisses at the door, promises of the traditional family Monopoly game that evening . . . That evening, however, he didn't

come home. He never even reached his office. They found him by chance on the other side of the city, lost, his pant legs rolled up boyishly, walking down the street and kicking stones aimlessly. He didn't remember having a wife and kids. He didn't know his address. He claimed to be twelve.

Even more inexplicable is the story of D. P. (33), a single mother, who, like every day, brought her kids to kindergarten. She dropped them off, kissed them, and promised to pick them up early that afternoon. A half-hour before the appointed time, the kids were already standing by the fence, dressed and ready to go, but their mother was late. The other parents started arriving. Finally only the two children and the teachers were left. It started getting dark, but no one came. They called the mother, but she didn't answer her phone. The kids had to spend the night at the kindergarten. They found the mother three days later in a distant northern city. She was acting bizarre, according to the authorities, she resisted arrest, scratched one police officer's face and taunted him with insults that had been popular twenty years ago, but which no one used anymore. This last detail is important, since to the question of how old she was, the woman, who was past 30, replied that she was in seventh grade. To the question of what she was doing in that city, she replied that she was on a class field trip. Of course, she couldn't recall her kids or family. The newspaper's own investigation revealed that the middle school where the mother had gone really had taken a field trip to that city twenty-nine years earlier.

They forcibly returned the woman to her city and took her home, expecting that the familiar surroundings would immediately bring back her memory. She acted as if she were in some stranger's home. She didn't touch anything. She asked where the bathroom was. She didn't recognize any of the clothes in her closet. When brought face-to-face with her own children, the psychologists could not detect any sign of recognition.

For now there is no clear explanation for what is happening. Scholars are working on several parallel hypotheses. One of the most intriguing suggests that this is a case of sudden reactivation of past events for inexplicable reasons and the opening of personal parallel time corridors. A powerful invasion of the past. They suspect it may be due to misuse of "regression therapy" which has become fashionable recently and which is being practiced illicitly by an ever-growing number of self-declared therapists.

Signs

More than 2,000 dead blackbirds fall from the sky over a small town in Arkansas on January 1, 2011. The reasons for these mysterious deaths are unknown. The report is from January 3.

Over the following days, reports of mysterious bird deaths start rolling in from various parts of the world—Europe, Australia, and New Zealand. Hypotheses include a bird plague, secret experiments with chemical weapons by the American military and so on. The man who announced that he would uncover the truth, a former U.S. army general, is found dead in a garbage truck. More and more people believe that the dead birds falling from the sky are a clear sign of the Apocalypse.

And on the coast of England, 40,000 dead crabs are discovered.

V. The Green Box

The Ear of the Labyrinth

It hadn't happened to me in a long time . . . I was looking through newspapers from 2010 and I ran across a short report, probably forgotten and buried by the incoming news from the following day. But for me it turned out to be one of those exceptional events that launched me back into that forgotten "emplanting" . . . Something I haven't experienced in years.

BULL LEAPS INTO CROWD, INJURING 40
AT A BULLFIGHT, THE ANIMAL IS KILLED.
Thursday, August 19, 2010, Tafalla

Forty people were injured in an unusual incident in Spain. The accident took place during a bullfight. The bull, which had just been led into the arena, looked around, then swiftly leapt over the barrier and began attacking the crowd. The unfortunate incident occurred in the city of Tafalla. The panic-stricken spectators tried to run away, but were hampered by the amphitheater seating. The infuriated animal lunged at various groups of terrified spectators. The toreador tried to hold the bull back by pulling its tail. It took a whole fifteen minutes to get the situation under control. In the end, they were forced to shoot the bull.

An amphitheater, of course, is a labyrinth. One of the most commonly found circular labyrinths, made of concentric circles intersected by transverse corridors. The bull lifted its gaze and recognized the Labyrinth—the ancestral home of his great-grandfather, the Minotaur. And since animals have no sense of time (just as children do not), the Bull saw his ancestral home and recognized the Minotaur within himself. He remembered all the days and nights . . . no, wait, that's human language, there were no days there, he recalled only that endless night, a sum of all the nights in the world. Once again, he remembered the only two faces he had ever known. His mother's face, as she held him in her lap. The most beautiful face he had ever seen. The face he had come closest to. And the second face—that of his killer. Also beautiful. Human faces.

Now his killer (likely a distant relative of Theseus) was standing down in the arena, in the center of the labyrinth. It wasn't the fact that the scene would repeat itself and he would once again experience the softness and vulnerability of his body, that sacred softness and vulnerability that only proved his essential humanity, no, it wasn't that that caused him to do what he did. There was something else. The sudden realization that if his killer was standing before him, then his mother's face must be somewhere nearby as well. Up there in the audience. Those two faces went together. The scene repeats itself. The labyrinth twists and turns back not only space. Time has coiled up, swallowed its own tail and if something can happen, can be changed, now is the moment.

I turn my back on the killer, clench all my muscles, and clear the barrier. Like a lost child, I see my mother in the crowd and race toward her, nothing can stop me now. If only I could press my face against hers again. If only I could snuggle up to her. I'm three. And I'm looking for my mother. Some other people are screaming and falling at my feet, but they're not my mother. I'll recognize her. I just hope I don't miss her, that she hasn't already left. Just a little farther, just a little farther. Now there's one who looks like her, but it's not her. What about that one? No. No. The howl that escapes from the cave of my throat is terrifying. The only word that in all languages—those of humans, animals and monsters—is one and the same:

Mooooooooooom . . .

The labyrinth of the amphitheater catches that cry, ricochets it between the walls of its corridors, diverts it toward the dead-ends, cuts it off, and sends it back slightly distorted to the labyrinth of the human ear like an endless

Mooooooooo . . .

And there's the switch. The tiniest of switches. The labyrinth has turned that short "o" into a long "ooh." If man had only known that it was the same word, that very same "Mooooom" . . . the history of the world and history of the death (I wouldn't be surprised if they turned out to be one and the same story) would be different.

A terrified creature is looking for its mother. Human or animal—the word is the same.

But the myth is repeatable and the death of the Minotaur has to happen again. Before finding his mother, before snuggling up in her lap, before returning to her womb, that most primordial, soft, and pulsating of caves. Because that would already be another (unacceptable) myth.

Death catches up with him right when he seems to have caught sight of a familiar shoulder and locks of hair hurrying away. It's the first time they kill him that way. From a distance. Without a sword or a spear. Without seeing his killer's face.

Without a Face

Without seeing his killer's face. If a *General History of Murder* exists, which includes not only historical events, but also murders in mythology, as well as in all legends, rumors, and novels, it would be clear what a warm and human act it is—to be face-to-face with the one who will kill you. Cruel, yes, but cruel on a human scale. Death comes from another person, with a specific body, hand, face. A face we can only appreciate today, when murder has become dehumanized, if we allow ourselves to borrow that notion. This is a relatively new phenomenon, perhaps dating back several centuries to the invention of gunpowder, a trifling span of time.

Even language has not yet gotten used to this. We say "in the face of death," but this is already a phrase from a bygone era. Death has lost its face and therein lies the new horror. There is no face.

Several random examples. Achilles killed Hector and that was an epos, it was history, a dance between the killer and the victim. A ritual, in which the victim has the right to his moves, his gestures, and his lines. (Now that's why a Homer of modern gunfire is impossible.) Even when Lycomedes tricked Theseus and was about to push him off a cliff on the island of Scyros near Euboea, there was again the touch of a human hand, presence.

What happened afterward? Here we're not even talking about the slaughterhouse of war. Kennedy is riding in his limo, he smiles, makes a painful grimace, slumps down. That pantomime of death, which we've watched stamped on film, says it all. Achilles has become invisible. Theseus, yet another mythical serial killer, is hidden in the crowd and shoots from there. You don't have time to get ready, to mentally say farewell to a few people, to make bequests, to leave behind your final words, to make smart remarks, to zing your killer with a cutting line, to fix your hair. The full-stop of the bullet, which arrives before the first word of the sentence. An anonymous piece of lead from an unknown perpetrator. There is something deeply unjust about that. Something that radically goes against every nature.

No animal would do that.

No Animal Would Do That

The animal in me. So here's the new moral law—side by side with "the starry sky above me." The basic question, the litmus test, the divider between good and evil—could what I've thought up be done by an animal? Step inside the skin of your favorite animal and find out. If it wouldn't do it, then you shouldn't do it, either, or you'll be committing a mortal sin. A sin against nature. All sins have already been committed. But at least the boundary of the natural remains.

Theseus was a matador. "Matador" means killer, borrowed from Latin. Every butcher in the slaughterhouse shares in Theseus's sin.

I add this ordinance, which is actually quite relevant, to the box:

ORDINANCE No. 20/2002

For reducing to a minimum animals' suffering during slaughter

CHAPTER 1: Animal Stress and Pain

Scientific research has shown that warm-blooded animals (this includes livestock) feel pain and the emotion of fear . . . Fear and pain are very strong causes of stress in livestock and stress affects the quality of meat obtained from this livestock. (*Of course, everything is done for the quality of the meat. Less suffering means better taste.*)

Animals will also shy at moving things, as well as darkness and they may refuse to enter a dark place . . . (*I'm sure of that, I know this from firsthand experience.*)

They are afraid of sparkling reflections, dangling chains, moving people or equipment, shadows or dripping water. (*Shadows or dripping water . . . that's almost poetry, no, it's a cave.*)

CHAPTER 7: Slaughter of Livestock

Preparing livestock for slaughter

Animals injured during transport or not yet weaned should be slaughtered immediately (*out of compassion*), but if this is impossible, then no later than two hours after being unloaded. (*Because the quality of the meat decreases, following the logic of suffering = bad taste.*) Animals incapable of walking should be slaughtered on the spot or conveyed by cart or platform to the proper place for immediate slaughter. When ready for slaughter, animals should be driven to the stunning area in a quiet and orderly manner without undue fuss and noise . . .

There are three main technologies used to effect stunning: Percussion, Electrical Shock, and Gas . . .

The most widely used method for stunning is the captive bolt gun. This method works on the principle of a gun and fires a blank cartridge and it propels a short bolt (metal rod) from the barrel. The bolt penetrates the skull bone and produces concussion by damaging the brain or increasing intracranial pressure, causing bruising of the brain. The captive bolt is perhaps the most versatile stunning instrument as it is suitable for use on cattle, pigs, sheep and goats as well as horses and camels, and can be used anywhere in the world . . .

Bulls: place the gun firmly against the forehead at a right angle 1 cm to the side of an imaginary line connecting the top of the head and a straight line between the eyes. (*What mathematics of death, what geometry of murder . . .*)

Calves: the gun should be placed slightly lower than with adult cows, since in calves the upper part of the brain is still underdeveloped. (*Man really has thought of everything*)

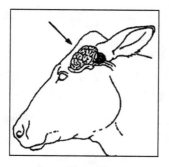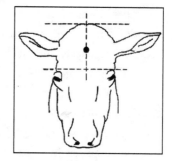

Fig.51. The correct positioning of a stunning gun.

(From "Guidelines for Humane Handling, Transport and Slaughter of Livestock" in accordance with the European Convention for the Protection of Animals for Slaughter.)

Now that's what I call an innocent, hygienic text, as cold and aseptic as the tiles of a slaughterhouse—washed sparkling clean once the job is done.

No animal would do that.

The Minotaur's Dream

I dream that I'm beautiful. Not exactly beautiful, but inconspicuous. That's what it means to be beautiful, to be like everyone else. My head feels light. My eyes are on the front of my face. I have a nose, rather than nostrils. I have human skin, thin human skin. I walk down the street and no one notices me. Now that's happiness—no one noticing me. It's a happy dream.

I walk slowly, avoiding the people coming toward me at first, I keep to the very edge of the sidewalk, near the walls of the houses. But a miracle has occurred. No one rushes to get away from me, no one screams in horror that they've seen a monster, children don't cower behind their mothers, the old folks don't cross themselves, the men don't draw their swords. I'm walking down the street. It's light out. I haven't seen this much light since I was born. One woman accidentally bumps into me. I'm afraid she'll scream. She turns around, looks at me from very close up . . . she doesn't recognize me . . . she doesn't scream . . . she smiles . . . and apologizes. No one has ever apologized to me before.

I see people sitting on benches. I sit down, too. Alone. I watch what the people are doing and do the same thing.

They sit and watch other people.

I sit and watch other people.

Then dusk starts to fall. I hear one little boy telling his father: dad, let's go home, it's getting dark. The words "dark" and "home" are the first worrisome thing in the whole dream up until now. The dark has always been my home, but now I feel homeless. For the first time I get scared that I'm lost. Which is ridiculous, since I have never gotten lost, I come from the Labyrinth, after all. And the more my fear grows, the more I shrink. A tall man leans down over me, grasps me with his large hand (I notice he's not holding a sword), and asks me if I'm lost and whether I know my address. I keep silent. And where is mommy, the man asks, can you tell me where mommy went? He shouldn't have asked that question. I can feel my jaw elongating, my skull growing heavy and hard, but I don't want to hurt him. Thankfully the dream is coming to an end, since the situation is getting pretty desperate. That's the moment in which dreams tear apart.

I woke up in the dark in my usual home. That was my happiest dream. One day with people whom I didn't kill, who didn't kill me, who didn't even notice me. There was no bad blood between them and me. I presume that people don't have those sorts of dreams. In their dreams, they wander through dark labyrinths and battle Minotaurs.

Irrevocable

From time to time I emerge from my refuge and go to Odeon, the art-house movie theater in town. Old black-and-white films are the only thing I feel like watching. I had read that they were showing a Dziga Vertov panorama and I didn't want to miss that. It was a cold January afternoon, dingy and slushy. As it turned out, five minutes before the film was supposed to start, there were no other takers. They could hardly be expected to show it just for me. Then I noticed two bums loitering around outside, shifting their weight from one foot to the other and smoking. I asked them if they wanted to come inside and watch a film and warm up. They looked at me mistrustfully, like people who were not used to getting such offers. One asked what film. I told them it was a classic, and he nodded, stubbed out his cigarette, and the two of them went in with me. I bought three tickets. The usher looked at us with the contempt of a full-blooded Aryan, but she didn't dare turn them away. As we went in, I glimpsed how they surreptitiously straightened up their coats and took off their winter hats. They settled into the back row, it was warm in the theater and from what I could tell they blissfully dozed off shortly after the opening credits. It was a silent film and the theater had hired a pianist to accompany the film just as during the 1920s.

An enthusiastic camera, still intoxicated by its own possibilities, climbs over the rooftops, changes angles, lies down on the train tracks. The whole madhouse of 1920s Russia, the drunks, the Pioneers, the bums on benches. And now comes the reason why I'm telling this story—a report about a slaughterhouse. The routine slaughter of a cow, and its subsequent "resurrection" through playing the film backward. The title appears: "Twenty minutes ago, this meat was a cow." It's as if the camera is calling: "Lazarus, come out!" And the sliced up pieces of meat turn back into an animal, beef turns back into cow. The intestines slip back into its belly, the steaks plaster its haunches . . . "And now we'll put on the skin." And it's as if the butchers' knives have become thick sewing needles, while they themselves are the tailors, dressing it in the skin, which they had stripped off only moments before, they scurry about, ridiculous in their backward movement. Even the pianist's music speeds up, the key somehow more major.

"And now we'll bring the cow back to life"—the title on the screen announces. And here, where you expect the culmination, the miracle, the "Ode to Joy" (the pianist's hands dash over the keyboard), instead we're in for a shock. The cow's death throes, rewound, remain death throes. That moment of dying, the electrical shock, the detuning of the body, the horror, the adrenaline, the whites of the cow's eyes, played backward only intensify the mortal agony, rather than bringing it back to life, as the cameraman had expected. And despite the fact that only seconds later the cow stupidly flicks its tail, it is nevertheless clear to you: the cow is irrevocably dead.

On my way out of the theater, I have to bring back from dreamland the two blissful bums, who have missed the incorrigible death of a cow.

Every year, 1.6 billion cows, sheep, and pigs, as well as 22.5 billion birds are slaughtered by humans for food. We are hell for animals, the animals' apocalypse.

A Tale of the Vegetarian Man-Eater

"Once upon a time, there was a man-eater who was a vegetarian."

"What's a vegetarian?

"A person who doesn't eat meat. Like you and me."

"And is a man-eater a person?

"Wellll . . . yeah, it looks like a person, but it's even scarier."

"Stop scaring the boy with your nonsense!" A woman's voice comes from the room next door.

"Mom, I want to hear the story about the vegetarian man-eater. Should I shut the door?"

"Shut the door, so we don't scare mom."

"But people are made of meat, right?"

"Yes, we're made of meat."

"So that poor vegetarian man-eater must've been dying of hunger."

"He wasn't only dying of hunger, but from putdowns, too."

"Wait, can you really die from putdowns?"

"Putdowns are the deadliest thing of all. All the man-eaters were making fun of him, calling him a fruit-eater and grass-grazer. Nobody wanted to talk to him. Because if you didn't eat people, you didn't have anything to tell your fellow man-eaters. And they were telling funny stories . . ."

"Scary . . ."

"Stories that are scary for men, but funny for man-eaters. Each would tell a tale more outrageous than the last and they'd bust a gut laughing . . . Meanwhile, our vegetarian man-eater just stood off to the side and didn't have any stories to tell. If he happened to go over to the group of real man-eaters, they would rib him mercilessly: hey, why don't you tell us how you battled three raspberry bushes and came back home all bloody. That kind of stuff. Or how many cabbages can you behead at once? And the poor vegetarian man-eater would slink off with his tail between his legs . . ."

"So they have tails?"

"That's just a saying. Then one lady man-eater, who was secretly in love with our man . . . with our man-eater, she went over to him and told him that he should try people meat at least once in his life, he might like it and get himself straightened out. And he'd best try precisely with a vegetarian . . ."

"Dinner's ready," my mother says, standing in the doorway.

On the Eating of Flesh

My father is a vegetarian. And a veterinarian. He simply does not eat his patients. I can see it now, how the waiters look at him when he orders some meatless dish. Just as the man-eaters looked at the vegetarian man-eater. I can still remember how one of our neighbors was always grilling him about why he refused to eat meat, had somebody been putting him up to it, had he joined a cult by chance, had he read something, how is it that everyone eats meat, but he's broken away from the collective, if you get what I'm saying? Come on now, man up, order a trio of sausages with a side of beans, or baked kidney pie or lamb's head. As for me, he'd say, when I grab that head, I first open up its mouth nice and wide and pull out that little tongue, mmm, then I split that little skull right open with a knife and, then, you slurp out the brains with a spoon! To say nothing of those yummy little eyeballs . . . Here my father would get up suddenly and say he had to go outside, I would run after him to puke in the bathroom. Just take that little lamb, it only eats grass, why don't you start with that . . . the neighbor would call after him.

Funny that socialism and vegetarianism don't go together. Like yogurt and fish.

We know that where the neighbor has been, the police are sure to follow. My father was prepared and when they called him down to the precinct, he explained to them in detail how the human anatomy was adapted to a vegetarian diet—a long gastro-intestinal tract, six times longer than the human body, unlike carnivores, whose tracts were only three times longer; flat molars, alkaline saliva and so on. He even quoted Plutarch and his essay "On the Eating of Flesh" to them, where it is said (he had copied this out in his notebook): "But if you will contend that yourself was born to an inclination to such food as you have now a mind to eat, do you then yourself kill what you would eat. But do it yourself, without the help of a chopping-knife, mallet, or axe."

They let him go.

My father was proud that he had managed to convince them with anatomy and Plutarch. While they had probably decided he wasn't worth the trouble, figuring he was slightly nuts, but ideologically harmless.

Anti-Anthropocentric Notes

During World War II, in the period between 1940 and 1944, in air raids on European museums, seventeen dinosaur skeletons were destroyed. I can clearly picture these double murders, the crushed dead bones, the toppling of these Eiffel Towers of ribs and vertebrae. No animal would do that. To kill someone who had already been dead for millions of years all over again, to reawaken that prehistoric horror in the black box of its skull.

Actually, has anyone ever counted the bodies of animals killed during wartime? Millions of sparrows, ravens, robins, field mice, torn-apart foxes, scorched partridges, rats, the moles' ruined bomb shelters, the lightly armored turtles crushed by heavily armored tanks—their giant likenesses . . . No one anywhere has ever made an inventory of such deaths. We've never really stopped to think of the suffering we cause to animals during wartime, during air raids. Where do they hide, what happens in the "wild" brains of our "fellow brethren in pain," as Darwin called them in his notes.

I love natural history, but not its museums. I don't see anything natural in them. In the end, they are more like mausoleums. What else could we call a place with gutted antelopes, Tibetan yaks, badgers, does, and rhinoceroses? I've never experienced pure, unadulterated joy from zoos, either. But everyone is always forced to visit them once, as a child, since parents are convinced that you're dying to see the elephant listlessly flapping its trunk or the wolf pacing anxiously in its cage, which stinks of carcass.

I'll never forget the elephant's heavy sorrow, which almost crushed me (yet another one of my fits), then the melancholy of the black panther stretched out on the dirty cement, or the undisguised tedium with which the tiger met and saw off its guests. On the way out, I recall, I was filled with animalistic sorrow. I can attest that this sorrow is far denser than human sorrow, it's wild, unfiltered by language, inexpressible and unexpressed, since language nevertheless soothes and calms sorrow, disarms it, bleeds it, just as my grandfather would bleed a sick animal. When they took me to the Museum of Natural History the next day, I had the feeling that the whole zoo had been slaughtered in a single night, stuffed and brought there. I've never gone into such tombs since.

Negligent Murders

Whole columns of ants, over all these years, which I've stepped on without noticing it. I have big feet, size 12, which increases their destructive power. And my guilt.

Miriam, or On the Right to Kill

We were talking, or actually, I was talking about the need for an anti-Copernican revolution, how important it was—and I mean vitally important—to oust man from the center of the universe, about death, and animals . . .

"I lived with a Buddhist for three years," Miriam said, splitting open a large mussel with her long fingers.

I love such beginnings, with no preface, raw, hard.

"It was a long time ago," she added, heading off my unasked questions. "Know what the most unbearable thing about living with a Buddhist is?" The mussel sank into her mouth, strong white teeth, pearls and the grains of sand between them, seconds until this magnificent meat grinder had made short work of the flesh. "The vow not to kill. That's the most brutal part . . ." Another mussel.

By the end of the second year, the whole house was swarming with cockroaches. Miriam watched the smug hordes creeping by only centimeters away from her. She had no right to lay a finger on them. She was in love and thus magnanimous. She held out for a whole year. In the evening, she would slip into her sleeping bag and pull the zipper up over her head, leaving only a small hole for air. One night she woke up and saw two cockroaches nestled in the beard of her Buddhist-lover who was sleeping soundly beside her. That was too much. The next day, while the Buddhist was at work (I was amazed that Buddhists work), she bought the strongest spray against such varmints and fumigated the whole apartment herself. It was true mass murder. Genocide! Miriam imitated the infuriated Buddhist, who had come back that evening, stood in the middle of the room, looking around at the dead cockroaches, their stiff little legs turned up toward the ceiling, he had stood there like the last survivor amid an apocalypse.

"Have you ever seen a Buddhist scream?" Miriam asked. "It's worth seeing. He screamed that I had shattered the whole chain of life, that the world would never be the same, that the karmic . . . He slammed the door and left. Actually, he already had a mistress."

For several minutes, the only sound was the cracking of shells and the cold rain outside. I was thinking about that last line and an inexplicable rage was building up inside me against that working Buddhist with his mistress, that shepherd of cockroaches.

"Anyway, the right to kill is inviolable," Miriam said slowly. Then she carefully placed the last mussel shell on the rocky mountains in front of her.

I will put Miriam's story in the green box, too, for balance. So we have one of every kind.

Through a Lamb's Ear

Man needs to shut up for a while and in the ensuing pause to hear the voice of some other storyteller—a fish, dragonfly, weasel, or bamboo, cat, orchid, or pebble. How do we know, for instance, that bees don't write novels? Have we deciphered even a single honeycomb? Or should we start with fish? What a huge part of evolution remains locked up in the fish's silence, what knowledge have fish accumulated over all those millennia before us! The deep, cold storehouses of that silence. Untouched by language. Because language channels and drains deposits of knowledge like a drill.

And so, the only storytelling creature, human, shuts up and steps back, yielding the floor to the organic and inorganic ones that have stored up silences until now. Actually, they've been telling their tales, but their muted, suppressed narrative has turned into mica and lichen, seaweed, moss, honey, the tearing apart of other's bodies and the torn-apartness of their own.

I have no idea how to make this happen. Maybe we just need to take the first step. All the world's classics, retold by animals for animals.

For example, we could retell *The Old Man and the Sea* through the eyes of the fish, that marlin. Now that's what I call anti-anthropocentrism. Its battle with the gaunt old man and the sea is no less dramatic. When it comes down to it, the fish is the character locked in a life-and-death struggle throughout the whole story. The old man's story is a story about the battle against aging. While the fish's is a story about death. The whole story through the voice of a fish, bleeding, gnawed clean to the bone, yet resisting to the very last.

A marlin can be destroyed but not defeated.

. . .

Muria (that's how she spelled her name, with a "u"), a fishing fanatic:

"In the morning, when I get up, I imagine what I'd like to eat if I were a fish, and that's how I sense what'll make them bite during the day. The whole trick is to turn yourself into a fish for a while. And you'll get hungry. Sometimes you're hungry for a worm, sometimes for corn, sometimes for a fly. And when I figure out what it wants to eat, what I want to eat that day, I stick it on the hook, cast it out into the water and start reeling them in like crazy. To the horror of the other fishermen, who had been laughing at me just a few minutes earlier. Then I toss the fish back right in front of their eyes. Which makes them all the more furious."

"Ugh, do you really feel like eating a worm first thing in the morning?"

"When I'm a fish, a worm is not to be missed."

. . .

"The history of the world can be written from the viewpoint of a cat, an orchid, or a pebble. Or lamb's ear."

"What's lamb's ear?"

"A plant."

"And do you think we would figure in a history of the world written by lamb's ear?"

"I don't know. Do you think lamb's ear figures in the history of the world written by people?"

Buffalo Shit, or The Sublime Is Everywhere

I remember how we walked through a historical town famous for its Revival Period architecture, uprising, fires, cannons made from cherry-tree trunks, history rolled down the narrow streets but my father was impressed mainly by the geraniums on the window sills, praising aloud those who had grown such flowers. Suddenly he stopped in a street and started hovering over something on the ground. I went to see what he had discovered. A pile of buffalo shit. It was standing there like a miniature cathedral, a church's cupola or a mosque's dome, may all religions forgive me. A fly was circling above it like an angel. It is very rare to see buffalo shit nowadays, my father said. No one breeds buffalos here anymore. And he spoke with such delight about how one could fertilize pumpkins with it, plaster a wall, daub a bee hive (of the old wicker type), how one could use it to cure an earache—you should warm it well and apply it to the ear. At that moment I would have agreed that the Revival-Era houses we were touring and the pyramids of Giza were something much less important than the architecture, physics, and metaphysics of buffalo (bull?) shit.

Even if you weren't born in Versailles, Athens, Rome, or Paris, the sublime will always find a form in which to appear before you. If you haven't read Pseudo Longinus, haven't heard of Kant, or if you inhabit the eternal, illiterate fields of anonymous villages and towns, of empty days and nights, the sublime will reveal itself to you in your own language. As smoke from a chimney on a winter morning, as a slice of blue sky, as a cloud that reminds you of something from another world, as a pile of buffalo shit. The sublime is everywhere.

Socrates on the Train

If everything lasted forever, nothing would be valuable.

—Gaustine

The world is set up in such as way that it looks obvious and irrefutable. But what would happen if for a moment we turned the whole system upside down and instead of the enduring, the constant, the eternal, and the dead, we decided to revere that which is fleeting, changeable, transitory, yet alive?

The train was passing through the hot stubble fields in late August, where they still use that barbaric method of stubble burning. The fields had been reaped and to make for easier plowing afterward, someone had set a match to them. I imagined the meadow birds' scorched wings, the running and squealing mice and rats, the burned up lizards and snakes. Storks were anxiously circling above the burning fields—we've got to get out of here ASAP, ASAP . . . Everyone wanted to run away, the world was heading toward autumn. At the same time, I was returning to the town of T.

In the end, man, if we still insist on seeing him as the measure of all things, is closer to the parameters of the fleeting—he is changeable, inclined toward death, alive, but mortal, perishable, constantly perishing.

I sensed that my imagination was running wild, I needed an opponent. I invented an opponent, clever, with a sharp rhetorical bite, I generously endowed him with qualities and gave myself over to my favorite pastime, Socratic spats.

"So, my dear sir, you propose that we replace the lasting with the fleeting," my opponent began.

"I suggest that we examine this possibility."

"Very wellll . . . Just say it aloud and you will hear how absurd it sounds—to replace the lasting with the fleeting. Illustrate it with a concrete example, isn't that what you always love to say, my dear fellow? Now then, imagine a nice, sturdy house on the one hand, and a tumbledown hut on the other. Would you exchange the house for the hut? In one hand, I'm holding gold, in the other straw. Which would you choose? Won't the straw grow moldy after the first rain?"

"Wait, wait, my most noble opponent . . . You speak wisely and take shameless advantage of your right to peek into my own misgivings. Yet let us look at the other side as well. Imagine a world, in which everyone agrees to a new hierarchy. In which the Fleeting and the Living are more valuable than the Eternal and the Dead. The opposite of the usual world, which we share today. And so, let us imagine what consequences this might have. Immediately many of the reasons for war and theft fall away. That which entices one to theft is that which is eternal or at least lasting, like a bar of gold, for example, or sturdy houses, cities, palaces, land . . . That is what's ripe for the taking. No one goes to war over a pile of apples or lays siege to a city for its fragrant, blossoming cherry trees. By the time the siege is over, the cherry trees will have lost their blossoms, and the apples will have rotted.

"And since gold will have lost all of its agreed-upon value (because that's exactly what it is, a contract value), it'll just be rolling around on the ground and no one will think to up and go on a crusade for it.

"And speaking of crusades, let's look at that side of the question as well. The religions that stand behind every crusade or holy war will suddenly have the rug pulled out from under them. The old gods were the Gods of the Eternal in all of its aspects. Is there a God of the Ephemeral? If there are Gods in the new constellation—and why not?—they will be exactly that: Gods of the Ephemeral. Gods of the Fragile and the Perishable. And hence fragile and perishable gods. Sensitive, feeling, empathizing. What more can we say? Mortality raises the price and opens our eyes."

"But isn't all of that so fleeting and unstable . . ."

"You're fooling yourself. Let's take that straw, which you've been clutching in your left hand since the very beginning of our debate. That straw used to be wheat, which used to be seeds, which used to be wheat, which used to be . . . And here, *nota bene*: the perishable reproduces itself. And that is its first advantage. While the gold, which you've been holding in your right hand, is made once-and-for-all, it won't give birth to gold even if you plant it and water it every day for two hundred years. Let me put it like this, para-doxically—the perishable is more enduring, precisely because of its death, than that which is imperishable and cannot reproduce itself." (I've completely forgotten about the opponent I created.) "What do you say to that, my friend?"

"Wellll, what happens to tradition then? To all of art, to your own pathetic scribbling?" (We've left politesse behind, my opponent is pissed off.) "Let me ask you this—that book you're writing, is it on the side of the ephemeral, or does it uphold the values of the eternal? How long do your own words last?"

"How long do words last?" I repeat this, because I don't know the answer. "Let us assume that they last as long as the breath with which you utter them. You exhale the word, it's so light, you fill its sails and send it toward the harbor of the Other. It might per-ish before reaching shore, it might sink along the way, shipwrecked against the flotilla of another's words. Whether that is fragility or unfathomable endurance, I cannot say." (I won't apologize for this outburst of lyricism here.)

"I'll ignore the lyrical explanation. So where does that leave your own identity, if you set store by the changeable?" He refuses to give in. "Where does that leave your forefathers, traditions, culture? All of that which was created from constancy? All of that which you call up so as not to forget who you are and where you come from?"

"And what has that identity of yours ever given you, ass-hat?" (Politesse has now definitely been left in the dust.) Blood and wars, busted butts, suicide bombers—there's your inheritance. There's only one true identity—to be a living creature among living creatures. To be ephemeral and to value the Other, because he is ephemeral as well."

"Man is the measure of all things, thus what man creates must endure so as to outlive him."

(Now I've got him—I invented him after all, I have the right to push him into a trap.)

"Exactly, man is the measure of all things. And everything that exceeds this measure and lasts longer and remains after his death is inhuman by its very nature, a source of sorrow and discord as a rule." (Are you listening to me now? He's listening, that's what I invented him for.)

"But . . ."

"We live in houses that will continue to live on even after we die. We go into cathedrals, where long lines of people and generations who are no longer with us have trod, as if on Judgment Day. All of this tells you: you pass on, but we remain. We've buried plenty before you, we'll take care of the ones you've sired as well. Think up at least one good reason why that which is built of stone should last longer than that built of flesh. I don't see any particular point or justice in that. We can only wonder what sense of time and the eternal the ones who came before us had, in the dark night of the primeval, living in their flimsy huts, outliving their flimsy huts, outliving their hearths, moving from place to place, measuring out their lives in days and nights, in lighted and extinguished fires . . . They truly lived forever, even if they died at thirty."

Things Unsuited to Collecting
(a List of the Perishable)

> cheeses – start to stink
> apples – shrivel up and rot
> clouds – constantly change their states of aggregation
> quince jam – gets moldy on top
> lovers – get old, shriveled up (see *apples*)
> children – grow up
> snowmen – melt
> tadpoles and silkworms – anatomically unstable

If we draw the line, it turns out that nothing organic is suitable for collecting. A world with a permanently expiring expiration date. A perishable, shriveling, rotting, deteriorating (and thus) wonderful world.

A Place to Stop

I can imagine the look on the face of the first person to find these notes. He'll probably think that some monster lived here. Indeed, inside me, the Minotaur shivers, afraid of the dark, but otherwise I look completely normal, I wear the body of a white, middle-aged man, a woman is carrying my child, I sometimes go to the seaside, alone, or travel abroad. I keep up what they call "a normal life" in the upper world. OK, fine, I do pass as quite withdrawn and reticent, but in my line of work, that absolutely goes with the territory. My books sell relatively well, which allows me the time and space to do my own things and guarantees me much-needed tranquility. I don't give interviews.

I used to be able to take part—a bit sluggishly, true—in lively conversations and at the same time to be somewhere else entirely, in a different body or memory. Sometimes this would show ever so slightly, one or two women with whom I was in closer contact always caught me. I got off the hook using the alibi of a writer. You can be absent as much as you like, they'll always understand when you want to be left alone or when you don't respond to repeated invitations. At first they keep calling, then they quickly forget you. Here people forget quickly, I don't know if I've mentioned that already.

Annunciation and Oysters

When I got word from my wife that she was pregnant, I was almost 2,000 miles away from her. I was just preparing to eat an oyster for the first time in my life (me, who had once been able to be a slug) in an old French castle at the opening of a ponderous (and tasteless) writers' festival. I had never tasted oysters before. Just as I had never had a child before. We had been trying for a few years. So the two things were both happening to me for the first time—the annunciation and the oyster. A French journalist was holding a big oyster in her hand and explaining to me in bad English how to sprinkle it with lemon and suck it out of the shell. I was also holding an oyster in my hand, watching the squirming little body, in my other hand I was clutching a piece of lemon like a laser gun, trying to awaken the killer in me. I thought the lemon would kill it. The oyster's body, fragile and slimy, resembled both a vagina and a fetus, swimming in its embryonic fluid. At that moment the cell phone in my pocket started buzzing to tell me I had a message, this dulled my hesitating conscience, decisiveness was transmitted via some invisible neural synapses, the muscle fibers contracted, their movement reached the three fingers of my right hand that were squeezing the lemon, and the oyster-embryo writhed beneath the paralyzing lemon juice. I closed my eyes and swallowed it. At that moment, my grandfather passed by, swallowing his living medicine, and patted me on the back. I took out my phone. The text message read: "I took a test, it said YES." Short and sweet, without unnecessary drama. My wife always catches me at the scene of the crime. I thought I felt the oyster move inside me. I felt nauseated and made a dash for the bathroom. I felt like Cronus, having just swallowed another one of his children. I've never tried oysters again.

The End of the Minotaurs

Someone's walking around inside me. Someone's gotten lost in my belly. That's what she said one winter afternoon, as we were sitting quietly in the room, trying to hear the snow piling up outside. It sounded beautiful and timeless. Lying back in the rocking chair, she had opened up *Ancient Greek Myths and Legends* and placed the book on top of the protruding oval of her belly, like a roof.

It's so close, only centimeters away from us, I thought to myself, behind this wall of skin, yet days, weeks, and months have to pass before it arrives.

I wanted to remember all of that, the chair, the window growing bright with snow, the beauty of that phrase, the whole antiquity of dusk in winter. There is no season more ancient than winter. I grabbed a sheet of paper and scribbled out a few phrases, mostly for the sake of mnemonics. Despite this, something like a poem came out. Which nevertheless had its own logic, insofar as poetic techniques are a kind of mnemonic device. Is Homer's hexameter not, in fact, a mnemonic trick, a memory tool? I was trying to describe that night and to enter into the cave, the burrow or house of that belly. And I saw that the places had been switched around. That which was roaming around inside was not the Minotaur, but rather that which would kill him. Let's call it "Theseus" for the sake of clarity. The umbilical cord is there inside like Ariadne's thread. So then where is the Minotaur? The answer lay in the anxiousness of the inquiry. The Minotaur was me. Let's turn that phrase around, so I can't hide in its tail end. I was the Minotaur. Theseus—he, she, it (the gender doesn't matter) - was coming to kill me with all the innocence of predestination. There was nowhere to hide, I could only meekly await his arrival. That poem was called "The End of the Minotaurs." I should look to see where I tucked it away.

She was born early in the morning in winter. It was dark. I was walking back home, the way out of the hospital passed through a strange tunnel. I felt as if I were coming out of a womb, as if I was going down the child's path. A newborn father. It had been a long time since I had walked around that city at five in the morning, before sunrise. The neon signs were going out, the first streetcar passed by, I looked at the number. Seven. I told myself that this meant everything would be all right. It was exactly 5:07 A.M. A man was opening up his newspaper stand, I asked for every single one of the daily newspapers. He looked at me sleepily and bewildered. After all, nothing all that special has happened today, he said, puzzled.

Oh yes, it has. I paid, took my pile of newspapers, and walked away, happy.

What were the headlines from that day? Was the world's nursery ready to meet that child?

. . .

First winter.
First snow.
First wind.
First dog.
First cloud.

For the eye of a child.

For the eye of every newborn—rat, fly, or turtle—each time the world is created anew.

In the beginning, they speak the language of all living creatures, cooing like a dove, gurgling like a dolphin, meowing, squawking, bawling . . . The linguistic primordial soup.

Dgish, anguh, pneya, eeeh, deeeya, bunya-bunya-bunyaba, batyabuuu.

God does not give language to newborns immediately. And that's no accident. They still know the secret of paradise, but they have no words for it. When they are given language, the secret has already been forgotten.

Her first steps, she's wobbling like a royal penguin. As if walking on the moon. She reaches out to grab onto the air. So concentrated and smiling to herself, so fragile. When you look at her, she falls.

While I'm writing about the world's sorrows, Portuguese *saudade*, Turkish *hüzün*, about the Swiss illness—nostalgia . . . she comes to me, at two and a half, and suddenly snatches away my pen.

Sit here and open your mouth up wide, she says. Then she gets up on tiptoe and looks inside. Wow, it's really dark inside you, I can't see a thing . . .

Come on, let's play dust motes. You're the daddy dust mote, and I'm the baby dust mote.

VI. The Story Buyer

The Baby Carrier

Here's the deal, why shouldn't I tell you? I'm not afraid. You get pregnant here and around the seventh month you've got to cross the border into Greece. You suck in your belly, wear baggy clothes, that's why it's better to choose colder weather. You light up a cigarette while they check your passport, to keep calm and cool on the one hand, and to not give away that you're pregnant, on the other. Of course, the guy who's taking you across has greased some palms, but you've got to do your part, too. So you cross the border. You sit on the outskirts of Athens for two months in some windowless room, like a closet. You don't go out anywhere, so as not to run into any trouble. You just lie around, watching TV and eating like a pig. They feed you well, because the goods have got to be healthy. So you carry it to term, they have gotten in touch with the buyers, they say you're a relative, they find you a doctor and you give birth illegally. Your guy takes the money and that's that. I just don't want them to show it to me when it's born, so I don't get sad. If I see it even once, it's all over, I can't give it away and I'll screw up the whole deal. I support my other kids with this gig, I've got four waiting for me at home. I'm only doing it for them. How much do they sell for? Around five or six thousand, for one they gave me 8K, it was a boy, boys cost more, I get ten percent. I've sold four and raised four, that's the breakdown. But this one now is the last one, end of story. Hey, it's kicking, it knows we're talking about it, stop kicking, kid, you're life's gonna be a hundred times better there. Sometimes I dream about them and light candles for them.

I bought this story in late October, near the Greek border. When I offered her money, the woman looked at me in astonishment. She couldn't figure out what exactly I was paying her for. I've got nothing to sell you, she said, plus I'm not gonna have any more kids. I replied that I had just bought her story. I'm not sure she understood. She took the money and turned it over in her hands, as if expecting me to ask for it back, then turned around, took a few steps, squatted down, and burst out sobbing. I thought to myself that only now had she begun to sell her children. When she started telling about them. Without a story, it was all nothing but business.

Telling stories is part of Judgment Day, because it makes people understand. But what the point of understanding is remains unclear. I put these stories in the box, too.

The Story Buyer

In the past I could emplant, now I'm forced to buy. I could introduce myself this way, too: I'm a person who buys up the past. A story trader. Others might trade tea, coriander, stocks and bonds, gold watches, land . . . I go around buying up the past wholesale. Call me what you want, find me a name. Those who own land are called "landholders," I'm a timeholder, a holder of others' time, the owner of others' stories and pasts. I'm an honest buyer, I never try to undercut the price. I only buy up private pasts, the pasts of specific people. Once they tried to sell me the past of a whole nation, but I turned it down.

I buy all sorts of stories—about abandonment, about unfaithful women, about childhood, about travelling and getting lost, about sorrow and unexpected deliverance . . . I also buy happy stories, but there aren't many sellers of those. From the first word I can tell fresh from rancid goods, true stories from those of fibbing shysters who only want to make a quick buck.

Most people sell their stories for a pittance, some are even dumbfounded that I offer them money for something that doesn't cost a thing. Others are thankful to have someone to take on the burden they had previously been carrying alone.

What's in it for me? Thanks to an earlier illness and to the purchased stories, I could now move through the corridors of various times. I could have the childhood of everyone I had bought one from, I could possess their wives and their sorrows. I could pile them up in the Noah's Boxes in that basement.

The Olive Oil Trader
(the Whole Truth about Mr. G.)

1.

I've never met such a gentleman—and I've met plenty, believe you me—who respected women as much as the ever-so-gallant Mr. G., he was so respectful it was downright worrisome, I've never met a man who could sit calmly next to a naked woman, a woman who was ready for him, after he himself had prepared her, a woman soft as clay, feeling her skin burning and hearing her crying out for him and not laying a finger on her, not driving his stallion into her, as was written somewhere, I read a lot, not letting his horse run free, not drawing his sword, not releasing his arrow from the taut bow, I have not met and will never again meet such a man, who, faced with such an opportunity, would speak of how easily we drink from the cup of sin, as if it were an infusion of chamomile or mulled wine, and how we covet what is not ours like a fig tree growing in the middle of the road, dear God, how Mr. G. could talk, cleverly and outlandishly, peculiarly and prettily, our men don't talk that way, they simply stick their hands up your skirt, grab your tits and push you up against the wall. I don't know if that saintly man is still alive, does the gentleman know anything more about him, since he is asking?

Oh, the gentleman is so courteous, but must one pay even for that nowadays?

2.

It was rape, I'll tell you flat out, rape, pure and simple, without physical communion, I know that bit about physical communion from the late Judge R., may he rest in peace, he spent more nights with me than with his lawfully wedded wife, we had physical communion, that's what he called it, I didn't mind, it was the same thing, it just sounded fancier, so unlike the late judge, Mr. G. and I didn't engage in any physical communion, yet despite that I've never been so roughly and brutally raped, I had to suffer all his crackpot ranting about infidelity and sin, the likes of which I hadn't even heard from my husband . . . you call a woman over to your house, strip her naked and then look her over as if inspecting sheep, you condemn her, as if you yourself weren't the one leading her into sin, and in the end you throw her out . . . I've never felt so bruised and degraded after any other man, I got up, went straight over to Judge R. and told him that Mr. G. had tried to rape me and lead me into . . . I fixed him good, I don't know what exactly my dear judge did or how he did it, but the very next day, in the darkness before dawn, Mr. G. slunk out of town, and no one ever mentioned him again, probably because in every house there was someone who had passed through his iron bed   all these years and you, sir, are the first to ask about him, why do you want to know . . . had we spoken of money, thank you, thank you.

3.

That's exactly how he was, the Venerable G., sir, if you want an honest answer, incidentally I don't know if he had an ecclesiastical title, he had devoted himself to tempting women, but not all women, only wives, only faithful, obedient wives . . . and when they ended up in his bed sooner or later, he would not lay on a finger on them, he would start asking them why they were there, what they expected of him, what had prompted them to abandon their husbands and children, he talked about morality, oh yes, he was big on morality, he was; the woman would be lying undressed in his iron bed, and he would wag his finger in her face, talking, looking her over, asking . . . I've already reached the age when I have nothing to hide, so I'll admit it, I was there, too, never judge wives too harshly, sir, we are wretched creatures, they force you into bed and you start giving birth every year and a half, as if racing against the cow in the barn and the pig in the pen, while Mr. G. was not like the local men and he wasn't a local, he didn't stink like onion, he didn't swear at animals and children, he didn't spit on the floor, and he read books . . . all the wives were crazy about him, I swear, so he didn't really need to do much at all to land them in his bed, with all the risk that entailed back then . . . When it was my turn to lie in that cold room, I meekly listened to all he had to say, because sin really was circling over the bed, but when he was done I asked him straight out why he did this, wasn't it equally unnatural and sinful not to lie with a woman whom you had called over, who had come to you, and who had stripped herself bare of everything, her husband, her children, all of Divine Law . . . he was amazed that I had the courage to ask him anything at all in my state, then replied that he was a natural scientist studying sin and infidelity, he wanted to isolate it in its purest form, to distill it, and when he saw that I didn't understand much of his scholarly fiddle-faddle, he said—and I quote: You, woman, are the olive from which I press sin like olive oil.

More than forty years have passed, but to this day those words give me chills, sir . . . his eyes when he said that looked like two dark-green olives, and again I tell you that I cannot judge him, the Venerable Mr. G., something terrible must have happened to him to make him do such things . . . he was an abandoned soul . . . never go into an abandoned house or visit an abandoned person, there are only owls and snakes there—that's exactly how he was, if you're looking for an honest answer.

Oh no, I no longer need money. But what exactly is he to you, sir?

. . .

What exactly is Mr. G. to me? And what am I doing way back here in the year 1734? I'm buying stories under the guise of olive trading. What makes me better than Mr. G.? And aren't we talking about one and the same olive oil?

An old woman told me a story that her grandmother had heard from her grandmother about some guy who had possessed all the married women in these parts. That in and of itself wouldn't have grabbed my attention if it hadn't been for the name she uttered—a name that has been dogging me for some time now.

Gaustine. The person who would easily cross over eras like a shallow river and would always find a way to send me a sign from one time or another. I will never really be sure whether he existed for real or whether I've thought him up, or whether I myself was thought up by him. His latest move, I must admit, has surpassed all of my expectations. For several years now a book under my name (in German translation) that I never wrote has been circulating around the web: *Ding, Kunst, Kant und Zeitgenossen* (Wieser Verlag, 2005). You can look it up.

I'm waiting for his next book, under the name Gaustine, in which the main character will have my name.

I once Googled him. Immediately some Angelina Gaustine came up, who is known to have died exactly in the year 1900 at the age of 70 and who is buried in the cemetery in Paoli, Indiana. The source was the diocese's death records.

In one family tree, a certain Lucinda Gaustine, born 1853, also turns up. In another place, there's Molly Gaustine with a question mark after the name. Somewhere in Oregon we find one B. Gaustine. But everywhere the name exists only as a surname and never as a first, given name. Only his children were recorded in these books. A common, disappeared father.

After returning from this story (it was a rough journey, I had to transfer from voice to voice, it was a third-generation story, and after all, it's becoming ever harder for me to reach my erstwhile empathy), I dug into the archives around the place of the story, made various inquiries and indeed found confirmation. In one "Common Book of Births, Burials, Weddings, Debts, and Other Unusual Events," the name Gaustine came up. The very same person had arrived in the town precisely in 1700 and three years later was written off "without the right to return to the city." With three strange little crosses in the book's margin, which in those parts marked encounters with the Evil One.

The Underground Angel

The story of the guy born with angel's wings. The night before his birth, a messenger appeared in a dream and told his mother, okay, so this is the deal, woman, your boy is a gift from God, he will be an angel in human flesh. And as the rumor in town had it, the boy with the angel's wings would possess incredible strength. "Strength" here was taken literally—lifting weights, beating everybody at wrestling, going head-to-head with a bear or slinging two bags of flour over your shoulder. Or lifting up a full cask of wine with your teeth at town fairs like the famous Harry Stoev. The only condition was that the mother not tell anyone.

Now I'm imagining that boy like a classical angel, so different from everything around him, like the seed of an Italian pine or some other plant not found in these parts, blown in on a Mediterranean breeze. A gangly, skinny—here they'd say "wimpy"—boy who would be the target of taunts. His mom wasn't supposed to say anything, but she got scared that her son would be different, so she started blabbering about it left and right and his wings disappeared.

As kids we would secretly wait to catch a glimpse of him. He was a miner. Always somber and dirty. I would imagine him with big, limp angel's wings dragging along behind him, black from the coal dust. He walked slightly hunched over and never took off his shirt. Perhaps the wings had kept growing under it? And he had to clip them every morning. Just like he had to shave. Or like how my grandma would clip the chickens' wings so they wouldn't flit over the fence, so they wouldn't leave the yard. He wouldn't leave it, either. His mother had chosen the son over the angel.

As a child I despised that blabbering mother who had deprived her son of such power. But now I understand her. She refused to allow him to be taken away from the human species. Unlike Pasiphaë, the Minotaur's mother. The miner-angel was morose, withdrawn, never said a word. As if by killing the angel within himself, in the end he had managed to obliterate the human as well.

The underground angel's son was a few classes ahead of us, unusually tall, he went to Sofia to play basketball, then left for America.

The Underground Angel's Son

My father was a miner. In the dark, at five in the morning, he would go out to the mine. They would bring him back by truck at dusk. Both in the mine and outside—in the dark. He didn't remember what day was. Only one time he didn't go to work and lay all day in his room with the curtains drawn, he couldn't stand the light.

That's how I remember him, he would come home at night, gloomy, not saying a word, on the table a big salad and a bottle of brandy. As if he weren't here at all. I've heard that story about the wings, maybe it's true, mute as an angel. He would turn on the TV, but not watch it. He would eat the whole salad, and drink half the bottle. He never said anything. He'd go to bed. And start all over the next morning.

The happiest day of my life was when the coach from the city came to see which of us would make good basketball players. They picked me because I was already a beanstalk, tall and wiry, with hands like shovels. My mother started bawling, my dad just patted me on the back. I got the feeling that he wanted to say something, he took a breath, but he hadn't spoken in so long that the mechanism down there was most likely rusty, he cleared his throat, something creaked in it and he went to bed. The next day I took my duffle bag and left for the sports boarding school in the city. I trained like crazy, because I knew what awaited me if I was forced to go back home. I stayed late after practice, lifting weights, jumping rope, practicing free throws, everything . . . I didn't have an ounce of talent for that game, actually I didn't have an ounce of talent, but I just kept busting ass . . . like a miner. And I made the team, because I was ripped, I gave my all, I didn't spare my strength. And when some guy showed up after 1989 from some amateur American club to buy up cheap Eastern European players, I didn't hesitate to go. I knew I had no chance playing basketball there, I'd never make the cut. I just needed to get as far away from here as I could, from my father, from his bottle and his sullenness.

If I'd stayed, I would've turned out like him. I left, played for a year or so, they sent me packing—they really put up with me longer than they should have—so I started driving one of those big, long trucks, as long as a train, with smokestacks up on top. Lots of work, but good pay. You can't find a wife with a job like that. I take off early at 5 A.M., then sleep at a truck stop somewhere in the evenings. Busting ass from darkness to darkness. Then I sit down, drink four beers, eat two Big Macs, and sleep like the dead. Every day. One night I dreamed about my father. He was driving my truck. And in the morning they called to tell me how it had happened.

H.K., age 48. He had come from Dallas to bury his father and settle his estate.

Malamko the Cab Driver and His Happiest Day

Swarthy, curly haired, a bit over twenty, wearing a pleather jacket, an incarnation of Michael Jackson from the '80s. And, of course, a picture of Michael himself up by the mirror. This story starts with my getting into the cab. As if he was only waiting for a listener.

Bro (this is my role and name in this story), if you only knew what a babe got into my taxi today! Pushin' forty, but a babe, I'm tellin' ya. Maybe she was 38 or 39, who knows. A hottie. When she got in my cab, I felt downright ashamed to be driving this old Opel.

We're at a stoplight. I, too, cast a glance over the car, the threadbare upholstery, the cracked dashboard, the overpowering scent of vanilla coming from the pine-shaped air freshener.

That woman was not meant for this car, Malamko goes on. She needs a Cadillac, pink. And she's got tits on her. So she gets into my cab and says drive wherever you want, that's what she says. She's just gotten a divorce from her husband. She tells me everything, from beginning to end. How they got married, how many years they were together, how he turned out to be a slug. She's like, he turned out to be a slug. I dunno what a slug is, bro, but it's gotta be bad. A snail, I say. Huh? A slug is a snail without a shell. Really? Well, what's so bad about a snail without a shell, hmm . . . And he'd been messing around with some other women, but she'd found out—in short, he'd screwed up big time, royally. A huge tragedy, like something straight out of a Turkish soap opera. And so I'm just nodding, bro, and driving, I don't even know where I'm going. I can see she's in the midst of a spiritual crisis, so I just drive and listen. And the more she talks to me, the more she's checking me out. She's givin' me signals, right that minute she's giving me signals. I get this kind of stuff. Stop here now. We'll see each other again, she says, you can be sure of that. Then she starts digging around in her purse, that goddamn, slug-sucking son of a bitch took my cash! She's cursing, but even cursing fits her to a T, like a fancy necklace, like a brooch, a bona fide babe no matter which way you look at her. No worries, I tell her, money doesn't matter. Pay me back next time. What's your name, hon, she asks me. I'm like: Malamko. Let me give you a kiss, Malamko, she says, and leans over and grabs my head and plants one on me right here (pointing to his cheek) before I know what's going on.

He looks in the mirror to see if there's still a trace of that kiss. The stoplight has turned green, the drivers behind him start honking. I'll give you a call soon, she says, slams the door and disappears. Now there's a real woman for you, bro, the real deal.

Silence. But how's she gonna find me, I don't know. She didn't take my number or anything. Maybe she remembered the number of the cab and will call the dispatcher to ask. There's no other Malamko working for us.

He falls silent. This question gnaws at him. This is my place to intervene, as a bro.

Listen, Malamko, I begin in my deepest voice. When a woman wants to find someone, she'll turn the world upside down. In such cases, only clichés help. I'm probably quoting some novel, some bad literature, God damn it. Let it do some good in consoling a handsome young Gypsy.

(The truth is that I'm thinking about how that woman is getting free rides all around Sofia with that sob-story about the slughusband. But who am I to ruin the happiest day of Malamko's life? And the fact that I'm even thinking this and he's not makes me a ten-times bigger loser. Lucky Malamko . . .)

I'm a really lucky guy, eh, Malamko says after a short pause, as if having read my thoughts in the mirror. Such a pretty woman, and she likes me, Malamko, of all people. Who cares if she's 30 or 35, she might be even younger. I'm a player, I don't go looking for faults.

I gave him the biggest tip I've ever given. Actually, it wasn't a tip, I bought the story.

I add it here now, in the capsule of this book, who knows, maybe that babe will read it or someone else will tell her that Malamko is waiting for her, she should give him a call. Let literature do some good, goddamn it.

The Story Seller
What exactly are you? A writer? I'm always running into writers. My grandfather was one, it must be karma. A month ago I was invited to a wedding. And who do you think turned up at the same table? Can you guess? They put me right next to Salman Rushdie himself. Yes, yes, the man himself. With the little round glasses and the goatee . . . To tell you the truth, I've always thought that the

people they show on TV, the most famous ones, don't actually exist in real life, they must be some kind of computer animation or hologram. Don't you doubt the existence of Madonna or Brad Pitt even a little? Anyway. I sat down next to him, we shook hands, he said his name and my mouth hung open. The writer? As if a whole slew of celebrities lurked behind this name. He was even a bit flustered and mumbled something—you could say that, yes.

Know what I felt like the whole time? Like cannon fodder. Jesus Christ, I thought this guy didn't even dare poke his nose outside. I must admit I haven't read any of his books, but I watch TV from time to time and read the newspapers, for God's sake. I mean, they burn this guy's books, he's got a death sentence, a fatwa. And those dudes who issued it, you know they aren't messing around. So I had this strange feeling at that wedding, both proud and on edge. And I was constantly looking around to make sure none of the guests at that joyous event made any sudden movements. I was ready to dive under the table any second. I was more scared than he was, he's surely gotten used to it. I wonder if he had anything under that dress shirt and bowtie? I mean a thin, elegant, cutting-edge bulletproof vest, with fibers made from a totally new and lightweight material. I thought about asking him, but decided not to. I could just pat him goodbye on the back and see for myself. Actually, the guy behaved very decently. He never once asked me what I thought of his latest novel. Begging your pardon, since you're a writer. Insofar as I know them (present company excluded, of course), they never fail to ask that question. They have it in their heads that the world lives and breathes with their books. I was afraid that he might ask me and realize that I hadn't read anything of his. But now there's a great writer, he didn't even ask. Either he's sure you've read it or he doesn't care. He was quietly cutting his steak, spearing his carrots. He exchanged a few pleasantries about the joyous event, about how adorable the newlyweds were, how they were made for each other, blah blah blah . . . Small talk you could make at a wedding with any ordinary neighbor to your left or right. I thought that writers talked more, well, you know, only about important things, about life and death . . . Anyway. I was a friend of the bride, he had known the groom since childhood. We both swore by our people. And in the end, I told him one of my stories. I never did figure out whether I'd really impressed him or if he was just pretending. I don't know, people with glasses throw me. I'll follow his writing from now on. Do you think he'll use it?

I finally managed to get a word in. Writers are never innocent. They're as thieving as magpies. Still, it's important who steals from you.

But no, I gave him the story as a gift.

Well, then we'll wait and see.

If you'd like, I could tell it to you, too.

I am curious.

But you do understand that it is already sold.

Didn't you say it was given as a gift?

Yes, that's right . . . given, sold. We didn't sign a contract. If you really like it, you just need to work out with him who's going to use it. I'll sell it . . . in exchange for two large Four Roses.

So, for eight roses, I laughed . . . Deal. (That's how I met the story seller.) And after the first bouquet of roses landed on the table, the story began.

. . . and His Story

Naturally, it's about a woman, the storyteller began slowly. I appreciated that opening a la "naturally, a manuscript," but for a moment I wondered whether he wasn't trying to resell other people's stories, trying to foist off Eco on Rushdie, hence sowing the seeds of unrest and discord in literature. I let the story unfold.

I had to get away from her if I wanted to live. I had to leave her, leave the city in the most literal way. I wandered around Europe for several months. To forget a relationship, some try promiscuous sex, I tried promiscuous geography. I picked cities at random, usually travelling by train, I changed stations and hotels, all the other tourists were in groups or couples, I wandered alone around the squares, which at a certain point all started to look the same. I looked like a person who wanted to abandon his own abandonment around some corner. Like someone looking for a distant and unknown place to release the cats of his sorrow, so that they would never find the way home. Do you know how hard it is to get rid of cats? They possess an incredible homing instinct, astonishing memory. Once my grandpa tried to get rid of all the housecats that had multiplied in the house and yard, he stuffed them in sacks and let them go a few miles outside of town, near the graveyard. When he got back home, the cats were there waiting for him. That bit about the cats is a bonus, I didn't tell it to Rushdie, the storyteller said, taking a sip of his second Four Roses.

I soon realized that Europe was far too close, it was full of this woman, it reminded me of her. I needed more space, empty and unfamiliar. So I caught the first plane to the Americas. I needed to get lost like Columbus, but amid long-since charted lands. We don't ever stop to think how difficult it is to get lost nowadays. Almost as difficult as it was not to get lost back then.

When I got home a year and three months later, I spread the world map on the floor and connected up all the places I'd been with a marker. It was a real round-the-world journey, I traced the route with my finger, saying the names of the towns and megalopolises aloud. The best mantra for forgetting a woman.

Sofia, Belgrade, Budapest, Wrocław, Berlin, Hamburg, Aarhus, Bremen, then down to Rouen, Dijon, Toulouse, Barcelona, Malaga, Tangier, Lisbon, across the Atlantic and up to Long Island, New York, Ontario, the North Hudson Bay, and back down to Minneapolis, Chicago, Colorado Springs, Pueblo, Phoenix, San Diego . . .

I got up, put the map on the wall, and only then noticed . . . The lines of my journey perfectly traced out a letter. Her letter. A big, clear M. An exquisite monogram of a foolish man. The cats had beaten me home.

It wasn't a bad story, even if he had swiped it from a third party and already sold it once (certain phrases like "the cats of his sorrow" and others were definitely not his own). The bouquet of roses flourished. He looked satisfied, like a man who had managed to sell the same goods twice. But I, too, was satisfied with the deal, because I had bought two stories for the price of one—the one he had told me and the previous one, about his meeting with Rushdie, which I suspect is even more made-up than the second one.

Two Men Bet about Whose Wife Is More Faithful

First, they decide to check up on one wife. The man announces that he'll be going away for a few days. He and the other man hide in the yard and wait. The husband has even gotten a gun from somewhere. The first night—nothing. His heart lightens up a bit. But the very next night, once the darkness has become impenetrable, the woman steps out of the house, opens the door and a man slips inside, silent as a shadow. No lights go on inside, however. The two friends go over to the window, the scanty moonlight reveals the movement of two bodies, but even that is enough to see what is going on. How the woman is winding around him, what movements, the husband is downright thunderstruck, he has never seen her like that, the dirty bitch. His friend also looks on, open-mouthed.

We're going in, the husband says quietly, and they slip into the house like thieves. The next scene is such a classic in cinema, literature and real life, that I don't know how to describe it. The husband has opened the door, taken a step inside and to the right, standing with his legs slightly apart for support, that's what he's seen them do in the movies, and is pointing the gun at the tangle of bodies that is now lying there stunned. His friend is standing six feet away from him, his stance slightly ridiculous, because the situation itself is quite ridiculous, he doesn't know where to look. He feels uncomfortable looking at his friend's wife, because she is naked and had been having sex just moments earlier, it's uncomfortable to look down, as if he himself has been caught in the act, he's too embarrassed to look at his cuckolded friend, so as not to embarrass him all the more. In a word—awkward. The lover, who has been caught red-handed—or rather red-panted, in his red-and-black striped underwear—keeps glancing from one man to the other, as if not yet sure who is the husband, the one with the gun or the other one. The woman's body is a complicated mixture of slowly waning desire, rage toward the intruders who barged in out of the blue, and growing fear. Sometimes seconds have immeasurable lengths and volumes.

The cuckolded husband is the one who had to make a decision. Matters (and the gun) are in his hands . . . It is up to him how everything will unfold, but he still doesn't know what to do. He only knows that he needs to decide quickly, time is not on his side. The man has never before found himself in such a situation, he knows them only from movies and books. And none of that is helping him now. He pulls himself together. He points the gun at the man. That's right, squirm, you dirty little rat. The rat has nestled into his very own bed. He has even left his watch on the nightstand.

People kill someone just for setting foot onto private property, those kinds of signs are everywhere, so what should happen when someone enters into the holiest of holies, not just your home, but your bedroom, and not just into your bedroom, but into the woman you sleep with? On the other hand, what fault of it is his, he didn't force his way in, someone let him in, what's more, someone even called him over, gave him a sign. Isn't that someone the guiltiest party in this situation? The guiltiest one—the woman. That is the radical decision, the adulteress must atone for her sin with death. Jesus, what melodramatic lines, is this Greek theater or a second-rate bourgeois play? To kill your wife over nothing, okay, well, it's not anything, but she's still your wife . . . And after he kills her, then what? Decision-making has never been his strong suit. Ever. If he has to pick out a pair of slippers from the store, his whole afternoon is shot. Black or brown? After he has mentally counted all his pants and divided them into two piles—those that go with brown and those that go with black—then he glances at the furniture in the room, because it would be good for the slippers to match it as well. After all of that, an hour has already gone by and he's decided on the brown ones. But, horror of horrors, there are two types of brown slippers—with braid and without. On top of everything, there is darker and lighter braid. That's how bad it is with slippers, but here we're talking about murder and doling out justice. Who is guiltier in a case of fornication?

He lifts his gaze from them and sees, as if for the first time, their wedding photo above the bed. How could they do this right beneath it? It occurs to him that it would be very effective if he were to shoot their wedding picture, he imagines how the glass would shower down on their heads. What a metaphor. You, woman, have shot dead our married life itself, so our past gets a bullet to the head. Where should he aim, though—at himself or at her? We're talking about the picture, but still. If he shoots at his own portrait that will be suicide of sorts.

The next moment, he turns and does the most unexpected thing before everyone's astonished gazes—he pulls the trigger and shoots his friend. No external witness, no crime.

Scheherazade and the Minotaur

Usually stories are told by the one in the weaker position. This is clearest with Scheherazade. One doomed woman tells story after story to gain night after night. The thread of the story is the only thing leading her through the labyrinth of her doom. Inside the stories she tells, the most frequently tendered coins to buy someone's life are again stories. It's enough simply to recall the first—about the poor merchant who accidentally kills a genie's son with an olive pit, and three passing sheikhs each buy a third of the merchant's life from the fearsome father (here we really are talking about direct trade) by telling (selling) him stories. "*O Genie, thou Crown of the Kings of the Genies! Were I to tell thee the story of me and this gazelle and thou shouldst consider it wondrous wouldst thou give me a third part of this merchant's blood?*"

If your stories are good and you really do impress me, replies the genie, then it's a done deal. And it's a done deal. The genie gives them the merchant's blood, and Shahryar, who is listening to the story, gives one more night to the storyteller, Scheherazade. Blissful times. "By Allah, I will not slay her, until I shall have heard the rest of her tale." But the story is endless. Just as the labyrinth is endless.

It's obvious that that's where Scheherazade got the idea from. You set off down the corridor of one story, which sends you off toward another, which leads you toward a third and so on . . . She has moved the labyrinth of stories into Shahryar's bedroom. And—now here's the secret—upon going inside, she has brought along her own executioner, she has sneaked him inside without him suspecting a thing. The two of them are there, but she holds the thread of the story, its thin opium leads Shahryar through the galleries and corridors. If the thread snaps, this mass murderer of women—because that's what he is—will wake up, realize where he is, and all will be lost.

Where does the storyteller's strength come from, even if it is the strength of the weaker one? Is it from his power over that which he tells? To hold in your hands, or rather, on the tip of your tongue, a world in which you can dole out death and put it off whenever you wish. A world that can be so real or so fabricated as to duplicate the real one, to become its double. If in one, death's sword is hanging over you, you can escape down the redeeming corridors of the other.

Almost no one remembers or pays attention to how *One Thousand and One Nights* begins. In the exact same way as the myth of the Minotaur starts. With an infidelity. Pasiphaë, Minos's wife, betrays him with a bull (Poseidon is peeking out from behind it). For their part, all the 1,001 stories begin thanks to the unfaithful wife of Shah Zaman, Shahryar's younger brother, ruler of the Persian city of Samarkand. He sets out on a journey, realizes he has forgotten something, goes back and catches his wife embracing a slave. In one case, the lover is a bull, in the other a slave—always taboo bodies. For now, this infidelity costs only the couple involved their lives. Then the younger brother sets out to where he had been going—to visit his elder brother, Shahryar. There his brother's wife's infidelity is indeed on a mass scale, involving ten concubines and as many slaves. Shahryar decides to avenge his brother, himself, and the whole male world. Then the serial killing of women begins, along with the series of fairytales.

Night. Everything happens at night from here on out. In the eternal night of the Labyrinth, where the Minotaur lives, or in those thousand and one nights in Shahryar's royal palace. Night is the time for stories. Day is another world, which has no inkling of night's world. The two worlds should not be mixed.

A Place to Stop

Some books need to be equipped with Ariadne's thread. The corridors are constantly intertwining, crisscrossing one another. Sometimes I can see my grandfather going into the Esprit store on Friedrichstrasse with me, touching the cotton shirts distrustfully and muttering that he wouldn't for the life of him buy anything that thin, which the wind could leapfrog through. Another time, when crossing the Doctor's Garden with my daughter, a man wrapped up to his eyeballs in a scarf with his collar turned up high, nods at me as we pass. An episode I would have ignored if Aya hadn't tugged at my sleeve and pointed out his strange two-horned shadow on the snow. The Minotaur had gone out for a walk in the labyrinth of the winter garden.

VII. Global Autumn

Howl

Elenaa, Elenaaa, child of the wild desert, Amooour . . . A drunken song wafting through the night from the panel-block apartment building next door. We sang it as school kids at summer camps, but to this day I still don't know which Elena and what desert it's talking about. The obligatory kitsch that each and every one of us needed, some sort of romantic exoticism, an oasis amid the only possible desert here, in which the sand has been turned to concrete. The same song now, thirty years later, at three in the morning, drifting over with drunken longing from a group of friends celebrating nearby. This is the alternative Bulgarian song in the cosmos. Youth has passed away, socialism has passed away, yet the demons of erstwhile desires have remained, drowned in the alcohol of that which never happened. Those erstwhile school kids have grown old, they've gotten beer bellies, they've married themselves an Elena a piece, but something has gone wrong, something just isn't what it should be . . . Meaninglessness has entered the uncertain Troy of the body via a wooden horse. That's what all this howling in the night is about . . . I hate them and feel close to them in all their helpless sorrow and absurdity. Sometimes I feel like I want to add my howl to theirs. If I had a small, loyal pack of friends, I'd surely howl with them, happy and disconsolate amid the city's eternal concrete fields. Amid its wild desert, Amooour . . . But I don't have that pack. So

I howl quietly, oh so quietly, and ostensibly with such subtle irony that I can barely hear myself.

The Saddest Place in the World

To the Angel of Inexplicable Nighttime Noises,
who watches over those crying in the bathroom,
those cutting themselves in the kitchen
and those smoking on balconies at three in the morning.

Revoltingly lonely. That's how I had been feeling over the last few years, that's the most precise definition. A while back I saw it written in black marker on a telephone booth: "I love people and that makes me revoltingly lonely." I added it to the collection of persistent phrases that I run through my head during fits of . . . revolting loneliness.

I went to take a walk around the neighborhood during autumn's late, joyless afternoon. The scent of rot. The scent of overripe, falling plums, inebriating, with a whiff of mash. The brandy that will never be. Scattered watermelon rind, already drained by an army of wasps, then sucked dry by a procession of ants. I was breathing it in, no, I was swilling it down, with the doggedness of a man who has decided to get sloshed in some grimy neighborhood dive.

I was looking at the beat-up, rusting, wrought-iron casings of the glassed-in balconies. The poor man's pathetic trick for enclosing your only balcony, putting up windows and curtains, turning it into an aquarium, reclaiming a few more square feet, adding another room to your panel-block apartment, putting your stove, hot plate and pepper roaster out there, planting dill, parsley, onion, and even a tomato plant in square plastic pots, turning it into a kitchen and a winter garden all at once. Frying peppers in the evening in that shop window onto your miserable life or smoking in your wife-beater in the inexplicable sorrow of the wee hours.

I cut through a schoolyard, with battered basketball backboards, their hoops missing, overgrown with weeds. Grass was sprouting up through the cracked asphalt where a few kids were fervently kicking around a ball, dude, you're a fucking faggot, one of the kids, not more than ten, yelled, then the "faggot" told him to go fuck himself and the game continued. It wasn't so much the words themselves, but more the doctoring of the voices, the rasping, the straining of throats to produce something growling and threatening that made me get the hell out of there. Smashed water bottles, a scrap of newspaper that read: "Sozopol has become a second Jerusalem. Miracle-working relics of St. John the Baptist were discovered there yesterday: three knucklebones from the right hand, a heel, and a molar belonging to Christ's cousin . . ." The pseudo-mystical kitsch of Bulgaria's backwaters.

It has turned into a ghetto. Or maybe it always was. Nothing has changed—except for the creeping rust everywhere; the panel-block apartments are thirty years older, irreparable. Back in the day, everybody was always saying: it's too late for us, but let's hope that at least the kids will live a different life. The mantra of late socialism. I now realize that it was my turn to utter that same line.

The boxes have to contain a little of everything. Most of all something of those whispered, buried, hidden things. Something of that which didn't make it into the shot, which didn't last, but vanished, dried up like an autumn leaf, which started stinking like fish on a hot afternoon, went sour like milk, wilted like a pissed-on geranium, rotted like a pear . . .

I passed by a power substation. They needed to be recorded, photographed, documented: the rusty sign reading "Warning: High

Voltage" and the death notices with pictures of the deceased hung all around it. As if all those people from the death notices had illegally rummaged around in the power substation (of life?) and the electric shock had swept them away. Death notices and want ads. From these want ads, pasted up on the crumbling plaster, you could reconstruct the entire unwritten history of the last twenty years. Of supply and demand. I took out my notebook and started copying them down.

A company is looking for elite dancers to work abroad. Young women needed to work for Italian families. Apartment for rent for two female students, non-smokers. Learn English in three weeks. I break curses, cast spells to improve your love and professional life. A cure for hemorrhoids and hair loss. Lost dog. We buy hair.

What's up, douchebag, someone clapped me on the shoulder. The phrase dated back twenty years ago, the gesture, too. Let's put it down in the catalogue of vanished words and gestures, I instantly filed it away. I turned around, a vaguely familiar face, most likely a schoolmate: Ooh, Señor Schlong . . . My own answer surprised me, I had never used that form of address, but now the situation somehow naturally called for it. From that point on, the conversation shifted into the genre of "two old acquaintances chat, while asking themselves 'who the hell is this guy?'" A rhetoric of flanking maneuvers. A feast of general and diluted speech. Skillful avoidance of the minefields of concrete facts and names. You can't think of his name, you have no idea what he does for a living, you don't even know whether he's mistaken you for someone else, thus causing you to rummage around in the bottomed-out sack of your memory in vain. At that moment the omnipresent question "How are you?" comes to the rescue. And everything falls into place—the army of adages about the unrelenting passage of time, the kids are growing up, we're getting older, you haven't changed a bit, you're exactly the same (who the hell are you, for Christ's sake), well, that's the way it goes, isn't it, okay, I've gotta run, okay, let's get together some time . . .

I note this encounter as well (everything is important). Saying farewell to someone whose name you can't even remember, someone you'll write down as Señor X, that eternal X of the unknown perpetrator. No matter how hard you wrack your brain all day, you won't come up with his real name, but paradoxically, this is precisely what keeps him alive in your mind for some time. We cannot run away from the ones we've forgotten.

Farewell, Señor X, farewell to all those I've forgotten, and to all those who have forgotten me. May your memory live on forever.

Description of a Phobia
(Side Corridor)

A friend of mine was terrified by dolls' gazes. She would fall into an actual stupor if she ever met their glassy eyes. They certainly did have creepy stares, those dolls from back in the day. It turn out that this fear has been described and has a name, it's called pediophobia.

My fear is even more terrible, because the threat can be anywhere. I've never found it in any nomenclature of phobias, so that's why I'll duly add its description here. Let this be my humble scientific contribution to the endless List of Fears.

I have a phobia of a certain question. A nightmarish question that can literally jump out at you from around the corner, hidden in the toothless mouth of the neighbor lady or mumbled by the clerk at the newspaper stand. Every telephone call is charged with this question. Yes, it most often lurks in telephone receivers:

How are you?

I stopped going out, stopped answering my phone, I started shopping at different stores so as to not fall into the trivial acquaintances of everyday life. I wracked my brain trying to hammer out defensive responses. I needed a new Shield of Achilles against bullshit. How to come up with an answer that doesn't multiply the banality, that doesn't get bogged down in clichés? An answer that doesn't force you to use ready-made phrases, an answer that doesn't lie, but which also doesn't reveal things you'd rather not reveal. An answer that does not predispose you to entanglement in a long and pointless conversation.

What spurious tradition of etiquette has given rise to it, how has it slipped through the centuries, that hypocritical question. "How are you?"—that is the question. (The sublime "To be or not to be" has been replaced by that pitiful inquiry, now there's proof positive of degradation.)

How are you?

How are you?

How are you?

How are you supposed to answer that?

Look, the English have pulled a fast one and made it into a greeting. They've defanged it, taken away its interrogative sting: *Howdoyoudo.*

"How are you?" is the banana peel so courteously placed beneath your feet, the cheese that lures you toward the mousetrap of cliché.

How are you—the weak, enfeebling poison of the everyday. There is no above-board answer to this question. There isn't. I know the possible answers, but they repulse me, understand? They truly repulse me . . . I don't want to be that predictable, to answer "fine, thanks," or "hanging in there." or "getting by." or . . .

I don't know how I am. I can't give a categorical answer. To give you a fitting reply, I'd have to spend nights, months, years, I'd have to read through a literary Tower of Babel, and to write, write, write . . . The answer is an entire novel.

How am I?

I'm not. End of story.

Let that be the first line. And from there, the real answer begins.

List of Available Answers to the Question *How Are You*

So-so.

The most common answer in these parts. "So-so" means things are not so good but not so bad, either. Around here, you never say you're doing well, so as not to call down some huge calamity on yourself.

Still alive and kicking.

In other words, I'm not doing well at all, but I'm not going to sit down and bore you with complaints, 'cause complaining is for sissies. This is the manly answer.

Let this be as bad as it gets!

This is said around the table, when you've gathered the whole gang together and you're drinking toasts, munching on your salad, and sipping your brandy . . . I've always wondered what "as good as it gets" would look like. I don't mean to be harsh, but I would guess it hardly looks any different.

We're fine, but it'll pass.

A waggish answer from the socialist era, someone clearly got fed up with the absurdity of the question and the system, in which complaining openly would only bring you grief. Hence the popular joke from that time:

"How are you, how are you?" The general secretary of the Communist Party jokingly asked.

"We're fine, we're fine," the workers jokingly replied.

A l'il sick t'day, dead as a doornail t'morrow.
The whole phony concern of the question "How are you?" collapses.

Any better would be criminal.
An answer again along the same lines, the brainchild of someone displeased with the essence of the question.

Not very how.
A classic, Eeyore from *Winnie-the-Pooh*. But it, too, is now thread-bare from use.

Putting one foot in front of the other.
Nothing happens, I'm not looking forward to anything, I somehow get by, I keep pushing on through. Whom and what keeps getting pushed on through and gotten by isn't quite clear, the day, or life, most likely. The day is hard to push on through, like a donkey that's dug in its heels on a bridge and won't move an inch, like a hefty buffalo that has settled down for his noontime nap and refuses to budge.

One thing I'll never forget from my childhood are the old men sitting in front of their houses or gathered in front of the general store on the little square in the late afternoon, puffing on cheap cigarettes and digging around in the dirt at their feet with sticks, the day's unknown and unlettered philosophers. In those parts, life is short, but the day is endless.

Still breathing, but that might change.
A sly variant version on the preceding answer, but its meaning or meaninglessness is more or less the same.

Losing brain cells . . .
The sincere and merciless response given by my nephew and his high school classmates in a sleepy, backwater town.

How Are You

Somewhere, a brilliant idea pops into your head, the words come of their own accord, you can hardly take them all in, you immediately look for a pen and paper, you always carry at least three pens with you, you dig around in your pockets, can't find a single one . . . You try to remember the phrases, you use tried-and-true mnemonic devices, taking the first letters or syllables from every word to forge a new keyword. You hurry home, dropping everything, chanting this word over the rosary of your mind. Right in front of your building, a neighbor stops you with that awful question "How are you?" and starts telling you some story, you open your mouth to say you're in a terrible rush and at that moment the keyword flits out of your mouth like a fly and disappears into space as if it had never existed.

Here's How

I'd been feeling more and more foreign in this place over the past few years. I started going out only at night. As if at night the city regained something of its style, its legend. Perhaps late at night the shades of those who had lived here during the 1910s, '20s, '30s, and '40s would come out. They would wander through their old haunts, banging into the newly built glass office buildings like sparrows that have accidentally flown into a room, looking for peace and quiet in the park in front of St. Sedmochislenitsi Church, strolling around the Pépinière, or hustling down Tsar Liberator Boulevard, passing by the other shades. I wanted to walk through that old Sofia like a shade among shades. At first I seemed to be succeeding. When I would stop by Yavorov's house, sometimes I could hear a couple arguing from behind the dark windows.[1] Once a window was lit up.

---

1   Peyo Yavorov, the most famous Bulgarian poet from the early twentieth-century, whose short and turbulent marriage ended in their double suicide, 1913–1914.

Lately the shades have left this city as well. This is a forsaken city, a city without a legend. And the more people pour into it during the day, the emptier it seems. Its own dead have abandoned it. And that is truly irreparable.

One evening, as I was wandering through this dark, beat-up, deserted city, I stumbled across a fight. I had never seen one so close up before. They were wailing away on one another as only people in these parts can, crudely, with no sense of style. They were thrashing away, that's the word for it, pummeling faces, about seven or eight young guys around twenty years old. I now realize that my only experience with fights is from movies and literature. And how different the picture actually is. It had nothing in common with the battle between Achilles and Hector. Nor with Rocky Balboa, nor with Jackie Chan, nor with De Niro in *Raging Bull* . . . Ugly stuff. Then one of them pulled out a knife. I knew I had to intervene, but I didn't know how. I stepped out into the open and yelled something. Someone shouted at me to get the hell out of there and they kept fighting. Yes, I was scared, there were lots of them, they were young, strong, ferocious. Where are those snoozing cops when you need them? Then an idea occurred to me. I picked up a broken paving tile from the sidewalk and hurled it through the nearest shop window on the street. It was a cell phone store. The alarm started howling. The fight stopped instantly. They looked at me stunned that some dweeb had dared to interfere. I could read their minds, as if their bloodied heads were made of glass. Suddenly all of them were ready to jump on me. But they realized what I had actually just done, the alarm was shrieking and in less than a minute the strapping private security guards would show up, who, unlike the police, wouldn't just sit back on their heels. They hadn't totally lost their grip on reason, so both gangs quickly got out of there. Nevertheless, the guy with the knife made sure to jab me, just like that in passing, as he made his getaway. I managed to raise my arm to protect myself, so the knife struck a little below the elbow. Nothing serious. I sat there bleeding meekly in the warm June night, sitting on the sidewalk amid pools of other people's blood, waiting for the security guards.

Afterward, I had to pay for the window.

I'd better get out of here quick. I'd better be someone else. Someone else, somewhere else.

Empty Space

If you turn to the back pages of the European newspaper you're reading, there, on the map showing the weather forecast, you'll see an empty space—between Istanbul, Vienna and Budapest.

The saddest place in the world, as the *Economist* called it in 2010 (I clipped out the article), as if there is truly a geography of happiness.

I wrote about this for a newspaper. An innocent piece, which stirred up a backlash on the Internet, and I received threats—the first since I had started publishing. (No one wants to be told he doesn't exist . . .) I didn't take the hint. I wrote a few more pieces, more ironic than anything else, about the fact that 1968 never happened here. About how we don't exist, how we're so nonexistent that we have to do something really over-the-top to be noticed, like Georgi Markov being jabbed with a poisoned umbrella on a bridge in London. To get mixed up in hazy dealings with Turkish terrorists, an assassination attempt on the Pope that later, proof or no proof, will be called "the Bulgarian connection." To steal Charlie Chaplin's dead body, to hold his corpse hostage. The Internet forum was already abuzz with threats, the mildest of which was that I'd be trailing my guts out behind me like a beat-up dog. I still didn't pay much attention, dismissing them as the work of anonymous nutcases with inferiority complexes. One night the telephone rang, the message was brief, but it was no longer just about me, they knew exactly what to do. That was the final straw, I decided to drop everything, take my daughter and leave.

Somewhere else, somewhere else . . .

Advice from the Nineteenth Century

Your bile is stagnant, you see sorrow in everything, you are drenched in melancholy, my friend the doctor said.

Isn't melancholy something from previous centuries? Isn't there some vaccine against it yet, hasn't medicine taken care of it yet? I ask.

There's never been as much melancholy as there is today, the doctor said with a throaty laugh. They just don't advertise it. It's not marketable, melancholy doesn't sell. Imagine an ad for a slow, melancholic Mercedes, S-class. But getting back to the point, I'll recommend something to you that you'll say is straight out of the nineteenth century: travel, stir up your blood, give your eyes new sights, go south . . .

That sounds pretty Chekhovian, doctor.

Well, Chekhov knew what to do, after all he wasn't just some ignorant writer, but a doctor, the doctor laughed.

He's right, of course. I had exhausted my personal reserves of meaning. The doctor read a lot, I'm sure that he secretly writes stories similar to those of his mentor, Chekhov. What I really love him for is the fact that he has never taken advantage of the opportunity to foist them on me.

I'd better travel, I'd better travel . . .

As a Beginning and End: Berlin

Eighty percent of Bulgarians had not
left their native country before 1989.

. . .

Being abroad is like being in space, a woman I know said as I was preparing to leave, you don't age as quickly there. When you get back, we'll already be little old ladies, while you'll still be forty-something. How awful, I thought to myself then, to still be young, when the women you thought were hot have grown old.

What was in the beginning? Not the chicken, not the egg, nor the darkness upon the face of the deep . . . Now, in the middle of my empty and unorganized room, I look for something to write in. There's that damn notebook. Seen from the outside, the moment is solemn, a new life in a new and unknown city. Which words are fitting, the first words for such a moment? I hurry so as not to forget them.

Bread, apples, toothbrush, honey, mouse, corkscrew . . .
In the beginning was the list.

The first night under the oppressively high ceilings of a Berlin apartment. I lay there, remembering all the ceilings and all the rooms of my life.

The St. Matthias Cemetery in Schöneberg, near the Turkish market. On the one side the vendors' shouts—kilo-euro, kilo-euro . . . *Buyurunuz!* Here you are. On the other side, a few yards away, the absolute silence of the walkways and the dead under the grass.

My father, whom I took with me for a few months, never managed to get used to the size of the apartment and asked to sleep in the kitchen, the smallest room. He never managed to get used to the size of Berlin, either. The only place he wanted me to take him was that Turkish market and the cemetery next to it.

There he could always exchange a few "Bulgarian" words like *arkadaş* (friend), *çok selam* (many greetings), *aferim* (bravo), *mashallah* (bravo), *evallah* (bravo again) . . . and to buy himself some "Bulgarian" cheese and a roll. Afterward, he would sit on a bench in the cemetery across the way, where the dead didn't speak German anymore, so he could chat with them a bit and throw crumbs to the pigeons. I would leave him there in the morning and go pick him up in the evening.

I would bike around the afternoons of Grunewald. Huge, heavy houses. Another time, another Germany. A monolith that has weathered catastrophes.

You don't come to Berlin for fun. In February 1918, the Bulgarian poet Geo Milev came here to patch up his shattered head and stayed a whole year. Auden arrived in Berlin in 1928, driven here by despair. Eliot came here to lick his wounds, after his first book had been rejected. Russian emigrants, fleeing the revolution, settled here in Charlottenburg. When the elderly writer Angelika Schrobsdorff was asked why she left her cozy home in Israel at such an advanced age to come live in Berlin, her withering answer was: "Who said I was coming here to live?" And to be maximally clear, she added: "Berlin is a more comfortable place to die."

One day, while we were poking around the Olympic Stadium, two German officers in Nazi uniforms suddenly jumped out in front of us. We were startled, then we spotted the camera behind them. They were shooting a film. One of the assistant directors signaled to us to quietly slip away, but Aya started bawling at the top of her lungs and the stadium resounded with her screams. Cut! Cinema's whole machinery fell silent. For a few minutes, World War II was subject to a compulsory lull.

And since things happen simultaneously, I imagined how precisely in those two minutes during that battle in Hungary, a woman took advantage of the inexplicable lull in military operations to go out onto the street and drag a wounded soldier into her home.

What remains in the end—a wintry Berlin day in a high-ceilinged room, almost empty, on the edge of Charlottenburg, a sense of emptiness, monumentalism and minimalism. Here, where Arvo Pärt lived for a year, I'm now listening to his "Für Alina," every note breaks away, circles around the empty room, you can hold it in your hand before it disappears. Aya will take her first steps in this room, here she'll say her first word: *Nein*.

What else. The sky above Berlin, the saddest bakery in the world at the very end of Kurfürstendamm with wedding cakes that nobody buys, Savignyplatz's autumn with its leaves falling endlessly over the pizzeria, the lakes of Grunewald, the glass dome of the Reichstag set ablaze by the sunset, the early dusk of November, the widows of Wilmersdorf who survived the air raids, exhausted from the peacetime they must die in, the late autumnal crocuses along Halensee, the Chinese women selling tulips in the subway, Christmas Eve, when we leave the table uncleared following some custom, so that our dead can come and eat their fill. Anxiousness over whether they'll find the way, and consolation in the fact that even if the place is different, the heavens are not.

I did everything possible to make a life for us there, but my melancholy, instead of scattering, only deepened. I grew ever gloomier and more withdrawn. In such moments I wanted to spare others my presence—my daughter most of all. I started accepting all sorts of literary invitations, even for second-rate festivals and residencies in other countries and cities . . . Before I left, she gave me her favorite dinosaur. I've always kept it with me.

I imagine how some day in the future, when she is telling stories to her own children, she'll start with the line: "My father and the dinosaurs disappeared at the same time . . ." which is a good beginning, or rather, end.

Global Autumn

Now here I am. Following an autumn all over Europe. In the beginning a chestnut in Berlin fell just a few feet from me, then several fall leaves slowly fluttered down in Warsaw, enough to set fire to all of Europe, I watched it landing over Normandy, I walked beneath the seemingly ablaze (or rusting) chestnuts of Sibiu, stood stunned before a burning blackberry bush in Wrocław, walked in the buffeting wind in Gent and watched the endless November rains through the windows of an attic room in Graz.

Cities that look empty at three in the afternoon
> Graz
> Turin
> Dresden
> Bamberg
> Topolovgrad
> Edirne
> Mantua
> Helsinki
> Cabourg
> Rouen

The wounded Jesus from Caen, Normandy, in the church knocked askew by the bombings in 1944. All that's left of him is his head with the crown of thorns, his wooden torso is scorched, his arms blown off by shells. He has no legs.

The marble Jesus with a shattered right hand in the half-destroyed church on Ku'Damm.

Europe's maimed Jesuses.

The small towns of Normandy gasping under the historical shell of their own past, of fortresses and cathedrals. A dozen centuries ago, they were grand; now they are provincial. There's a cause for historical melancholy for you. The only thing left for them is to nobly bear both their fame and their oblivion. Falaise is a town of 8,000 with an enormous chateau and fortress wall. The birthplace of the man known as William the Conqueror to some and William the Bastard to others. After seven o' clock the town is deserted, I almost said "devastated." It smells of hay and herbs. No fortress wall can stop the merciless cavalry of the hours.

Rouen. First scents. Of lilies . . . strong and devout along the city's abbey. And immediately a memory of my grandma's house, the lilies at the back of the yard, on the way to the outhouse. Everything seen is projected somewhere there, in the lost country of childhood. The ideal city lies there, the heavenly city, which has already happened to us, and in all of our later wanderings, we can only note its likenesses—sometimes more felicitous, sometimes not. The second scent I add to the catalogue is that of urine, again here by the cathedral. The homeless people who sleep nearby are already gathering up their cardboard bedding.

Alone, I stroll through the Saturdays and Sundays of the world, which is always very family-oriented on those days. And everyone is laughing, they're laughing, it's unbelievable. With the lightness of laughter that takes pleasure in life. Laughter for no visible reason. Not throaty, obliterating, sardonic or hysterical laughter. Rather the laughter of lightness that you're enjoying a nice day, rolling around in the meadows of the world with other people rolling around carefree.

In one edition of the *Süddeutsche Zeitung*, I saw a picture of the already elderly Horkheimer at some celebration at Frankfurt University in distant 1952. A round face, grinning awkwardly, holding a carnival stick with a paper ball hanging from its end. As if the aging philosopher was feeling slight guilt at having been swept up in the festivities and some fear that, at any moment, his friend Adorno would appear and give him a stern and judgmental look. Hey, I'm not even enjoying myself, the grinning Horkheimer from the photo seems to be saying in his defense. And please let that be taken as an extenuating circumstance mitigating my guilt.

The best thing about provincial European museums of fine arts is that they do not show us the high points—despite the fact that they all have a Renoir or two, a Monet, and, of course, a Picasso, who keeps the whole museum industry afloat—but they do show us the intensity of a life without geniuses. The art of good, second-string paint-slingers, who, to be frank, are more interesting to me now. The seventeenth and eighteenth centuries were swarming with artists who didn't stand much of a chance.

I stood for a long time, disconsolate, in front of a painting by Tilborch, "Banquet Villageois." Feasting peasants, captured at the very end of the celebration, breaking up into groups. Such sorrow, coming up from below . . . the deep sorrow of the belly. The stomach is sated, yet joy has not come in any case, or has already departed. Sorrow from the seventeenth century.

Directional signs in the Museum of Fine Arts in Rouen
ROMANTISME ➝
IMPRESSIONISME ➝
NATURALISME ➝
CUBISME ➝
TOILETTES ➝

As I make the rounds of the world's museums, I seem to meet one and the same group of old men shuffling stiffly and fragile old women with white hair, curious in their late meeting with the world's art. At first, I used to think how tragically late this group is. Then I slowly began to realize, drawing nearer to their stiffness and fragility, that the meeting was right on time. From the eternity of the old masters toward another eternity—such a smooth transition.

I'm standing on a square in Pisa, looking at faces. I'll never get tired of it. After the hunger for faces which I experienced in those basements and ground-floor apartments and lonely afternoons, I find the human face our creator's greatest accomplishment.

People have gotten more beautiful. No, it's not just another sign that I'm getting old. Or at least, it's not only that. People really have gotten more beautiful. The women in particular, of course. Especially the women.

Rome—an abandoned city. Sunday.

I will add these to the list of cities' first scents: asphalt melted by the sun in the late afternoon (a scent from childhood), the heavy scent of roses and a hint of rot. If something in nature can be pushed to the point of kitsch (since culture has done its fair share on that front), it's the rose. The city is full of roses. Is it to cover up all the death that has accumulated throughout the centuries? All graveyards smell like roses.

The sunset on this day will catch me on a hill, in the garden of a monastery founded by the Knights of Malta, with oranges rotting on the grass and ravens pecking at the fruit's flesh. Momentary epiphanies, which will disintegrate in the next instant. Which raises their value a hundredfold. For a few minutes, the sunset *of* the Roman Empire and the sunset *over* the Roman Empire mean one and the same thing. The nocturnal barbarians can be heard, racing along on their Vespas and Piaggios.

You don't quite connect with some cities, just like you don't quite connect with certain women. You meet them either too early or too late. Everything is set for your meeting, but some random whim makes you suddenly turn down some other street.

And Sunday again, all the Sundays in the world, in the morning, somewhere in Europe . . .

The bells wake me up and, half-asleep, I try to guess exactly where I am. I recall all the mornings in the world, starting like this, chanting the rosary of cities and towns—Graz, Prague, Regensburg, Vienna, Zagreb . . .

Every place has a small square, a cathedral and a hotel behind it, just one bell's ring away. I look around the room. It's Ljubljana, as the thick green folder of Hotel Union confirms, with its gold Secession-style inscription reading "1907"—the year it opened. The bells are ringing, some gentle, bright force hurries me to get dressed and go down to the street. Bells and the body likely have some very old conversation of their own tied to all the joys and sorrows, weddings and deaths, fires and uprisings, floods and parades that bells announced over centuries past. Run out onto the street as soon as you hear them. I mingle with the crowd, trying to dissolve into it, obliterating my own identity. Now, I tell myself, I am only here, in this city, on this square, with these people, on this Saturday or Sunday. I want to be a part of all this, to enter the cathedral humbly, to cross myself at the entrance, sometimes I do it Orthodox-style, sometimes Catholic-style, I don't know which one is more proper, forgive me, O Lord, I pick up the hymnal, open it up to some page, I don't understand the words, I listen to the singers' voices, the organ's response, is that what God's voice would sound like, full, warm and stern all at the same time. I feel protected and calm, a part of everything. Except with a slight feeling of sinfulness that I've tasted only one day, not even a full day, but only a single morning of a life that doesn't belong to me.

The woman who was crossing the square in front of the cathedral in Cologne on that overcast afternoon, godlessly and majestically screaming at somebody over the phone . . .

The Angel of the North near Newcastle with airplane wings.

. . .

Why didn't I write down more names? The names of all the places I've been. The names of cities and streets, names of foods and spices, women's names and men's names, the names of trees—a memory of the purple jacaranda in Lisbon, the names of airports and train stations . . .

I'm sitting in front of my notebooks like an aged Adam, who once had given out names, but who now merely waves after them, watching their tails disappear in the distance.

Memory of Hotels

I'm developing a peculiar kind of memory for those memoryless places, hotels. The ideal hotel room should not recall anyone's previous presence. Cleaning the room after the guest checks out is above all about erasing the memory. The bed must forget the previous body, new sheets must be put on and stretched tight, the bathroom must be shined to a sparkle. Every trace of a prior human presence—a hair on the sheet, a faded lipstick stain on the pillowcase, is a disaster. Only oblivion is aseptic.

The heavy plush rooms, as long and narrow as train compartments, at the Royal Station Hotel in Newcastle. The windows open vertically from the bottom like on a train. As if at any moment the hotel's whistle will blow and it will take off. British workaday asceticism. It's not easy to have invented the water closet a few centuries ago, yet out of loyalty to tradition to scorn the mixer tap. I think this as I try in vain to adjust the hot and cold water.

The Royal Victoria Hotel in Pisa, a room with heavy, lusterless mirrors, high ceilings, and two enormous, old, carved wooden beds. Prolonged dithering over which of the two to choose and the vague sense that I can see upon them the bodies of everyone who has lain there for the past 200 years, thin, translucent, as negatives.

The hotel in downtown Helsinki, behind the train station. Tall, with windows that open only a few centimeters, so that a human body cannot squeeze through and jump from there. A feeling of claustrophobia and of being denied a fundamental right.

You have salmon for breakfast, then asparagus soup, bananas, and oranges, which you used to dream about, so what's this melancholy again, what could you be missing?

Nothing. Only that hunger.

The cheapest hotel in Paris—the Acacia in the Eleventh Arrondissement . . . The whole evening I listen to the bed in the room above me creaking in a precise, robust iamb. A thought crossed my mind and I wrote it down: the cheaper the hotel, the more furious the fucking.

A hotel from the fifteenth century in Old Prague, on Ostrovni 32. How uncozy the Middle Ages are for the human body . . .

The big hotel in Sibiu, light-blue rooms, a glassed-in bathroom, bad breakfast.

Hotel Vensan in Rouen, right in the center of town, a room over the boulevard, the unbearably heavy bordeaux of the fabric wallpaper. Among the brochures—a discrete flyer for an elite night club "Madame Bovary." I'll spend the night with *Bouvard et Pécuchet*.

The starless hotels of Normandy and the most starless of them all—Hôtel Bernières with a shower and toilet bowl in the wardrobe.

The bed-and-breakfast in Bairro Alto, Lisbon, with the wooden window shutters buffeted in the evening by the ocean wind. The butcher's shop across the street, the clothes on the clotheslines, the crumbling ochre of the façade. The small *papelaria* for notebooks, paper, newspapers, and pipes, with a Pessoa faded from the sun on the door. A sudden memory of the town of T., which is precisely on the other end of the continent.

The Bible in the Catholic hotel in Wrocław. Next to the Beatitudes, next to "Blessed are the poor in spirit . . . Blessed are those who mourn . . ." which are anything but beatific, the female hand of a temptress had written in the margin: "I don't mean to meddle, but if you're bored, call Agnieszka, telephone 37475 . . ." (I'm not going to give you the whole number.) Thus, she had added one more bliss to those blessings. That "I don't mean to meddle, but" was magnificent . . .

I didn't call that night, but I carefully wrote the number down, along with the whole note. I wonder what Agnieszka is doing now, all these years later. Does she still manage to peddle some belated bliss, or do I need to cross out that (emergency) phone number as well?

Lists and Oblivion

What do you call the obsession with constantly making lists, with thinking in lists, with telling stories in lists? What kind of disorder is that?

I rush to write everything down, to gather it up in my notebook, just as they rush to bring in the lambs before the thunderstorm whips up. My memory for names and faces is fading ever more quickly. That's the most likely explanation. That's how my father's illness was at the end. Somebody with a big eraser came and started rubbing everything out, moving backward. First, you forget what happened yesterday, the most distant, out-of-the-way stuff is the last to go. In this sense, you always die in your childhood.

My father would go out and wander the streets, lost like a child in an unfamiliar city. Good thing it was a small town, people knew him and brought him back home. Most often they would find him at the train station. He would be watching the trains. Once when I was home for a short visit, I followed him and watched. Whenever a train stopped at the station, he would get up and head toward the open doors, then his gait would slow, he would stop, look around like a person who has suddenly forgotten or is having second thoughts about the point of his journey and finally he would totter back to his place with uncertain steps. The scene would repeat itself with every train.

My worst nightmare is that one day I will be standing just like that at some airport, the planes will land and take off, but I won't be able to remember where I'm going. And worse yet, I'll have forgotten the place I should return to. And there won't be anyone to recognize me and bring me back home.

Labyrinth and Choice

The labyrinth is someone's fossilized hesitation.

The most oppressive thing about the labyrinth is that you are constantly being forced to choose. It isn't the lack of an exit, but the abundance of "exits" that is so disorienting. Of course, the city is the most obvious labyrinth. Barthes points to Paris as a model: "the labyrinths of the center and the outskirts built by Haussmann."

I've been happily lost in that city, but here I'll add just one disorienting afternoon. The time when I stood between two streets, wondering which one to go down. Both of them would have led me to the place I was looking for. Incidentally, there was nothing particularly unusual about the streets in and of themselves. The problem was, as always, no matter which one I chose, I would lose the other one. I could only have been satisfied in that quantum physics experiment that shows how a particle also acts like a wave, passing through two openings at once. The minutes were flowing past, and I was standing there, shifting my weight from one foot to the other. I must have looked terribly lost, since an elderly woman stopped and asked me if I needed help.

What did I do? I headed down one of them, the street to the right, but I was thinking about the other one the whole time. And with every step, I kept repeating to myself that I had made the wrong choice. I hadn't gone even a third of the way before I stopped decisively (oh, that decisive gesture of indecisiveness) and turned down an alley toward the other street. Of course, hesitation seized me with the first couple steps and again after a few meters, I practically ran down the next alley to the first street. And then again, seized by hesitation—back to the other one, then back to the first. To this day I don't know whether with that zigzag I gained both streets or lost them both. In the end, completely exhausted, like a marathon runner in a labyrinth, my heart pounding as if to burst, I sank down onto a bench.

Chamomile Harvesters

I never travel alone. It's only that my companions are not visible to the naked eye. I'm like a human trafficker, sneaking whole columns of people across the border. Some of them are no longer alive. Others, on the contrary, are far too alive and curious, touching everything, asking about everything, getting lost, wandering away from the group. The metal detectors at the airport don't catch them.

In the most unexpected and untimely places around this continent, even in the impersonal territory of the airport, that separate country, unexpected faces crop up. As I'm sitting there sipping my tea in the Munich airport, it is suddenly filled to the brim with Gypsy tinkers, boisterous and brightly colored. The police don't notice them, nor do their silver bracelets, heavy tin pans, and copper kettles set off the metal detectors. There's that friend of my grandma's, too, the old Gypsy woman Rusalia, with her tulip-printed headscarf and an enormous wooden rake, going to harvest chamomile. The tea I'm drinking is chamomile, that's the key. Chamomile doesn't grow here at the Munich airport, I want to tell her, but Rusalia doesn't look at me. Then I realize that I, too, don't exist for her, just as the police, the metal detectors, and even the whole huge terminal don't exist . . . It hasn't been built yet. In its place stretches an endless field of chamomile.

As a child I was afraid of all those noisy Gypsies. Adults would scare us with them, saying they would whisk away naughty children in their big saddlebags. I wasn't naughty, but who knows, mistakes happen. But I wasn't afraid of old Rusalia. She would come into our house, sit down and talk with my grandma the whole afternoon. I would hover around them, listening. Rusalia loved my grandma, because she was the only one who let her into her house and talked to her as an equal. My grandma loved Rusalia, because she had travelled far and wide, and she respected everyone who had seen the world. Every summer, Rusalia would tell stories about the world, and my grandma would listen and spin, the stories becoming part of the fiber being spun from her distaff. Why do you invite them into the house, a neighbor woman would always chide her afterward, you can't trust those Gypsies, while she's bamboozling you with tall tales, her people are sneaking around, snatching some chicken or swiping some tomatoes from your garden. Let them swipe away, my grandma would say, they've got souls, same as we do, plus we've got tomatoes galore this year.

The voice over the loudspeaker announces that my flight is delayed, pulling me back to the Munich airport. There is no trace of the Gypsy Rusalia with her big wooden chamomile rake and her colorful people. My tea is gone, too.

As long as I live, Rusalia will go to harvest chamomile at the Munich airport, her people will clatter their pans behind her, and on those endless afternoons my grandmother will spin and listen to stories about the world.

Description of a Finnish Family of Poets at Lunch in Lahti

This could be a painting by Vermeer.

A handsome, very elderly Finnish poet, with an elongated face, as old age does to some faces, very blue, already fading eyes (one with a slight tic), has difficulty moving his hands, there's a constant smile on his face (could that be a tic, too?), a sweet and uneasy smile, as if he were apologizing for his age. The elderly woman next to him is probably his wife—and enormous hat with a brim edged with strawberries, with a bit too much rouge on her cheeks, as elderly ladies are wont to do . . . She discretely keeps an eye on her husband's movements, ready to come to the rescue at any moment. For now, he is doing fine on his own despite that tremor in his right hand, which always causes half the contents of his spoon to spill back into the bowl.

Next to her sits their son, also a poet, as he was introduced to us, around 40, thin, lanky, with glasses and teeth jutting forward, not as handsome and refined as the father. It's strange that sometimes parents are more beautiful than their children, you always expect it to be the opposite. The daughter-in-law, in contrast to the whole family, is plump and dark-haired, most likely a foreigner. And the two charming girls of four and six in their blue suits, torn between table manners and the natural law inside them.

The conversation falters, but this is a picture in which conversation is unnecessary. Fascinated, you watch life itself in its elegant vanquishing of old age. There was love, love gave birth to children, those children have given birth to their own children. There surely have been cataclysms, too, but now here they are together for Sunday brunch, at the table of honor in front of all these writers gathered from around the world who most likely have never read a single line by the great Finnish poet and who surely will not remember his impossible name. To enjoy the respect of people who are seeing you for the first time, even for just one lunch, and to share it with your loved ones. What more could you ask for?

And now the Finnish poet does something that jerks him out of the picture. His trembling hand drops the spoon, it hits the edge of the bowl with a bang, scooping up a bit of asparagus soup as it falls, spilling it on his white shirt, splashing a few mischievous droplets onto the cheek of his astonished wife, and landing with a clatter on the stone floor.

The host rushes to pick up the spoon, as if this were the most important thing, and hits his head on the edge of the table in the process, the four-year-old girl can't contain herself any longer and bursts out laughing, her mother shushes her, but this only makes matters worse, without a pick-up note the little girl replaces laughter with shrieking, the old poet's son helplessly turns first toward his mother, then toward the children's mother, but does not receive any instructions from either one. The wife is trying to clean the stain on the poet's shirt with a napkin. And the poet himself? He keeps smiling in that innocent, apologetic way, like a little boy who has gotten up to some serious mischief.

If some invisible Vermeer is painting this picture and it is exhibited in the next century, pay attention to the dark spot in the lower right corner, right where the spoon fell. If you look at it long enough, like a Rorschach test, you'll see the little devil of old age and his malicious grin.

Sorrow Makes Bones Brittle

I went to Finland mostly because of my father. I took advantage of a kindly invitation to a literary festival. I had had an intimate connection to this country since childhood, without ever having been there. My father had gone there by chance on his first and, as far as I know, only trip abroad back then. Finland, you might say, lived in our living room—six Finnish cups made from sturdy light-green glass, which we took out for guests. Setting them on the table always kick-started my father's story. For us, it was like a fairytale, a Nordic saga, and an adventure novel all rolled into one. How they were each given only five dollars apiece, how they each illegally smuggled in a bottle of cognac or vodka, how afterward, with all the concomitant fear and shame, he had traded his bottle for the glasses we were drinking from, for the Finnish ashtray that was also sitting on the table, and for cloth for a dress for my mother. Here my mother would take the dress out of the wardrobe, bright and colorful, with big, withering roses, and everybody would click their tongues. Finland was the country of my childhood that came closest to that mythical country known as "Abroad." The country of my father. Of fathers.

It just so happened that my visit to and initiation into Finland came about exactly thirty years later, right when I had become a father myself. And during the very same week when my father got the results of a "routine" test. At first, I decided to not go on the trip, but then it occurred to me that it was no coincidence that it had come about right at this moment, that it was fate, and that this trip would all but set some healing processes into motion.

I boarded the plane with an excess baggage of sorrow. It was the middle of June, the endless white nights. I was dwelling in some strange melancholy. It wasn't the country I had imagined. It seemed to have aged since the time of my childhood. I was walking through the streets of Helsinki, but I wasn't completely there. My daughter had just been born, and my father had just gotten a terrible diagnosis. When he had walked these streets, he had been twenty-five, I was already thirty-nine. I would never be able to match his eye for the world. I had already visited quite a few countries, the senses grow accustomed, the eye merely registers, the feeling of déjà vu builds.

And one night, my body gave out.

There is a lot of symbolism in breaking down in a country you have been inventing your whole life.

Past midnight, sometime around noon . . . It's equally lightish-dark. In the dusk of the room I try to figure out what time of day it is and where my body is. I have no sense of either one. I feel light, hovering a few feet above the bed, nothing hurts, this is either heaven or . . . Those are either nurses or angels. They are speaking an unintelligible language—angelic or Finnish? I have no sense of a body, which would be wonderful if it were not slightly worrisome. With great effort I turn my head to the left and see the bag of liquid dripping into my arm. OK, got it, there are no IVs in heaven. My last memory is of riding the bike I had rented, mulling some things over, and suddenly there was a bright light ahead of me, turns out I was in the wrong lane, I swerved to get back into mine, then the sound of brakes, then . . . the room.

I slowly regain consciousness. The nurse on duty comes in from time to time with a syringe and a single English word, which is nevertheless sufficiently clear: "Painkiller!" She stops for a moment at the door, announces "Painkiller," as if introducing some very important gentleman who will come in any second, forces the air out of the needle and plunges the syringe somewhere into my absent body. I try to explain in my broken English that nothing hurts. But she shakes her head and says something I don't understand, in her Moomintroll-speak.

Sorrow makes bones brittle . . .

I have an almost cinematographic memory of being wheeled to the operating room. I'm lying on a moving stretcher and the long fluorescent lights above my head frame the empty shots of the film reel. I think to myself that if the stretcher were travelling at a speed of twenty-four frames per second, it would start some film rolling that is now invisible to me. The corridor is empty and echoes slightly. We pass through a floor that has a small café. A mother in a hospital gown and robe and three little girls, whom the father has clearly brought for a visit, are eating cake and drinking juice. I remember every movement in slow motion. I must look frightening, with my leg elevated, a slightly soaked bandage, an IV. The three little girls stop chattering, I hear the sounds of forks dropped onto plates as they innocently turn their heads in my direction as I pass by. I try to smile, the three little girls with pink shirts, straws, juice, their vague sympathy, mixed with curiosity and a bit of fear . . . The mother says something and the three of them immediately, albeit with displeasure, turn their heads away from the passing stretcher carrying some bandaged up thing. I hold this frame in my mind while the anesthesia overtakes me. You never know what your last vision before you cross over might be.

I open my eyes a crack and see the slightly blurry silhouette of Ritva, who immediately livens up when she notices I'm awake. She has stood by my bedside for hours. Once upon a time, back in distant 1968, she had been in Bulgaria for seven days. The best seven days of my life, she always says. I was twenty—young, leftist, and in love. Those three things never came together for me again, Ritva says. We must paint a strange picture for the doctors. A woman of sixty and an immobilized man of forty. The only thing we have in common is a year—1968. The year when she was happy is the year I was born. Without a visible connection between the two events.

What worries me most at the moment is a terrifying hypothesis. I can't raise my head to look. So I try to move my leg. Nothing happens. I can't feel anything from the waist down. Suddenly I imagine that the sheet there is empty. I feel myself falling back into that thick milky whiteness I had just swum out of. When I swim out of it again, it is because of a searing pain. My eyes jerk open. Ritva is again standing by me, I tell her it hurts, she calls Nurse Painkiller. I gradually realize that the pain is coming from my leg, so it must be there in its place and I can even move it. It hurts, thank God. It's there and it hurts.

A week or two later, a cast-encased survivor, I'm lying at home, physically feeling the hours and minutes. I lie there throughout the summer of that year, serving it out like a prison sentence, without knowing for sure what crime I've committed. But that's what all convicts say.

Triple fracture to the left ankle, two plates, seven pins, two cracked ribs, again on the left side. I stare at the ceiling for hours, the recumbent one's only sky, and remember all the ceilings I've lain beneath. The high one in Berlin and the low one of my childhood. The constellations of flies on it. The bare light bulb wrapped in newspaper, that sole lampshade.

I recall the endless afternoons with which we were so generously endowed in that "once upon a time" of childhood, when I would again lie with my eyes open and stare up fixedly until the barely visible cracks and bumps in the ceiling started to change into strange mountains and seas upon which I set sail to distant lands. A few years later, the mountains and seas would magically transform into female hips, thighs, breasts, and curves. The more uneven and imperfect the surface, the more ships and women it hid.

And thus my journeys naturally came to an end . . . I returned to the saddest place in the world, shattered. All that remained from several years of hotels, airports and train stations were a couple of notebooks filled with hastily jotted impressions. Now, as I page through them distractedly to kill time, I finally realize it—melancholy is slowly swamping the world . . . Time has somehow gotten stuck and autumn doesn't want to give way, every season is autumn. Global autumn . . . Traveling doesn't cure sorrow, either. I need to look for something else.

The saddest place *is* the world.

VIII. An Elementary Physics of Sorrow

These notes are stored on old punch cards from the dawn of electronic computing devices, which have long since fallen out of use.

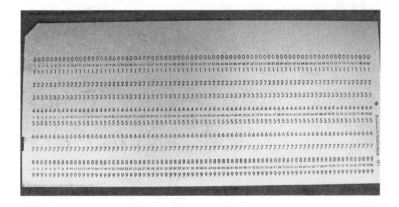

Quanta of Equivocation

One of the most mindboggling things in the physics of elementary particles is how important the very act of observation is on their behavior. According to the Copenhagen interpretation, as early as the 1920s quanta act like particles only when we observe them. The rest of the time, hidden from our gaze, they are part of a scattered and supposedly disinterested wave, in which we don't know exactly what's going on. Everything there is possible, unforeseeable and variable. But once they sense we're watching them, they instantaneously start acting as we expect them to, orderly and logically.

The world is the way we know it to be from the old textbooks only because (or when) it is under observation. Or as Idlis, Whitrow, and Dicke put it in the mid-twentieth century, "in order for the Universe to exist, it was necessary for observers to appear at some stage." I'm watched, therefore I am.

OK, fine, but if no one's watching me, do I still exist? I live alone, no one comes over, no one calls. On the other hand, there's always one big invisible observer, an eye we should never forget. The Old One, as Einstein called him. Maybe that's precisely what quantum physics or metaphysics is telling us. If we exist, that means we're being watched. There is something or someone that never lets us out of its sight. Death comes when that thing stops watching us, when it turns away from us.

The world behind our backs is some kind of undefined quantum soup, says a Stanford physicist—but the second you turn around, it freezes into reality. I like that definition and never turn around too abruptly. I think about that teacher from kindergarten who threatened to pour my soup down my back if I didn't eat it all. Then I would've found out what quantum reality is.

I write in the first person to make sure that I'm still alive.

I write in the third person to make sure that I'm not just a projection of my own self, that I'm three-dimensional and have a body. Sometimes I nudge a glass and note with satisfaction that it falls and breaks. So I do still exist and cause consequences.

If no one is watching me, then I'll have to watch myself, so as not to turn into quantum soup.

Someone must constantly be watching and thinking about the world so that it exists. Or someone needs to be watching and thinking about the one who is watching and thinking about the world . . . Crazy stuff. Can I take on that round-the-clock duty?

The physics of elementary particles rehabilitates randomness and uncertainty. Now that's why I love it. Whereas Einstein himself was horrified precisely by this and grumbled in his letters: "The theory says a lot, but does not really bring us any closer to the secret of the 'Old One.' I, at any rate, am convinced that He does not throw dice." I, at any rate, am convinced that the Old One—just like the local geezers who spend their afternoons playing backgammon—nevertheless loves throwing dice.

One remark. Quantum physics—perhaps so as not to turn entirely into metaphysics—avoids delving into the question of who that observer could be in order to have such a status. Are we including anything here but the eye of God? Does the eye of man count as capable of maintaining the world? Does the eye of a snail, a cat, or a violet figure in the equation?

Well, we mustn't forget, after all, that quantum physics explains things on the micro-level. But how can we be sure that God isn't an elementary particle? It's quite likely that he's a proton, electron, or even a boson. God is a boson. It sounds nice. It sounds like God is a bison, Aya would say.

However, He's most likely a photon—which has a dual nature like all quanta, but a rest mass of absolute zero. And that's why it can move at the speed of light. When we say that God is light, we don't even realize how deeply we've gotten into quantum physics. Or else he's a neutrino, maybe even faster than light and capable of unexpected transformations. That which the old Evangelists/physicists described as the Transfiguration of the Lord was a transformation of the neutrino. But I still would like Him to be an ant, a turtle, or a *Ginkgo biloba* tree.

That which has not been told, just like that which has not happened—because they're of the same order—possesses all possibilities, countless variations on how they could happen or be told.

Alas, the story is linear and you have to get rid of the detours every time, wall up the side corridors. The classical narrative is an annulling of the possibilities that rain down on you from all sides. Before you fix its boundaries, the world is full of parallel versions and corridors. All possible outcomes potter about only in hesitation and indecisiveness. And quantum physics, filled with indeterminacy and uncertainty, has proved this.

I try to leave space for other versions to happen, cavities in the story, more corridors, voices and rooms, unclosed-off stories, as well as secrets that we will not pry into . . . And there, where the story's sin was not avoided, hopefully uncertainty was with us.

A Question from the Quantum Physics of Reading

Has anyone ever developed a quantum physics of literature? If there, too, the lack of an observer presupposes all manner of combinations, just imagine what kind of carnival is raging among the elementary particles of the novel. What on earth is happening between its covers when no one is reading it? Now there are questions that deserve some thought.

Experiments

That popular experiment with the electron, in which it acts like a wave and passes through two openings at the same time, gives certain grounds for believing that it is possible to be in different places at the same time. But, as the Gaustine in me notes, we're not talking about electrons weighing 180 lbs. and standing 6'2". (If this were so, my grandfather would have stayed in both villages—the Hungarian and the Bulgarian one, bringing up both of his sons, living out both of his lives . . .)

Luckily, the things I'm concerned with have no weight. The past, sorrow, literature—only these three weightless whales interest me. But quantum physics and the natural sciences have turned their backs on them. If Aristotle had known that the formal division of physics and metaphysics would definitively and artificially partition the universe of knowledge, he surely would have burned his work himself. Or at least he would have combined the parts of it.

A while back, under one of my pen names, I published a novel based on the atomism of Leuccipus of Miletus and Democritus of Abdera. Ultimately, it turns out that they discovered quanta way back in the fifth century BC. Lots of time needed to pass for everything to be forgotten. I liked those pre-Socratics, those first quantum physicists, who coolly and boldly painted a picture of a world made only of atoms and emptiness. Endless emptiness and countless atoms floating around in it. I wanted to transfer the model of atomism to literature and to discover whether the encounter between individual atoms of classic literature would produce new matter for the novel. *An atomic novel of opening lines floating in the void.*

This was a wholly serious experiment, but it was taken more as a postmodernist joke, grasped in terms of its metaphorics rather than its physics. Physicists don't read novels. Which disappointed me greatly and caused me to withdraw from publishing for a decade or so.

Here's what I'm interested in now. Can going back in time by recalling everything down to the last detail, with all senses engaged, bring about a critical point? Can it flip some switch and cause the whole machinery of the Universe to start going backward? It's on the edge in any case, so the only redemptive move is backward. Minute by minute, during this hour everything that was an hour ago will happen. The entirety of today is replaced by yesterday, yesterday by the day before, and so on and so forth further and further back, we slowly step away from the edge with a creak. I don't know whether we can meddle in those impending past days. We'll have to relive our prior failures and depressions, but also a few happy minutes among them. There's no getting around . . .

. . . the new injustice of death. Those, who at the moment of the reversal had already lived eighty years, will live another eighty, backward. Those who had lived not as long, say thirty, forty, or fifty years, will have to be satisfied with that same amount. But let's note that they will be heading toward their own youth and childhood. Ever happier at the end of their lives, ever younger, ever more adored. Happily wobbling on their unsteady little toddler's feet, having forgotten language, cooing and gurgling, until the day comes for them to go back home. Thus, I, born on January 1, 1968, will be able to die again on January 1, 1968. That's what I call complete universal harmony. To die the hour and minute you were born, after passing through your whole life twice. From one end to the other and back again.

G. G.
January 1, 1968–January 1, 1968
Lived happily for 150 years.

(Everyone can insert their own name and date here.)

They claim that life arose on earth three billion years ago. With this mechanism, we can guarantee at least three billion more years of life. If someone else has a better offer, then be my guest.

Another gravity is pressing in on us, one not found in classical physics, one which must be overcome, the gravity of time. That gravitational delay, which Einstein described back in 1915, doesn't work for me. In 1976 NASA confirmed that in the microgravity of space, time really does slow down a teeny bit, and this gave rise to the legend that people don't age in space. The myth of eternal youth was again on its way to being revived. A dozen or so aging millionaire matrons must've glanced up at the sky as if toward an eternal sanatorium, calculating how much a stay there with their beloved fox terriers would cost, because what's . . .

. . . the point of being young if your pooch is pushing up daisies? This legend even reached us, I remember it vaguely, but being all of eight years old I hardly paid any attention to it. In 2010, they actually measured that time lapse with an interferometer. Yes, there was a slowing of the cesium atom (that's what they used), but it was insignificantly small—over a few billion years there's a delay of a hundredth of a second. Those who had hoped to stay forever young in 1976 surely hadn't lived to see this highly disappointing result.

My goal isn't to slow time by a few hundredths of a second over a billion years, which I don't have at my disposal in any case. And not in outer space, which I have no particular soft spot for (even the bus makes me car sick). I want to bring back a slice of the past, a pint of drained-away time right here, within the confines of one insultingly short human life.

New Experiments

I practice concentrated and close "observation." I realized relatively early on that the shorter the time period I want to recreate (replicate), the better my chances. I gave up on the idea of my whole childhood. For some time I tried one chosen year. To remember that year in detail, to reconstruct it personally and historically, leaving nothing out.

I picked the year of my birth, because the infant has a more limited and pure world, which in that sense is easier to reconstruct, with fewer extraneous noises. So here's the new 1968. By happy coincidence, I was born in its first days, so the two stories, mine, small and piss-soaked, and its, grand (and also piss-soaked), could unfold in parallel. The wet cloth diapers, the January cold, my mother's warm skin, the first signs of spring in the Latin Quarter, nighttime colic, summer in Prague, the international youth festival in Sofia, "brotherly" troops in Czechoslovakia, first tooth . . . Everything was important. After a few months I was lying on the floor exhausted, crushed by the world's entropy. I realized that it was beyond my strength and stamina to build—as if from matchboxes—a year in its real dimensions with all of its scents, sounds, cats, rain, and newsworthy events. I've kept the draft of that failed experiment.

I need to narrow the range of the experiment. I decided on a month from another year, August 1986, I'm eighteen, my last month of freedom, after which my mandatory military service awaits me. A month, in which you say farewell to everything for two years—actually for forever, but you don't know that then. You let your hair grow long, you try to get to home base with your girl. Late at night, when your parents are asleep, you sneak out with a friend into the city's empty streets, you go to the river and look at the dark windows of the panel-block apartment buildings, on the verge of yelling "Sleep tight, ya morons!" à la Holden Caulfield or whatever it was he said . . .

. . . but in the end you don't do it. At the end of the month you go to the barbershop farthest away to get a buzz cut. You watch your hair falling to the floor and you try not to start bawling. You leave the barbershop already a different age, crestfallen, freaked out, sporting the hat you had prepared in advance, and you take the shortest route home. A few days later you'll have to show up at the appointed place in some strange city—with a shaved head and a bag filled with all the things from the list of what a recruit needs. I've kept that list in one of the boxes.

That was more or less the month from which I needed to reconstruct every moment and sensation with all of their subtlest oscillations. It wasn't so easy. Yes, there was fear during that month, but it was thousands of variations on fear, in some of them it looked like a radical dose of daring. Yes, there was sorrow, but the atoms of this sorrow moved quite freely and chaotically (sorrow's state of aggregation is gaseous) and in the best-case scenario I could only follow its twists and turns, the smoke that smoldered nearby. I lit up my first cigarettes, I now realize, to give a body to this sorrow, bluish, light-gray, vanishing. I remembered everything clearly, but I couldn't manage to get back into that former body. What I used to be able to do—entering into different bodies and stories with the ease of a man entering his own home—now turned out to be out of reach.

* *

LIST

OF RECOMMENDED ITEMS, WHICH THE NEW RECRUIT
SHOULD BRING UPON ENTERING THE ARMED SERVICES

1.	Long-sleeved shirt	[2]
2.	Long pants	[2]
3.	Short pants	[2]
4.	"Hero's T-shirt" [tank top]	[2]
5.	Footwraps of unbleached calico [socks]	[2]
6.	Hand towel	[1]
7.	Handkerchiefs	[2]
8.	Cloth collars	[5]
9.	Toiletries	[2 sets]
10.	Brushes for polishing and shining shoes	[2]
11.	Spool with white thread	[1]
12.	Spool with black thread	[1]
13.	Darning needles	[5]
14.	Safety pins	[5]
15.	Cloth bags [or plastic]	[3]
16.	One day's supply of food and water	

* *

Epiphanies

It happened when I least expected it.

It was a late winter afternoon, the snow was melting. A few days before I completely stopped leaving the basement. I was walking ever more slowly, looking at the houses, the Sunday's empty streets, January . . . It occurred to me, for the first time with such clarity (the clarity of the January air) that what remains are not the exceptional moments, not the events, but precisely the nothingeverhappens. Time, freed from the claim to exceptionality. Memories of afternoons, during which nothing happened. Nothing but life, in all its fullness. The faint scent of wood smoke, the droplets, the sense of solitude, the silence, the creaking of snow beneath your feet, the vague uneasiness as twilight falls, slowly and irreversibly.

Now I know. I don't want to relive any of the so-called events from my own life—not that first event of being born, nor the last one which lies ahead, both are uncozy. Just as every arrival and departure can be uncozy. Nor do I want to relive my first day of school, my first time having fumbling sex with a girl, nor my joining the army, nor my first job, nor that ostentatious wedding reception, nothing . . . none of that would bring me joy. I would trade them all, along with a heap of photos of them, for that afternoon when I'm sitting on the warm steps in front of our house, having just woken up from my afternoon nap, I'm listening to the buzzing of the flies, I've dreamed about that girl again who never turns around. My grandfather moves the hose in the garden and the heavy scent of late summer flowers rises. Nothing is determined, nothing has happened to me yet. I've got all the time in the world ahead of me.

In the small and the insignificant—that's where life hides, that's where it builds its nest. Funny what things are left to twinkle in the end, the last glimmer before darkness. Not the most important things, nor . . . there's no way for them even to be written down or told. The sky of memory opens for that minute as dusk falls on that winter day in a distant city, when I am eighteen and have miraculously been left alone for a minute or two, crossing the army base's enormous parade grounds. A parenthetical note for those who have never been soldiers: you're never left with a free minute, that's the way it's set up. A soldier with free time on his hands is nothing but trouble, that's what they say. I've trimmed the grass around the parade grounds all day with a nail clipper—those were my orders. I've carried stones from one pile to another. In the morning. Then in the afternoon I've returned the stones to their original place. At first you don't get it, you think the world has gone mad, you don't find that even in Kafka. But the majors don't read Kafka, to say nothing of the sergeants. You've come here directly from literature, you're carrying Proust in your gasmask bag. Hey, Proust, get over here double-quick! Hit the ground! Twenty push-ups!

Anyway, that moment when I was left alone on the enormous parade grounds under an empty sky, amid the cold air saturated with the first scent of winter, of wood and coal smoke sneaking in from the nearby village, the falling dusk and anticipations, alone for the first time, somewhere else for the first time, slight cold fear, cold clouds. And precisely that meeting of hopelessness and anticipation (my year in the army had only just begun), mixed with an endless sky, strange and beautiful, beautiful in a strange way, made that minute eternal. I knew that it couldn't be retold.

Of course, I could list off several other golden camels in the endless caravan of minutes, three or four, not more, but I'll try to retell only one of them. Late summer, I'm standing in front of the house, the sunset is endless in those flat places, I'm six, the cows are coming down the road, first you hear their slow bells, the shepherd's calls, the mooing to announce their return to their calves, the calves' bellowed response . . . this is crying, I know it even then. Like the bawling cry that always escapes from me the minute my mother comes back from the city at the end of the week to see me. Relief and accusation are never closer together than in that crying. As close as the crying of a calf and the crying of a child when they have been abandoned for a day or weeks. I missed you so much, I'm so mad at you. I'll never forgive you, cows and mothers . . .

In that minute, the memory is so clear even now, in that minute so densely packed with sounds, cows, and scents, suddenly everything disappears, a strip slices the horizon at its most distant point, time draws aside and there, at the very back of the sunset, there is a white room with high ceilings, one I've never seen before, with a chandelier and a piano. A girl my age is sitting at the piano with her back to me. Her light hair is tied in a pony tail, she is getting ready to play, she has raised her hands slightly, I see her pointy elbows . . . And that's it.

I have never been happier, more whole and peaceful than in that minute, on the warm stone at the end of my sixth summer. As the years passed, I started counting the winters, as my father and grandfather did, they knew it was right for a person to depart in the winter, during the summer there is too much work to bother with dying. I promised myself then that I would find that girl. I kept looking for her in all those places and years I passed through. No one turned to me with her face. I can feel myself giving up over time. Getting used to it. Old age is getting used to things.

Migration of Sorrow

Empathy is unlocked in some people through pain, for me it happens more often through sorrow.

The physics of sorrow—initially the classical physics thereof—was the subject of my pursuits for several years. Sorrow, like gases and vapors, does not have its own shape or volume, but rather takes on the shape and volume of the container or space it occupies. Does it resemble the noble gases? Most likely not, as much as we may like the name. The noble gases are homogeneous and pure, monatomic, besides they have no color or odor. No, sorrow is not helium, krypton, argon, xenon, radon . . . It has an odor and a color. Some kind of chameleonic gas, that can take on all the colors and scents in the world, while certain colors and scents easily activate it.

The more important thing is that its gravitational field is negligibly small, to continue the analogy with the gases. From this it follows that invisible fronts, cyclones, and anti-cyclones of sorrow hover around us. Their migration, their movement from one place to another is a remarkable fact. The blindness that causes us to pass over this fact is astonishing. Sometimes I'm overcome by a vague sense of sorrow, which doesn't seem to be mine. Sorrow from Northern Africa, let's say. Not local, strange, faded by the sun, yellow with grains of sand from the desert, like that yellow rain that fell last year, leaving opaque blotches on the window. I could sketch out a geographical map of the migration of sorrows. Some places are sad in one century, others in another.

What little success I've had with these experiments lies in the fact that for very short slices of time I've been able to attract a stray cloud of sorrow from some past afternoon, mine or someone else's, to walk alongside it, and sink into its nicotine. Like a smoker, who, even after many years without cigarettes, will always recognize the trace of smoke.

Quanta of Aging

I'm not talking about old age. I'm talking about the first signs. Not about night, but about dusk. About its irresistible incursions and the first fallen fortresses.

Once, when Aya was three, she came home from kindergarten in tears, because a boy had told her that fathers get old. Fathers get old, she said, sobbing. She glanced at me for a second, fully expecting to hear me disavow this and since I couldn't think of anything—I'm terribly slow-witted when I have to lie—she burst into tears again, even more hopelessly.

There is a grammar of aging.

Childhood and youth are full of verbs. You can't sit still. Everything in you grows, gushes, develops. Later the verbs are gradually replaced by the nouns of middle age. Kids, cars, work, family—the substantial things of the substantives.

Growing old is an adjective. We enter into the adjectives of old age—slow, boundless, hazy, cold, or transparent like glass.

There is also a mathematics of aging, a simple set theory.

We change the world's proportions over the years. Those younger than us grow ever more numerous, while the number of those older than us declines menacingly.

Aging requires a certain audacity. It may not be audacity, but resignation.

At eleven, I started a secret notebook in which I wrote down the first signs of aging and death. Death and children is an unjustly neglected topic, I've never been as close to death as I was then. Over the years, we've grown a bit distant and cold, although I've always kept my eye on it, just as it has on me, of course. Here are the things, from different years and in no particular order, puttering around in that box.

Cardiac exam. Sooner or later, everyone ends up lying here, the nurse says soothingly, as she attaches wires and clamps to my whole body. The noises, which I hear amplified in that way for the first time, are revolting. The discovery that the heart is a frog, judging by its croaking. My death will come like a stork, I write down upon leaving.

(41 y.o.)

I grow old . . . I grow old . . .
I shall wear the bottoms of my trousers rolled.

I love these lines by Eliot and I am afraid of them. That devil-may-care whistled tune of old age, which actually hides nothing. So humbly humiliated, so unheroic, rolling up the pant legs hiding the sagging white skin and the telltale blue veins. Just the ankles.

My left ankle is a frightful sight, shattered and stitched, with the years the scars will only deepen.

(53 y.o.)

Today in front of the mirror I noticed that my left half is aging more quickly than my right half. I haven't shaved in a few days (I don't have anyone to shave for anymore, as my father used to say) and can clearly see how the left half of my beard is almost completely gray, while the right side has only a few gray hairs. Besides that, my left eye has starting visibly drooping in the outside corner, the eyelid muscles can't hold out like they used to, when I gaze at something for a bit longer I notice some traitorous involuntary twitches. I wonder if such a difference is visible in my body as well. I look it over carefully, but can't seem to find a visible difference between the left and right sides. OK, that's if we don't count that shattered left ankle, which is quite different and swollen, as is my broken left wrist. And one ear that's ever more hard-of-hearing, precisely the left one.

I'm not even aging evenly.

(49 y.o.)

They say that as we grow older, our dead start talking to us ever more often. We lose the sounds of the world, so that we can hear other sounds and other voices more clearly and without interference. For now, I'm still only hearing noises.

(38 y.o.)

How would you describe the noise in your ear, my doctor friend asks.

I don't know . . . it's not that simple . . .

Come on, now, aren't you a writer?

Well, I'm the most uncertain of them (even though this, too, is uncertain) . . .

Is it like the sound of the sea? The doctor tries to prompt me.

I guess you could say that, but sometimes it is wild and sounds like crashing surf, other times it's more like wind in the late October woods, what I mean is, the leaves are dry enough and some of them have fallen, which affects the frequency of the noise. Sometimes, when there are high frequencies, it sounds like a washing machine on spin cycle two floors away, a thin howl . . . Sometimes it's like moooooo, but the calf is young and hoarse . . .

While I list off these sounds, my doctor's face grows ever more bewildered, rather than clearing up. What can I do, things are never so simple and unambiguous. Once I almost read a nurse the riot act when she made me describe the color of my urine. "Is it the color of beer?" she asked. There are so many different kinds of beer, for Christ's sake, there's light beer, dark beer, red ale, white ale, live-culture beer, non-alcoholic . . . You can't just roll them all together like that . . .

I can't stand categorical people.

(29 y.o.)

It hurts right here, something down on the left, maybe it's my appendix.

Stop with the self-diagnoses, if you please. The appendix is on the right. There's nothing that could be hurting there on the left.

What do you mean nothing?

Just that. There's nothing there.

Well, it's precisely that nothing that's hurting me.

(64 y.o.)

The hope that if you start telling your life story backward toward childhood, it will set some mechanism into motion and fool the direction [of time] . . .

Funny version. A guy decides to quit smoking using regressive hypnotherapy. He starts going backward toward the time before he started smoking, to awaken the memory of his clean lungs. The hypnotherapy is so successful and the regression goes so far back that he not only quits smoking, but also starts wetting his bed and not being able to say "R."

(43 y.o.)

In her *Pillow Book*, Sei Shōnagon gives two lists—Things that inspire sorrow and Things that drive away sorrow. The things that drive away sorrow in the early eleventh century, the Heian Period, include old tales and the sweet chatter of three-to-four-year-old children. I copy it down several times: old tales and the sweet chatter of three-to-four-year-old children, old tales and the sweet chatter . . .

(990 y.o.)

I remember clearly how we read back then. The whole ecstasy of that youthful reading, it wasn't reading, but galloping, racing through books. We sought out the racehorse of action, direct speech, short, muscular expressions. We hated the ritardandos, the descriptions of nature, who needed them . . .

Now I feel the need to stop, like an old man winded by climbing up a slope he used to take in three bounds. The hidden pleasures of slowness. I love to linger long over some "It was a pleasant May morning, the birds were shouting with song, the dew glowed beneath the sun's soft rays . . ."

(69 y.o.)

Our lifelong, round-the-clock jabbering seems to have a single, solitary goal, which we never say out loud. To bamboozle death, to send it off on a wild goose chase, to make a feint at the last moment. But death isn't moved by words. It is most probably deaf (like me). This is the source of its supreme impartiality.

(85 y.o.)

The years are a rushing river, flowing day by day
In its currents youth and childhood are swept clean away . . .
The years they are like song birds, flying south in fall
But unlike birds the years will never return to us at all.

(9 y.o.)

We grew old before we grew up . . .

(35 y.o.)

He started traveling, in fact, fleeing from old age, but ironically it was precisely there, in other places, where his first signs of aging appeared.

One morning at age thirty-five he saw his body in the large, mirror-laden bathroom of a Greek hotel. He had never examined it so closely before. He had a good, healthy, normal body. Not counting the broken arm, whose white plaster cast was starting to look weather-beaten. That morning, he saw the first signs of aging. Extremely faint, yet nevertheless clear. It had started years earlier, why hadn't he paid attention until then? He told himself that he would remember the day. That he would remember that hotel in Thessaloniki. His body, white and soft, had started to go slack, the skin had started growing thin, becoming translucent with thin blue veins. It's old age, he said to himself, just as a year or two earlier he would say to himself: it's love. That's how age happens sometimes, in just a few minutes one morning, at some foreign hotel. After that he would keep tabs on his body in hotel mirrors, that's precisely where old age would be waiting to ambush him.

(34 y.o.)

My grandfather had no time to notice that he was getting old. He had too much work to do . . .

(27 y.o.)

I went to a writer's funeral. While alive, he had hay fever. Now he was lying there, piled with flowers, looking as if he would start sneezing any minute. An orchid was sticking its tip right up his nose. But clearly he was already cured. I noticed, and I think the others noticed as well, the unfamiliar elderly women with blue hair and chrysanthemums at the other end of the funeral parlor who were truly upset. His former mistresses. The deceased had had a weakness for women. Now they were getting their fifteen minutes of fame. Invisible their whole lives, veterans of secret love affairs. From the army of the anonymous, unlike his official wife and his official mistress. In the end, old age has made everyone equal.

(50 y.o.)

Little Red Riding Hood and Old Age

The fairytale can be told this way as well:

The little girl went to her grandmother and started asking:

Grandma, why do you have such big (and sagging) ears? The grandmother kept silent.

Grandma, why do you have such big (and faded) eyes? The grandmother said nothing.

Grandmother, why do you have such a big (and wrinkled) mouth? The grandmother started sniffling softly.

Oh, how cruel Little Red Riding Hood was! And the grandmother—because this time it really was her—took off her glasses, wiped away the two telltale tears and managed to rasp out an answer that exhausted all the questions asked thus far: It's old age, my Little Red Riding Hood.

And opened her toothless mouth in a frightful laugh.

(60 y.o.)

The old hostel near the train station in Leipzig, overflowing with high school students brought here for the book fair. The elevator, which stops with a creak on my floor, the opening of the door and the bright light from inside (the lamp on my floor was out). A group of girls, juniors and seniors, laughing, pretty, Lolitas, without having read *Lolita*.

"Going up?" they ask through their laughter.

"Going down," I reply softly. It sounds so tragicomic that a new volley of laughter follows. A full four seconds before the doors close, parting me forever from that lovely company. Four seconds in which they and I share a common floor. An awkward and beautiful pause, given to me thanks to someone's benevolence, a pause that I parsimoniously hide away in my notebook.

(51 y.o.)

That repeatability of life . . . That sticky, exhausting, murderous, revolting, yet inevitable and sometimes marvelous repeatability of life.

(65,103,039 y.o.)

While climbing the hill in this city, intoxicated by the colors and scents, I feel my strength slowly leaving me, my body going soft, the muscles in my thighs traitorously trembling (is it visible through my pants?). Not wanting to admit I've been beaten, I simply stop and examine a burning-red blackberry bush up close. Then I see an elderly man, did I say elderly, actually, he is my age, embracing a young woman in an innocent summer dress. He is wearing a nice light-blue sweater, old age piles on the clothes, but still it is autumn after all and he is absolutely in season. She is young and is still in summer. Their meeting is the meeting of two seasons. She—generously reaching out her hand from one season, he—standing unsteadily on the edge of the other. A difficult balance, possible only for a short while, a month or two. A few years ago I would have laughed at the man, now he receives my full understanding and a few pangs of envy.

I watch this couple as the day, which is leaning toward its end, obligingly offers me the threadbare metaphor of its sunset. I watch with the full indiscreetness of the situation, then turn my back and slowly head down the hill, having forgotten that just a short while ago I had been planning to get a coffee at the top.

I walk down, thinking about all the European towns huddled like chicks around such a fortress-hill. The hills of Graz, Ljubljana, Zagreb, Thessaloniki, Rome's seven hills, which I've always confused with the teats of that she-wolf, as if she were lying on her back, hills as wolf-tits. I see myself running across them, always at sunset, at different ages.

I remember hurrying to catch a sunset in Lisbon, running up the steep alleys of São Jorge, I reached the top with my last ounce of strength "and suddenly it's evening," as that poet wrote. Everything swam before my eyes, I passed out, when I opened my eyes three elderly ladies and a stern-faced nun were leaning over me. I hadn't blacked out for long, as the ocean was still glowing beneath the final glimmers. I let myself lie there for a few seconds, my eyes swimming, like a sunset marathoner who has collapsed just before announcing his news . . . But there is no news. I'm growing old.

(58 y.o.)

Animals eat up time. They lick at it like the blocks of salt they're given, they nibble away at it like a donkey nibbles at blades of grass, they suck out its fruity marrow like wasps . . . The twentieth-century donkey, the eighteenth-century donkey and the thirteenth-century donkey do not differ in any away. Could it be the same with people? No. I can recognize a face from 1985 and tell it apart from faces from the 1970s and the 1990s, to say nothing of previous centuries.

(793 y.o.)

Aya, at three and a half, draws a picture of me in pen. She hands it to me, takes another a look at me, thinks of something and quickly takes the paper back. I forgot to draw those lines on your forehead, she says.

And thus we age.

(42 y.o.)

Telomeres get shorter and cells die every second . . . The truth is that science is still searching for the mechanism of aging . . . The most important cells, brain cells, never regenerate . . . I am a walking graveyard. Perhaps that's why I so devotedly tour all the cemeteries of every city . . . there is harmony in bringing together your own, second-by-second death with the death of the world.

(66 y.o.)

Grandma, I'm not going to die, right?

(3 y.o.)

A Past-Time Machine

The last time I went back to T., I noticed some strange things. They had restored the monument from the 1980s on the town square. I could have sworn it wasn't there a week ago. I remembered that monument well. A man with a long granite garment, perhaps a cassock, an overcoat or a royal mantle. And with the most nondescript face you'll ever see. On all important historical dates it somehow inexplicably took on the features of the corresponding hero who was to be honored. On February 19, it became Vasil Levski, on June 2 Hristo Botev. It was also a Bulgarian tsar, most often Simeon, sometimes a monk from Mount Athos, sometimes a partisan guerrilla commander. It was most often saddled with the task of being Georgi Dimitrov or some other (local) communists. A universal monument. It had its overcoat, noble forelock, and high forehead—the minimum requirements for every hero back then. Now they've cleaned it up and I could even see that a fresh wreath of braided carnations with two red ribbons had just been placed at its base. I also noticed that the newspapers arrived a day late, the shop clerks had become sullen like back in the day, there was no Internet, while the stores sold only two types of salami and frankfurters.

Given all of this, plus my fruitless experiments on the elementary particles of the past, I was gripped by a gnawing suspicion, which I tried to defang by turning it into a supposedly made-up story.

He opened his eyes with the vague sense that he was awakening into another dream. Could his empathy, which has shown no sign of itself over the past twenty years, be reawakening? Outside he could hear the high school marching band, sounding exactly like it did back then, he could have sworn that they were playing the very same instruments he remembered from his school days. He himself had once played the tuba, standing in the back row next to Nasko with the cymbals, Nasko the Candy Nut with the Blubber-Butt, as his full nickname went. Mr. Blubber-Butt was always a split-second late, a hundredth of a beat behind, which was almost inaudible to the ears up on the platform, but which set Comrade Brunekov, the singing teacher, on pins and needles, and all of us in the band registered that alarming pause, that crack in the music. In the end, the cymbal would nevertheless crash and the simultaneous sigh of relief added yet another note to the march. But that was so many years ago . . .

Now the music was again thundering down below, all guns ablaze. In the end, it seemed that he had managed to do what he had been trying to do for years—to bring back part of the past, just a little slice, to enter into it and never leave it again. Your body can't escape from the memory and you remain in your childhood forever. To a certain extent, it's merciful.

He also might be going crazy, everything might just be in his head. He got up and slowly went over to the window. He stood there for a moment before drawing aside the tatty curtain, then abruptly yanks it away. Down below school kids really were marching around, in the same uniforms as fifty years ago, men and women in suits and long gray trench coats were standing around them. The marching band was doing its routine, while the sun showered its glimmering rays into the brass instruments, which had been shined with *putzing* polish in advance. He hadn't thought about *putzing* in ages. A little farther on stood the platform. He got dressed quickly and went downstairs. They were all real, three-dimensional, living, the men with crew cuts, the women cold-curled, they smelled of strong, cheap cologne, green apples, and once-ubiquitous "Ideal" soap.

They must be shooting a film, how could he have fallen for it? Somewhere here the whole cinematographic machinery would reveal itself. The trucks with the generators, the cameras, the dollies, and slider tracks . . . He carefully looked around. There was no sign of any equipment, they had hidden it that well. But still, a bearded director with a megaphone would have to appear out of somewhere shouting "Cut!" and making everyone go back for a second take. The demonstration continued, however, the music was playing, the band had marched quite a ways ahead. On the platform, bored people in dark suits waved to the enthusiastic squads of marchers. Twenty or so kids in blue neckerchiefs broke away from the parading ranks and, guided by their teaches, ran over to the platform holding bouquets of carnations. The dark suits took the carnations, patted the children on the heads and kept waving. There were carnations everywhere, just like back in the day, he thought to himself. They were perfect for every occasion—party meetings, demonstrations, weddings, and funerals. In the latter case, you had to make sure they were an even number. The set designers had done a good job. They clearly had a nice, fat budget, yet another one of those stupid co-productions. He couldn't help himself, he turned toward an elderly man wearing a suit that looked like it had been sewn in the '70s with a pin on his lapel.

"Excuse me, but what are they filming?"

"What are they filming? Who's filming?" The man looked around anxiously.

"Uhh . . . it must be some movie. What's with this . . . demonstration?"

"Don't you know? Today is September ninth."

That really was the date, but it hadn't been a national holiday for the past twenty years at least. Bewildered, he begged the man's pardon and stepped away from the crowd. He now noticed that his clothes also differed quite a bit from the others'. Against the backdrop of the sober brown of their trench coats and suits, their macramé sweater-vests, and the older women's headscarves, he looked as if coming from another, hostile—or so he thought—world. His short red jacket stood out like a sore thumb, while his jeans and sneakers, in all their casualness, looked strange amid the sharp creases all around him. He ducked off to the right, wanting to stroll for a bit through the deserted side streets. The warm September sun was shining. The faint scent of roasted peppers wafted from somewhere. Flags were hanging from some of the windows. On one corner, a swarthy grubby man of indeterminate age was selling funnels of sunflower seeds, just like back in the day. The funnel is an ingenious invention, his father had loved to say, the cone gives a sense of height and volume, yet the inside holds a much smaller amount, the ideal shape for commerce. He bought himself a funnel. It was made of a piece of old newspaper. Just like in the old days, he thought yet again on that day. Once upon a time, everything could be made from old newspaper—from a painter's cap to a lampshade. As a rule, everything could be made from everything you had at hand. He could read parts of words, numbers and percentage signs on the scrap of newspaper, which was certainly from back then, with that unmistakable ink and font. If this is a movie shoot, they really have thought of everything down to the smallest detail. He was the only thing that didn't fit the set at all.

Carried away by such thoughts, he didn't notice the two uniformed men who had been following him for the last few minutes, without bothering to hide it. When they suddenly jumped out in front of him, they gave him a good scare. Then he noticed that the uniforms they were wearing were not exactly like modern police uniforms. With those ridiculous jackets and big peaked caps, those belt buckles, well yes, they were gendarmes from the socialist era. This reassured him a bit, anything could happen in a movie, and could happen like in the movies, without any particular consequences. Your passport? I don't have it on me. It's back at the hotel. How long have you been here? Two days. We'll be forced to take your down to the station. You have not completed the obligatory registration with the local office of the Interior Ministry, you're sauntering about in provocative attire on a national holiday, not taking part in the event. He let them stuff him into the Lada, Jesus, where did they dig this thing up, and drove off. There most likely weren't any cameras in the car and he thought that here they would finally put their cards on the table. He smiled and with a wink asked the sergeant who was sitting next to the driver: When will they show the movie? The cops looked at each other, then the sergeant turned around and with a well-aimed swing punched the arrestee between the eyes.

The building they brought him to had just been built, but architecturally it recreated late Happy Socialism from the 1980s, roughly hewn marble, wood and frosted glass. Blood trickled down from his split brow. The man who came out of the building wearing a suit immediately ordered them to get him medical attention, a nurse appeared from somewhere, put on a Band-Aid, found some ice, and led him into an office with a leather couch.

"Sorry, they got a bit carried away. I had explicitly told them not to touch a hair on your head. They can be real brutes sometimes, just like back in the day. Just don't tell me you don't remember me"—the man across from him took a bottle of brand-name whiskey and two glasses out of his desk drawer with a practiced gesture.

There was something familiar about that face, soft, babyish, looking ready to start bawling at any minute.

"Baby Cakes, is that you?"

"It's me, Swift-Footed Stag."

My (I didn't know it was me, God damn it) schoolmate Baby Cakes, one of the gang back then, the eternal butt of our jokes, we didn't even give him an Indian name. He carried Chingachook's bow and quiver of arrows.

"So you've bought up the whole town of T., you're the one . . ."

"When did you get here, when did you learn all the gossip? Yes, I occupy several posts, mayor, party secretary, chief of the gendarmerie."

"And why did you have to arrest me?"

"Oh, I have more than enough reasons. But above all, I wanted to see you, shame on you for coming here and not giving me a call . . . Because of the good old days. You've rented out a house to write in, and just imagine the coincidence, the same one you used to live in. I'm happy that you look back fondly on those years."

"What's with that baloney downtown, are you shooting some kind of a movie? You haven't become a director, too, now have you?"

"No, it's far more serious than that. I've launched a project. In short, I'm turning time back thirty years. Nothing has changed here in any case. I'm creating the world's largest museum. A museum of the past, of socialism, call it what you will. The whole town, every day, round-the-clock, a total museum. Actually, 'museum' isn't exactly the right word, everything is live. Everyone keeps being whatever he was then, and we pay him for it. I foot the bill for everything. We don't pay them much, but we don't ask much of them, either. Just for them to stay the same. They're nostalgic for the olden days in any case. We've cut off the Internet, TV, we sell newspapers only from back then, actually we reprint the old editions in reverse order, we've imposed penalties for telling political jokes, we've reintroduced the people's militia, party meetings, demonstrations. I invited those who had been secret service informers to get back to work. I also pay a few folks who used to grumble against the government to keep doing it. Those sorts of things create atmosphere.

In short, you don't do a damn thing, you loaf around all day and take home a paycheck in the end. Just like back then. But I'm merciless if someone breaks the rules, my gendarmes are like the ones back in the day. You got a first-hand taste of that, incidentally. People are happy. Do you have any idea how bad unemployment in the neighboring towns is? Rich clients come here and order themselves a demonstration or a party meeting. Everyone wants to go back in time. I've built the ultimate time machine. I even have visitors from abroad. Come on now, cheers, and welcome back!"

"Cheers. So what about the whiskey?"

"From Corecom, the hard-currency store. Like I said, we've thought of everything."

"And why are you doing it? If it's for the money, there are more conventional ways of making a buck."

"I've got money, although I never turn it down. That's not the reason, though . . . Let me be frank with you," he refilled our glasses, "I don't feel like living in modern times. Nothing but shit . . ."

"There was plenty of shit back then, too."

"Maybe, but to me it smelled good. The world is already bugging out big time, there's no way you haven't noticed. I want to invite you to join in. I want you to come up with . . . days, everyday life. I know that's a tall order. The holidays are easy, those I can manage. But these folks need a script for daily life. I've already got some clients interested in that," He went over to the bookshelf and pulled out a few of my books. "I've got them all. You gave me the idea to a certain extent, I'm indebted to you."

"Oh no," I try to protest. "I never gave you the idea of bloodying up my brow."

"That whole inventory of socialism was a brilliant idea, along with the stories from back then, too. I use them as a handbook, we recreate a lot of those things. People drink Altai soda and cider, we brought back those old bottles of Vero dish soap. We've already got a few manufacturing workshops up and running here in town."

"This is a nightmare, okay, I'm going to wake up now . . ." I have the worrisome feeling that I can't control the plot of the story or even my own lines.

"No, this is a story that you just think you're writing, but actually, you're inside it. I've known you since childhood, you've always been a space cadet, it's not hard for you to flit off somewhere."

"Am I under arrest?"

"Let's just say you've been invited to join in your own project. Don't forget that it's your idea, I'm only the manager."

He takes a sip from the glass, I barely touch my lips to mine.

"We've got some more serious plans as well. The Doctor will arrive shortly, I've given him the Yellow House, we've fixed it up. He'll be doing experiments there. Regression therapy . . . regeneration of cell memory . . . a sanatorium for the past, gentle electroshock stimulation . . . He'll explain it to you better himself. But we urgently need fabricators of the past."

For a moment it crosses my mind that some Anti-Gaustine has implanted himself in Baby Cakes. And my every thought occurs to him sinisterly turned upside-down. For the first time, I want to stop, to give up, to jump ahead in time. Turning back is not always innocent. The past can be a dangerous place.

"Quite dangerous," Anti-Gaustine's voice adds. "Incidentally, the Yellow House is not far from here at all and if we open the window, we'll hear a very familiar . . ."

I didn't hear whether he said "voice" or "howl," because I got up and hurled myself through the window headfirst. That always helps with nightmares.

The Minotaur's Diary

I have no idea how much time has passed since I've been here. I don't remember whether I came in by myself or whether someone locked me in. The darkness is so thick that time has gotten lost. Only in darkness is there no time. I don't know how old I am. I've been forgotten. I feel like pounding on the door until they hear me and open up. There's only one unsolvable problem and therein lies the whole horror. There is no door.

Here's what I've discovered. It's so obvious that it's almost impossible to see. The deoxyribonucleic acid of every living creature with its double helix is structured like a labyrinth. A vertical labyrinth that unwinds in a spiral. The genetic instructions for all forms of life are written in a labyrinth. So that means it's the perfect form for preserving and transmitting information. That's why DNA has remained encrypted for so long. We are made of labyrinths.

DE
   OX
      Y
RI
   BO
      NU
   CL
E
   IC
      AC
ID

Deoxyribonucleic acid. Deoxy . . . An ox plods through the primordial soup of the world. I write it out over and over again until I lose myself in the labyrinth of that name.

Except that there's some mistake there, some bug, some hitch. Which automatically turns me into a Minotaur. I walk through the whole labyrinth of my own deoxyribonucleic acid to find that mistake. I am locked up in one, the other is locked up inside me. The labyrinth in the Minotaur.

Things that resemble a labyrinth

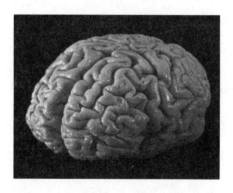

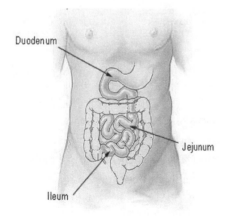

Duodenum

Jejunum

Ileum

The human brain. The cranial folds of all mammals.

A body's nervous system or a nerve taken individually with all of its branches, nerve fibers, axons, and so on.

The serpentine of the small intestine and the internal organs.

DNA

Banitsi, burek, saralias. All the winding, phyllo-dough sweets of the Orient.

The flight of bees, the language they use to communicate with one another, the interwoven figures. The language of bees is a labyrinth.

A forest.

The root systems of annual and perennial plants.

The structure of the inner ear with its membranous and bony labyrinth.

A city without a river that you find yourself in for the first time. The absence of a river is important. Otherwise the Ariadne's thread of its course easily shows you the way.

Secret routes taken on a walk with a mistress you are keeping hidden.

Doodles on a scrap of paper while having a boring phone conversation.

The pubis of a young woman. Here the labyrinth comes before the cave.

A ball of yarn.

The labyrinth sketched out by the reader's eyes.

If you look closely at a rose for a long time, you will see the labyrinth within it. And the horns of a beetle-Minotaur.

Good thing this darkness is here, this basement, so I can stay here, turning back time, running through its corridors, shouting, mooing The darkness helps me get used to it. When the one who is coming comes, I'll be ready. The transition will be truly smooth, from one darkness to another.

I remember, or I imagine that I remember, strange things. I remember afternoon, towns baking in the sun, deserted streets that grow crowded toward evening. I remember, and this is my earliest memory, my mother hiding behind a curtain and waving to me, I'm laughing, because I get the game, I head toward the curtain, I've just learned to walk, but she's not there. Sometimes I see rooms with high ceilings, a girl from behind, a cart disappearing into a field, an injured man in a strange city, a book in which I read my own story, full of mistakes.

I remember that I was once happy. It lasted about six minutes. It happened in the Kensington Gardens in West London, early in the morning. I can't find a reason for that happiness, which is proof positive of its authenticity. Any other kind of happiness is a conditioned reflex, like in Pavlov's dog. The stimulus comes and happiness is secreted, like gastric juices.

I was walking down the pathway, breathing deeply and sensing things with the body of a child. That is the key. With the body of a child.

I haven't gone out to the street in eighty-four days. I only slip out late in the evening to get the newspapers out of the mailbox, they're how I count the days. I don't want to meet anybody. I've stopped shaving, my jaw has gone stiff, probably because I haven't talked to anyone. Can your mouth atrophy?

I stop eating for some time. In any case, my supply of tin cans and provisions has been drastically diminished. I consider reducing my weight as part of going back in time. Children do not weigh 180 lbs. I feel better in this thinning skin. I'm looking more and more like that child-Minotaur. I don't know whether I'm a boy, the sickly thin person has no gender or age.

When Theseus came out of the cave, he was leading a child by his left hand. The myth has erased that child from its memory. Myths don't like children. Just imagine how incredibly awkward it would be. The hero Theseus with his short sword, Theseus who had defeated the giant Periphetes, the bloodthirsty bandit Sinis, the wild Crommyonian Sow, the hulking Cercyon, the cruel Procrustes, the Marathonian Bull, and so on, in the end sees a frightened child. Theseus tosses his short sword on the ground and leads the child out of the labyrinth.

That night he tells Ariadne: you know what, there was no monster there, just a little boy with a bull's head. And that boy somehow reminded me of myself.

(Theseus and I really do look alike, yet at the same time he is handsome. Perhaps he sensed that one and the same divine father was peeking out from behind both of us—at once god and bull. My brother begotten by a god, I by a bull.)

Ariadne doesn't pay attention to his words, but only hugs and kisses him, telling him that they have to get out of there right away.

The truth is, while looking for loopholes for the Minotaur in the story, I keep dreaming ever more frequently of my death in a basement, run through by a short, double-edged sword. The hand and the sword come out of the darkness of another time, they have travelled for so long that my human-faced killer is completely worn down from the journey, his arm is weak, and I myself have to help him with my own execution. To make a door with a sword in my very own body. My whole life I've been trying to lead the Minotaur out of myself.

But what if my killer (that which will kill me) doesn't notice me in the darkness and passes me by? What if I hide, like way back on that summer night when we were playing hide-and-seek and they forgot me . . . And I stand there hidden for a long time, while death goes about its business for years, a century. And what if outside there are now other people, a few generations have passed, and I won't be able to share the apple of a single memory with anyone? If that's the price . . . I hear myself yelling, howling, mooing like a bull in the corridors of that basement, because I no longer know which language is mine. I'm here, don't pass me by, here I am. Moooooo . . .

IX. Endings

The Storyteller and His Killer

Had the Minotaur perhaps thought to use Scheherazade's strategy? I see him with Theseus, the two of them walking together through the endless corridors of the labyrinth, with the Minotaur spinning endless tales. But what can someone who has been locked up in the darkness of a basement his whole life tell stories about? About a dream, in which he has a human face, about his mother's face, which never turns around, about his memories from an old bomb shelter where he lived amid piles of boxes and newspapers on the eve of some ending, which never came about in any case, about being trotted out at village fairs, about murders in bullfights and slaughterhouses, about the labyrinths of cities, where he "wandered lonely as a cloud," about all the books he has gotten lost in . . . Theseus walks beside him, the ball of string in his hand unwinding, Ariadne's thread mixes with the thread of the stories . . . Some things he doesn't understand, other things strike him as so unbelievable that his own feats and adventures pale in comparison. In the middle of one of the stories in which some ancient hero was wandering the corridors of a labyrinth to kill the monster, the Minotaur stops and says to Theseus: your ball of string has run out. But Theseus was so entranced by the thread of the story that he didn't even understand what ball of string he was talking about. You're here to kill me, the Minotaur reminds him. Now we've arrived at precisely that corridor of the story. If we continue on, you won't be able to go back, because your thread won't go any farther. But I don't want to kill you, Theseus answers. Someone forced me into this story. While you were telling me tales, I visited more places than all the ancient heroes combined. I want you to continue on with the story.

It passes through my own death, the Minotaur replies, but it's all the same whether you'll kill me for real or in the story you'll hear.

I see them walking along together through the corridors of cities and cellars, weaving parallel labyrinths from the threads of their stories, themselves entangled in them. And nothing can ever separate them again, the storyteller and his killer.

Police Report

(. . .)

A short, double-edged sword was found, in all likelihood an unusually valuable object from antiquity. An expert appraisal has been ordered to determine the precise period of its production, its value and provenance. There are no traces of blood on the sword.

Description of items found in the basement. Boxes filled with contents whose organizational logic is difficult to establish. Seven of them—filled primarily with clippings from newspapers and magazines. An old *halvah* box. Eight notebooks of varying thickness and with different sorts of bindings, almost entirely filled, have been found. Four large trunks filled with books in various languages. A gas mask. A computer and a dinosaur, which will be requisitioned for the needs of the investigation. (The dinosaur is a rubber children's toy). Fingerprints have been taken from all suitable surfaces. A literary expert must be appointed to examine the content of the notebooks. With an eye above all to what possible clues or leads could be derived from that material.

I am the appointed expert. As far as I know, the neighbors repeatedly called the police to complain of strange, random noises and howling (mooing—according to others) coming from the basement of the apartment building. Then for a week, no sounds were heard, the building manager went downstairs and found the heavy door to one of the storage units (part of a former bomb shelter) wide open. A sword was lying on the floor.

They asked me whether I had anything against working in the basement itself, since it would be a Herculean task to remove everything, besides the police had no free space. I agreed. I felt a strange sort of excitement, I had a complicated relationship with that writer, without having known him. I have always felt personally robbed while reading him.

I entered the basement on March 17 at 10 A.M. A strange feeling in the beginning that there was someone else there, watching me. I'm not afraid, the gaze is well-intentioned, if I can put it like that. I again peered into all the corners and niches, even though the police had done so before me. Nothing. Just a slug slowly crawling across the tin halvah box. I started reading. I stop, go back, go down a corridor that seems familiar to me, get lost, continue on. During the first month, I went out only once. Then never again.

What Is Left at the End

I'm back on that warm stone, six again, I step closer to the girl from the vision who is sitting in front of the piano with her hands raised, I've opened the door to the room, I'm leaning against the frame in my shorts, what's that ugly scar doing where my left leg was broken, a single beam of light passes through the heavy curtains, slicing the whole room in two, we are in two different halves. And then the miracle happens, the picture starts moving, the girl turns around . . .

At that moment, the Minotaur finds his mother in the crowd at the bullfight, my three-year-old grandfather sees his mother running back toward the mill,

a woman in Harkany receives a letter,

a man steps out of a poster, goes over to Juliet in front of the movie theater and the two of them set off arm-in-arm down the main street of T.,

Gaustine installs the biggest projector in the world and a night rain that doesn't get anything wet falls over the whole northern hemisphere,

my father and mother are watching from the balcony of a lit-up apartment on the top floor . . .

the girl and I are now on the same side of the beam of light, I see the edge of her face, she turns around . . .

Hi, Daddy.

Epilogue

I died (left for Hungary) in late January 1995 as an eighty-two-year-old human being of the male sex. I don't know the exact date. It's best to die in the winter, when there's not much work, so you don't cause too much trouble.

I died as a fruit fly, at dusk. The sunset of the day (of my life) was beautiful.

I died on December 7, 2058, as a human being of the male sex. I don't remember anything from that year. That's why I recalled the year I was born, 1968, day by day.

I have always been dead. And it's always been dark. If death is darkness and the absence of others . . .

I haven't died yet. I'm forthcoming. I am minus three months old. I don't know how to count that negative time in the womb. It's dark and cozy here, I'm tied to something that moves. In three months, I'll pass beyond to the outside. Some call that death birth.

I died on February 1, 2026, as a human being of the male sex. My father was always telling me that it was best to die in winter, I listened to him. I was a veterinarian my whole life. I once went to Finland . . .

I remember dying as a slug, as a rose bush, a partridge, as *Ginkgo biloba*, a cloud in June (that memory is brief), a purple autumnal crocus near Halensee, an early-blooming cherry frozen by a late April snow, as snow freezing a hoodwinked cherry tree . . .

I were. We was.

Beginning

My father and the dinosaurs died out at the same time . . .

Acknowledgments

This book was written in various places. It began near the Wannsee at the Literarisches Colloquium Berlin, where I had all the tranquility and sunsets in the world at my disposal; it continued on the banks of the Danube in Krems (Literaturhaus NÖ), the Wachau Valley in Lower Austria, between the river and the strictest Austrian prison; the final I's were dotted and T's crossed on the Adriatic, in Split (thanks to an invitation from KURS), in the labyrinth of Diocletian's Palace. I am grateful to the benevolent geography and my hosts in these places.

Thanks to Ani Burova, Nadezhda Radulova, Boyko Penchev, Miglena Nikolchina, Bozhana Apostolova, and Silvia Choleva for their valuable advice.

I thank Ivan Teofilov for his encouragement and shared faith in the wonder of language.

Thanks to Bilyana, who read and edited before there was even a book, and to four-year-old Raya for her patience and willingness to offer a story about cats and dinosaurs whenever she sensed that I was stuck.

Thanks to everyone who secured me the solitude necessary for a novel.